THE UNRIVALLED TRANSCENDENCE OF WILLEM J. GYLE

THE UNRIVALLED
TRANSCENDENCE OF
WILLEM J. GYLE

J. D. DIXON

THISTLE
PUBLISHING

To the good Doctor
Who found me before I found my voice;
And who
In darkest hour
Never blinked.

'The concept of good and evil has a double prehistory: namely, first of all, in the soul of the ruling clans and castes. The man who has the power to requite goodness with goodness, evil with evil and really does practice requital by being grateful and vengeful, is called 'good.' The man who is unpowerful and cannot requite is taken for bad. As a good man, one belongs to the 'good', a community that has a communal feeling, because all the individuals are entwined together by their feeling for requital. As a bad man, one belongs to the 'bad', to a mass of abject, powerless men who have no communal feeling.'

'We attack not only to hurt a person, to conquer him, but also, perhaps, simply to become aware of our own strength.'

-Friedrich Nietzsche

PART I:

WILLEM

The wishing well

E dinburgh has descended into the mist today. The lines are blurred, the faces are blurred. But it is all the same to him.

He has never seen anything accurately. He has never been able to. He has never felt the need. One of his mama's fancy men once told him that the inaccurate tells a far better story. 'Fiction is truer than any news story you'll ever read, lad,' he said. 'And half the news is made up anyway.'

All he can see now is the ground at his feet and the white mist. It is a shroud, a wall surer than any brickwork.

He can't see the mountain. He doesn't mind. It is a blank slate. It is inaccurate. His memory holds its curves, it holds its peaks. He can arrange them and rearrange them as he wills. Its flanks sweep into the ground, invisible for the moment. They carve a deep ravine before thrusting up once more. This last thrust is sheer and craggy, it is covered with briars. The briars count the mountain's age, they hold it close.

The last thrust shrugs off the howling coastal winds. The winds flow in from the Leith docks, they ruffle hair and feathers and make patterns of the mist. They groan as they run through the mountain's fissures, they herald the wake of a giant as old as the bones of the earth. He stares, always. He listens, he sighs and he smiles. At the mountain's bottom his feet take him past a castle. The castle is newly built by the world's clock, it is obscured by the same mist.

The mountain is not a real mountain. Charlie told him that it is an extinct volcano. It is one of many who breathed their last long before a city was built in their craters.

The mountain has a name. It is a name given by man and he never uses it. How do you name something so ancient, he wants to know?

He doesn't know how to frame the question, but he knows it hangs there. It hangs there like the mist. It obscures and it separates. Without form it is an obstacle and he cannot get around it.

The wishing well looms out of the fog. It is a cave set into the mountain's flank and around its front a low wall and an iron grate keep people from falling in. A plaque with writing carved into it tells tourists that it is dedicated to Saint Margaret. Its walls form a crown, it is shaped like a tiara with iron railings around its top and holly and ivy creeping all over. People throw their money in, their coppers and their silver. They close their eyes and their lips move, mumbling. Some are holy men, throwing entreaties up to god and his saint. Some are foreigners who can't read the plaque. They mime along with the natives, they throw their coins and laugh at the fun of it all.

The wishing well is alone today. No foreigners will brave the mist and the cold. The only holy men left in this world are old and tired. They will not come at this early hour.

A couple of rabbits disturb the mist's peace. They flee, they chase. They are white against white. Everything is white by the moonlight and the half risen sun. They are made distinct only by their motion. By their fast movements, so alien to the mountain's serene face.

The dancer and the ox

He was laid off yesterday and last night he broke a man's arm. The little Pole started it, he wanted a show. He wanted to star in a show and Willem had had enough.

'Come on, such big man, is that all you got?' The little man spat on the floor. The spit landed in front of Willem's feet, it lay in the darkness of his shadow. It quivered on the pavement. 'Big man, show me what Great British can do.' The little man's breath was onions and meat and lager, it frothed on his lips.

He circled to the left, he danced into the glare of a street light. His arms hovered forwards while Willem stood still, his shoulders bunched. The spit on the ground quivered, his breath quivered in his lungs and he squinted through the light. He didn't like to hurt people, his hands knew too well what they could do.

'Ha,' the little man laughed. 'Coward pussy. Son of bitch, your mum must have fucked a mouse before she had you. Bastard cunt, son of whore.' His left arm was a snake, lashing, pouncing. Both of his arms tensed and he lunged, dancing as he swung wide. One fist landed, it stung as Willem turned into it. Willem put his shoulder to the blow. He moved forwards and the little man bounced. He giggled, his voice was shrill and he began to dance once more. Another blow came and Willem put his hands up, he caught it. He twisted his wrists, he moved his hands and took a half step forwards. As he moved a loud crack rang through the street. It echoed and the little man squealed.

'Bastard, bastard,' he shrieked as he fell. Onto his knees, onto his back, squirming. 'Bastard, bastard,' he whimpered as he grasped at his left shoulder, rolling on the floor. 'You break, my shoulder, you break.' He was white, there was no blood in his lips. His eyes bulged. The spit was gone, he had landed in it. He rubbed it away, smearing it into the concrete as he twisted back and forth.

'Mam ain't no whore,' Willem mumbled. He turned his back, a light rain began to fall. It brushed his shoulders, unbunched now. It brushed his face and his cheeks. It made the pavement slick and it pattered through the lamp light.

The Pole was a runt, everyone said it. He was a man of wire and bristling anger. Willem once asked him what he was so angry at. 'The world, whole stinking world is fucked,' the little man replied. 'In a world like this, why just be angry at one thing? So many to choose from.' Charlie called him out on it a few times, he used to scream himself hoarse over the Pole's attitude. Every week or so there would be an argument, a fight, and management would step in. 'But he's the best welder in Edinburgh,' Charlie would shrug afterwards. 'How can you stay angry at a guy like that?'

The Poles were tight knit. They always stuck up for their own. But even they tried to shake him lose. He got into fights with the Scots and the Slovaks and the Albanians and the Lithuanians and they left him to it. 'Like kettle boiled too hot,' they said to Willem. 'Got to let the steam out sometimes. Just stand back, mind you don't get burned.'

Willem turned his back on the little man and the other Poles turned with him. 'Man had it coming, so much drink, so much rage,' they muttered. They pulled some more cans from their plastic bags. The bags were blue, they were thin and stretched under their load. Raindrops beaded on their skin, they got inside and beaded on the cans. One of the men passed a can to Willem, its cold bit into his fingers. He cracked the ring pull and suds sputtered at its rim.

'Drink deep, brother. It's been too long. And tomorrow's a new day,' they said. And then, 'come back with us. Such nights as this it's best to be with friends.' They were all laid off at lunchtime. The Poles, the Lithuanians, the Scots. Everyone, immediately. And that made them brothers, at least for the moment. The little man's cries grew dim as their feet slapped the pavement.

A cloud shifted overhead as they crossed the street, the rain stopped for a minute and a crow cawed its melancholy heart as the moon shone through. Willem slugged his beer, he swilled it around his mouth and swallowed.

'Mam ain't no whore,' he mumbled.

The rattling

When they arrived that morning Charlie had been acting funny. His eyes were too small, they were red around the edges. The site was nervous, the men and the machines were nervous and Charlie's breathing was too fast. He was in three places at once, running, always running.

'What does he run from?' the Lithuanians wanted to know.

'Every man runs from something,' the Poles said. 'His shadow chases him, and a man's shadow is his own business.'

But as the morning wore on the rattling grew worse. Their nine thirty tea break shook, it couldn't control itself. The tremors shook the earth, they got into the sandbags and the tool shed. Metal sang and people chattered with

the sound. By mid morning the scaffolding was loose at
the rivets, shaken by Charlie's panic, by the men's panic.
And then he called them, one by one and in groups. They
trudged into the foreman's cabin and the rumours let
loose.

The rumours silenced the rattling and stole their jobs.
They flattened everything on site as flocks of men downed
tools and slumped.

'Mam, I've been laid off,' he told her. He phoned her
straight away and she swore. 'I'm off for a couple of pints
with the lads. Then I'll be home. I love you.' The gates were
locked behind them and the Poles invited him to drink with
them for the first time in over a year. And he fought the
little man and broke his shoulder and went home with the
rest of them.

The gods of man part I

'Is fine for British man laid off. No work, get benefits.
Sixty pounds in a week, nice flat, all free. Sit down and get
fat, no problems. Poland is no money for this. No easy free
life for us.' The rambling went on, it clung to the walls in
their house. Cigarette smoke rose in plumes, the smell of
meat frying in the kitchen rose in plumes. It all mixed, it
clung and the rambling went on.

'This is why god is dead in Great Britain,' he said. His
name was Bratomil, he lived there and he dragged Willem
and the others back with him. To ramble and moan and
drink and smoke. He sat them down with cans of Tyskie and
the words formed in his throat. They grew angry, they grew
forlorn and everybody listened and formed their own words
and it all got mixed together.

Six of them sat around Bratomil. They slumped on a dead sofa, bowed in the middle. They slumped on shanty stalls, leaning against walls. The walls peeled and the words pealed and everybody laughed together in their bitter thoughts. They had red eyes and their hands were calloused from years of long work. Arduous work which united them. The loss of which united them still.

Another Pole agreed with Bratomil, he nodded when he heard god's name spoken. He slurred and he squinted and he drank deep before talking. He said 'yes, yes, you are so weak for god here. All those empty churches. British churches being bought up by Polish church, by Nigerian church. Now niggers pray and British don't care. Some even bought up by Muslims, used as mosques for those bastards. God is dead here, this is dead country.' He lost focus, he rambled, he took another sip and his can shone dully through the smoke.

Another man took up the narrative. He said that 'here everything goes to shit, you say please government, please, no work and I'm hungry. I'm cold and I can't afford my flat, I can't keep boiler going. And government says yes, yes, of course, how sad, have money. Have all this money. At home there is nobody to ask, nobody to tell you yes, how sad. There is no money without work.

'So who else to ask but god?'

They finished their cans and they finished their cigarettes and they wheezed heavily into the night. They stubbed their butts out into their empty cans, they flicked their ash into empty cans. The cans hissed, the warm froth grew around the ash. And soon every surface was an empty can, slowly drifting in the clinging smoke.

'And where does all this money go? British all so expensive people,' another continued. 'You!' he pointed at Willem. 'You British buy so much, you want so much. I tell you where money goes, these big sandwich places, these big coffee places, these expensive pubs with three pounds fifty beers.'

'British stupid with money,' Bratomil took the reins once more. His head nodded, his beer can dipped as his eyes grew wise. 'Polish buy cans from supermarket, six for four pounds. We make lunches at home, we buy cheapest ingredients and save our money. And now look! London spends all money, we don't know where, recession comes and no more jobs for us.' He swigged the last of his beer, he cursed in his native tongue. His curses stank, his breath was toxic. It wriggled around the floor, into the carpets. He spat into his can, savouring the noise of his puckered lips, of his harsh throat.

'Rozpierdol!'

The serpent's dreams

The mist hangs heavy as he walks through his hangover. From the top of the mountain you can see for miles on a good day. The deep hills to the west, the deep sea to the east. All of them are old beyond measure by any man's reckoning. But today the mist is hungry, it eats everything up. From the highest point you can only see a few houses at the outskirts of the park. These fade all too soon. They are tattered, they are nothing.

At five o'clock in the morning Willem is at the lowest point, streaming through the cold on his way to the site. His boots are wet with dew, his bones are shaking with the cold. He marches at a furious pace to ward off the morning. Tramp's gloves keep his palms in a cold sweat. His mama calls them tramp's gloves because they have no fingers. He wears them so that he can feel his fingers to work.

He drags himself through this world with his shoulders bunched. He dragged himself into this world and his mama screamed in pain.

The first thing the nurses noticed about his mama when she presented herself at the door to their ward was how pale she was. Even for a ragged little weegie she was pale. They could see blue veins tracing pathways across her neck and her bare arms. The pathways are still there. In her twilight they have sunk a little but they are still there.

The second thing the nurses noticed about his mama was how young she was.

'The poor wee thing, she can't be more than fifteen,' the nurses said to one another afterwards. They sat over over cups of tea at their station, sharing the day's news. 'Come on love, let's get you seen to,' the midwife said when his mama staggered in. She put her arm around the swollen child and brought her onto the ward.

Ten minutes later the doctor announced that there was a complication. 'We'll have to operate, we can't wait,' he said. He phoned down to the theatre to tell them to prep for a caesarean. 'Like Macduff, it's a just sign,' they told her afterwards. 'Who the fuck-' she wanted to ask, but the anaes-thetic was strong. She couldn't frame the question, it died on her lips.

From the outset his mama resented the scar on her belly. Like a long snake uncoiling, pink and raw, it crept upwards from her pubis, its mouth wide open and hungry. She would often dream that it was readying itself to strike. She would wake in a cold sweat, cry out to whichever of her blokes was sharing her bed that night and hope to find comfort in his arms.

The infant Willem would lie in his cot at the foot of the bed, awoken and scared by his mother's screaming. Her men would find it all too much. They would not return after such a night. She had to look time and again for a new pair of arms to comfort her through the small hours.

These are all just stories to Willem. They are make believe. But his mama's scar is real. He has seen it. It winks at him from her naval.

Of course it has faded with time. It has paled from red to pink to a shade almost as bright white as her natural colouring. It has also shrunk slightly as age has put a little flesh on her frame, as time has softened her hard skin to fit the weight of her years. And as the weight of her years has grown, little by little she has noticed that her nights have become easier.

The toiler

Willem went to work with his mama from the first. The men who came late at night only cared for his mother's company, they didn't want to care for the bairn. She had no friends or family able to keep him and she needed every last penny to keep their room warm and their bellies full.

Early each morning she would carry him to one of the offices she cleaned. The men who worked there wore polished shoes that scuffed the carpet. They drank coffee whose cups left light rings on every surface. The rings were eyes, they stared all night long until she closed them. And she cleaned and she tidied, putting those watchful eyes out of sight for a short while.

She was invisible and the men in the offices were invisible. They would still be waiting for their morning alarms to ring when she was putting on her gloves. She would be done by the time they arrived. Afterwards she would lift Willem up again and carry him first to one tenement block and then to another to clean stairwells for the council. The graffiti shouted at them both. The dirt lay thick and Willem often cried. The graffiti was too loud, it hurt his ears. The dirt caught in his little lungs.

The fear and the struggle caught them. The stories turn to memories and dirty men loom, they suck on cigarettes and laugh coarse air. More than once police had to be called. Drunkards and drug addicts and worse would be dragged away, the graffiti laughing along with their dirty chuckles. By the time Willem reached his fifth birthday the cleaning company had started to refuse government contracts. The graffiti was too loud, it won the battle. It turned into white noise, inaudible and unapproachable. His mama had her hours cut, but she found herself safer in her days.

And then the evenings would see them back in an office and then later on in a leisure centre, wiping sweat from cardio machines and weight stacks. Hoovering the carpets. Bleaching the heavy mats the customers used for aerobics classes. Cleaning out the washrooms, throwing away the pills and the needles with which the men made their muscles sing. And then, and then, and then, over and over again.

And then they would be back in their room, eating beans on toast and drinking orange fizz. Late night television would ring blue in the corner as she prepared herself for a visit and rocked the little lad to sleep.

The slow burner

When he was five the routine changed. 'Now you're a big boy, Willie, now you're nearly a man... my big brave boy's going to start proper school,' his mama crooned to him. She dropped him at his primary school at nine o'clock every morning. She was relieved of the burdens of playing watchman for a few short hours before she picked him up again at three. She could let her mind wander as she scrubbed floors and hung out laundry, she could allow herself to dream sweet dreams in the daytime to offset the nightmares of the serpent's sleep.

But it soon became apparent that her son's mind was stolid and set, unable to dream such dreams as she. Unable to jump the hoops required of the other children. Because of the manner of his birth Willem's mind was never quick. He had been starved of oxygen in those crucial minutes in which the snake scar first opened its mouth. It bit him too deeply, it stole his wits enough to put him a half beat behind the rest of the world. And no matter how desperately his mother tried he was never able to catch up with it.

He needed extra help. The state wrote to her telling her that the new government was requiring certain standards of all young boys and girls and that remedial education was needed to bring him up to par.

Special needs, she thought to herself. She was embarrassed, she didn't know where to look. *He's being sent to a special needs school.*

But St. James' wasn't a terrible place and the teachers gave Willem what he needed. What his mother wanted for him but couldn't give. She gave him warmth and encouragement and they taught him his letters and his numbers, how to say please and thank you and how to keep quiet when his head wouldn't give him rest.

He went to a few more places as he grew up, all intended to do the same. By the time he left school his shoulders were broad and his brain had mastered the basics. Without too much asking around he was able to get work as a labourer for one of the largest construction firms in the Lothians. And the Scots and the Poles called him brother and shared their cans as he earned his crust.

The thickness

He is too slow witted to have too much luck with the ladies, but every so often one of the kinder lassies shows him some pity and allows him a little warmth, a little encouragement. A girl from the pub. A friend of his mama's one time. A handful of others, hanging on his arm. And there was Celina, who haunts him even now.

He isn't happy. He doesn't really know how to be happy, he doesn't know what happiness is. Happiness requires wit and imagination. But he has a slight paunch from fried food and lager, he has thick muscles and skin browned from hard work and he has no worries in this life. 'You've made me proud, pal,' his mama often says to him.

Her voice is thick with the years and no words are wasted.

And then lunchtime came yesterday and this morning comes and his story starts with its low hanging mist. A deep mist whose cold steals the breath from his body with every other footstep. A deep mist whose thick fingers blur the outline of everything in front of him.

The first fall

The economy has crashed, he has been told. It happened last year and now it's caught up with us, he has been told. The men down south have spent all the government's money. They have borrowed too much and now they can't pay it back. Jobs are going to become scarce, he has been told. He doesn't understand, but why should he? He shifts bricks and mortar, he helps build houses with his thick callouses. This is his domain and it suits him nicely.

'But you've worked for them more than ten years,' his mama told him when he got home. He was drunk, he shrugged and said it didn't matter. There was no work. 'You go back down there tomorrow and you tell Charlie it's not good enough, tell Charlie you need your job and you deserve to be treated better!'

Charlie has been laid off too, he protested. But she told him to march down there anyway, to find out who was in charge and tell *them* that he deserved better. She told him to stand up for himself. 'OK mam,' he said. And when he woke up he pulled on his work boots and his tramp gloves and set out into the mist.

He likes walking to work. He likes it because all his work mates drive. He learned to drive but he never liked it too much. There was always too much going on. The lights were too hot. The other drivers on the road were too hot. Because his brain works so slowly he is happiest in his own company, away from any of that. When the world spins too fast around him he likes to pretend that he is on his own. Then he doesn't have to worry about anything at all, he can just let his mind drift into the trees and the rocks. He can let the crows and the pigeons take his thoughts and do what they will. Later, when his life has changed and he truly is alone in the world, when the ground beneath his feet has shuddered so hard he can barely stand, he will still enjoy the solitude of thinking his own slow thoughts, uninterrupted.

The Polish wife

'I never go to London. This many crazy people,' one
of the Poles announced last night. His English was getting
worse as he drank, his voice was growing harsh. 'This many
nigger, cut your throat. Fucking blacks and Arabs and cra-
zies everywhere.'

'And rent so high they break a man's heart,' another
man chipped in. Willem no longer knew who was speaking.
The room was dizzy and everybody was half asleep. His head
was thick with drink and smoke. His heart was tired with the
day's news.

'Two thousand pounds one month rent, not even bills
included. Here it is not even half this, and look,' he gestured around the room. He gestured to the window, to the
faded curtains. He gestured to the open lounge door and
the peeling hallway beyond. 'I live here, Bratomil live here.
With his wife, my wife, mother, children, how many others?'

There were four bedrooms and two bathrooms, a
kitchen, utility room and a lounge in their house. Fifteen
people lived there, three families in the bedrooms and
a young couple sleeping on the lounge's tired furniture.
The Poles cursed at the British, at their decadence. Every
so often a woman came bustling through and they cursed
at her too. She would glare at them all and sweep the
empty cans in to a bin bag. She would exchange a few
words in Polish with Bratomil. He would grow angry and
she would grow stern and the other men laughed. They
coughed and they laughed and the stories continued
through the smoke.

'Fucking bitch woman,' Bratomil rumbled. He smiled
at Willem. He nodded at the young woman, still smiling. It

was a joke, it was OK because he was smiling. 'Break my balls every day.'

'Don't listen to such bad man, sweet heart,' the woman laughed. She was joking too. It was all a joke and everybody smiled, they laughed and Willem found his heart growing a little easier. He looked at her, he lifted his eyelids a little. She was pale and pretty, she had deep eyes and her mouth was always pouting. She looks like Celina, he thought. Just like her. There is warmth in her grace.

'He is just mad I make more money cleaning big rich houses than he makes building them!'

Bratomil threw a cushion at her. It sailed, it twirled and it bounced off her bottom. She laughed her way out of the room as Willem mumbled 'it's all a joke.' He stood to leave, the room rushed as his knees straightened. They creaked and his head swam. 'Mam's expecting me,' he told them as he left. 'She'll want to talk about tomorrow.'

The Polish daughter

He used to drink with the Poles all the time. Before Celina came and went. A couple of nights every month they would invite him back to drink and smoke and eat fries and spicy sausage. He was an outsider in his own skin. They were outsiders in their own homes. They told him this, they told him that he was like them. He had thick callouses and the shoulders of an ox and they accepted him as a brother.

Then they said he broke Celina's heart and their doors were closed to him. They stopped being brothers until they were laid off. Then they shared the same fate.

'We are brothers again,' they said. 'Come, drink with us one more time.'

Celina's heart beat warm and strong. She said her name was short for Marcelina, which meant 'warlike' in her own tongue. She told him this and she laughed. Her laughter was a bark, it flashed through her eyes and dazzled him. 'You go to war with me, strongman?' she asked him. 'Life is a battle, you fight battles for my love?' He smiled, he nodded and she kissed him deeply. Her nose was long and thin and her hair was short and blonde and she was the most beautiful thing he had ever seen.

He still thinks about her sometimes. He remembers how she seduced him, how she pounced one night when the other men were asleep and he was about to leave. He remembers her smell, the cigarettes and the strong perfume. How that smell wafted around him as she fed him vodka, as she drank vodka herself and her cheeks burned red.

He thinks of her at night. He thinks about her little titties, about how he used to nestle his head into them. How they cushioned his head after a day's labour, how they smelled as she stroked his hair and his eyelids grew heavy. He thinks of her and he sighs, he turns over and bunches his shoulders.

He saw her for a few months. For the first few weeks it was all sex. Every second was sex and sleeping and cheap vodka. She was the only girl who ever wanted to spend more than a couple of nights with him. And then the sex gave way to longer evenings spent walking the streets, talking of everything. She let him think in his own time, she left him to form his own thoughts and listened patiently as they unravelled. He took her to the cinema sometimes. He bought her burgers on Saturday nights in town, he gave her chocolates to make her happy.

'You daft bastard!' his mama said when she found out. 'She's only using you to get a passport. She's no good for you, you need to find yourself a good Scottish girl. Men!' And he stopped seeing her, and the Poles turned their backs on him.

'You break a girl's heart,' her brother told him. They were at work. It was a few days after he had told Celina he couldn't carry on seeing her. The sun was setting over the rooftops and her brother was scowling at him. 'You fuck her then you throw her away. Pah!' He spat at Willem's feet and Willem didn't go out drinking with them anymore. Not until that last night when the company closed down and they were laid off.

'We are all thrown away, now,' they told him. 'Come, drink with us.' And he broke a man's arm and he sat in Bratomil's living room, worrying about tomorrow.

The fast sound

The site is completely locked up when he arrives. Overnight the world has been deserted. 'The mist has swallowed us all,' he mutters. The padlock is still on the chain even though it is getting on for six already. The lights behind the fences are off, the slag is still piled under tarpaulin and the new slabs are still bound with tight blue cord. He grows scared as he watches. The fear is hot and his eyes are hot. He knew Charlie and the others might not be here, but he was not prepared for this dead world.

To calm himself down a little he buys some breakfast. A cheap café stands on the corner near the site. Its doors are open and the warmth wreathes the street. Formica table tops reflect pools of electric light and the first few punters are lining up inside. They are bathing in the kitchen's bright warmth and the smells of frying meat.

He takes his place among them, queuing behind three other people at the counter. The man in front of him is wearing a cheap navy polyester suit with his name pinned at the lapel. It reads JIMMY, Customer Service Attendant. He shuffles away from Willem, scuffing his shoes on the lino. His eyes dart back and forth. They are fast and they make Willem nervous. 'Everyone is so nervous,' Willem mumbles. That thought calms him. If they are all nervous then they are all the same.

In front of the man in polyester a young couple is huddling over a pram. The boy is wearing a baseball cap, the girl has her hair tied tight at the back of her head. Her hair is red, it is as warm as the café's kitchen. The baby starts to cry and they try to ignore it. The screaming, the noise. He knows it too well. It is the same noise he hears whenever the world travels too fast around him. His ears echo with it and his eyes begin to dart as fast as the customer service attendant's. He is glad when the couple take their order and leave the café. The world can slow down again. The world can be at peace.

'Yes love, what can I do you for?' A middle aged woman with a large stomach and low, pendulous breasts is smiling over the counter at him. She is MARA, Customer Service Attendant, and her cheeks are ruddy with the morning.

'Sausage roll, ta, and tea.'

'Milk and sugar?'

'Aye. Two. Ta.'

'I thought they closed the site. Didn't expect to see any of you boys in here any more.'

'Mm.'

The lock and the chain

He takes his food outside. He sits on a bench facing the construction site and waits. As he waits he munches the hot, cheap pastry. The piping meat rolls through the mist, it steams in his mouth. It carries the kitchen's warmth and curls around his teeth and tongue.

He chews noisily. He eats with his mouth open, his tongue works the food furiously. People often comment on it. 'Hey, piggy,' they say. 'Want a trough for that?' He never gets their jokes but the tone in their voices is not lost on him. He knows they laugh at him, sometimes in fun, sometimes in spite. But now he is alone, happily alone and he can chew as loudly as he wants. He need not worry about upsetting anybody today.

As he sits eating he watches the front gates. He watches the chain, silent and padlocked. 'They were silly to leave it,' he mutters. If nobody comes to the site the lock won't get greased and it will rust through. It will crumble in the morning damp, in the night time storms. He could do it, if only he had his toolbox with its rag and its oil. But they are locked away inside.

He licks the last few crumbs of pastry from his palm. He licks the grease from his fingers, sips at his scalding tea and watches the lock and chain. His fingers began to itch. How useless, he thinks. How bloody useless.

The first haul

Last night's rain has made the pavements slick. It has started to rain again now, adding to the flood. The rain tickles him, it creeps into his jacket and patters gently on his cheeks. The traffic picks up as morning blossoms. Cars with flashing headlights cut through the mist. They are commuters leaving this neat little suburb to get to their offices in town. They trundle through the pale streets, splashing the curb as their tyres churn up water.

Willem finishes his tea. He perks up a little as the sugar and caffeine pull him out of his morning daze. He pulls his jacket tight. He pulls the collar up and digs his chin into the neck of his hoody. His fingers start to go numb as the empty tea cup cools down. The wet cotton of his tramp's gloves sticks, it is clammy with the rain.

By eleven o'clock nobody has come and his cap is wet through. The rain has grown stronger. The mist has been washed away and his hair gel has run out from under his cap, it starts to run in rivulets down his cheeks. He smells watermelon and sugar and his eyes sting as it streaks over them. His shoulders and thighs are soaked and cold water has started to drip down his back.

He sneezes once, twice, and fixes his eyes back on the gate. His mama has told him what to say when somebody comes and he is reluctant to leave until he has said his piece.

A bus passes. It sends a great wave from a large puddle. The water hits Willem's shins, it plasters his jeans against his skin. It covers his work boots and seeps in over his ankles.

'Hey buddy, what you doing out here?' an old man asks him.

'Waiting for the site to open.'

'If it hasn't opened by now it probably won't open at all today, sonny. It's getting on for lunch time.'

'I know. But still. I've got to wait.'

'Suit you, lad. Suit you,' and the old man trundles away.

'First haul of the day!' another old man laughs. He sits down next to Willem. He sighs as the bench takes his weight. A shabby overcoat hides his skinny bones and he carries a plastic shopping bag in one hand. He smells like he hasn't washed in a good few days. He smells like Jap when he swims through the canal.

The old man pulls a two litre bottle of cider and a packet of tobacco from the plastic bag. He unscrews the bottle, cursing a little as the carbonated fizz leaks over his finger nails. The nails are black, they are claws. He takes a deep swig and offers it to Willem.

'No ta, not in the morning. Not on a work day.'

'What work?' the old man cackles, wheezing into his fist. He takes a pinch of tobacco from the pack. He rolls a thin cigarette and asks Willem for a light. Willem has a nice lighter in his pocket but he doesn't like to take it out in front of strangers. It was a present from his mama on his last birthday. It is his and it is special and he only likes to play with it when he is alone and the world spins along without him. He carries a cheap lighter for everyday use. He takes it out. He clicks it, lighting the old man's roll up. It hisses in the rain, the paper and tobacco smoulder. He takes a cigarette out of his own packet and sticks it in his mouth. The two men sit, puffing, watching the rain fall.

The good eye watches

The left side of the old man's face is purple, like someone gave him a hiding a couple of days ago. The skin is tight, stretched against his cheekbones. It turns greenish yellow around his left eye and the lower lid is swollen shut. Blue veins streak upwards from his left eye, they snake across his temple. They are fat and they trace the years across his face. A mop of straggly grey hair folds them up when they climb too high. Then they are gone, lost.

'What happened to your face?' Willem asks. He is not a curious man by nature. Nor does he relish idle chat. He can sit happily for hours in someone's company without talking if they let him. But he wants to be a kind man and the old man looks like he wants to talk.

'Direct bugger, aren't you? Ha ha, you wee shit!' the old man thumps a knee and cackles. He takes a swig of his cider and begins to wheeze. 'I look like I've been through the wars, no?' he asks when he catches his breath. His breath is tobacco and porridge, it is thick in the rain.

'You look like someone did you over.'

'Well they'd have to have one hell of a hook. I've looked like this since I was a bairn. Purple and ugly on one side. And then a few years ago I got an eye infection and the damned thing closed up. Of course, the doctors just wanted to give me some pills. Well, I've had enough of doctors, I told them. They've been giving me the once over my whole life. And I've had enough of pills. Fuck them, I'll let it be, thank you very much.'

'But doesn't it hurt?'

'I've got my wee friend here for that,' he says, swigging once more from the bottle. It is so big that he has to support it with both hands while he gulps. His wrists are thin and his knuckles are sharp. His Adam's apple bobs as he swallows. It is bristly and thick and it quivers with the drink.

'Can you see?'

'Not with my left eye, not any more. But listen to me laddie: my right eye doesn't miss a trick! Not a single one!'

The long wait

The old man with the one good eye comes and goes several times as the day passes. Willem doesn't know where he goes each time. When he leaves Willem gives him no thought. When he comes back he says hello. He continues to stare at the closed gates, at the chain pulled tight and locked, at the rain as it gathers into puddles and little streams.

Other people come and go throughout the day. Some of them are old men, older even than the one eyed man. Their faces tell their stories as surely as his own purple cheek and blue veins.

Others are around Willem's own age or younger. Their stories are still being written. Their wrinkles are not yet deep. At one point a young lad of sixteen or so slumps down next to him. He has a rucksack strapped to his stomach and a vinyl sports bag in one hand. The sports bag is filthy. He dumps it at his feet as Willem budges over. He asks for a cigarette. He thanks Willem politely and asks him where he is staying.

'At my mam's. I always lived with her.'

'You're not on your uppers?'

'I don't know.'

'I mean you don't live out here?' The lad gestures around them.

'No. I work here. Or I did yesterday. I don't know that anyone works here today.'

'So what are you sitting about in the rain for?'

'I'm waiting.'

'What for?'

'I don't know. For something to happen.'

'Like what?'

Willem shrugs and the lad soon loses interest. He smokes his cigarette. He asks for another and goes on his way with a mumbled goodbye.

An hour or so later the sun begins to droop in the sky. It bleeds the sky. It sucks at the grey clouds until the street lights flicker on. As it sets a woman a few years older than him joins Willem on the bench. She asks him how he is doing. He tells her that he is doing just fine, but he wishes the rain would let up.

'Rod said I'd find you here. He said you had cigarettes.'

'Mm.'

'He said you have a job.'

'I don't. I did yesterday.'

'But not today?'

'No. Lots of people don't have jobs today.'

'That's the truth of it. But you got money?'

'Sure. Charlie paid me up to the end of the month. He didn't have to, he said. He said I didn't have a contract so the company didn't owe me a thing. But he's a good man, he said. Not like some of the others.'

She sits a little closer. She tells him he can touch her for twenty quid. She says she will touch him for forty. For a hundred he can put it in her, but he will have to find somewhere for them to do it. And he would have to wear protection. Just because she lives under the stars doesn't mean she can't keep herself clean.

He watches the chain fade into the night. It dissipates as he thinks about the woman. It is gone and he imagines her breasts, the warmth between her legs. He has paid for it before and he enjoys being in the arms of a woman. But he is cold and wet, he doesn't feel like it today. Today he would rather just be by himself with his thoughts.

'What are you, some kind of poof?' she asks. He tells her no, he doesn't think so. He is just a little too cold to think about anything like that right now. She asks him if she can at least have a fag. He takes one out for himself and gives her the packet. There are five cigarettes inside and she thanks him as he lights one for her.

The vigil ended

'So you're back off to your mama's then?' the one eyed man asks him. Willem nods. He is soaked and half frozen and the evening has set in.

The commuters in their cars are clogging the streets once more and the buses have more and more faces pressed against their windows. Their faces glisten, they watch as the world around them is drowned. They watch as the bus sends up sheets of water. Their worlds are blank and tired and they are mirrors. The world glistens and they are blank and tired.

'Don't suppose I could trouble you for a bed for the night?' Willem say no, there are only two beds in his mama's and they are both taken. And she doesn't like him to bring company home.

He stands up from the bench. His knees creak. They are tired and his eyes are blank. He brushes some of the water from his shoulders and thighs and limps off down the road. His knees ache with the cold and his trousers cling to the insides of his thighs. He walks like a cowboy, swinging his ankles wide, not bending his legs at all.

'Not even a sofa?' the one eyed man calls after him. Willem pretends not to hear. He is tired.

'No bother, lad. You wait, you wait and see! My world is big, I've got a path before me. Goodnight and god bless, lad!'

He passes a big hardware shop. It looks more like a warehouse than a shop. Smart cars are parked in front of it and behind it. Smart shoppers carry bags through the rain. The rain has washed the mist away, it beads their plastic bags. The cold sucks at the plants they carry in ceramic pots. Willem briefly considers buying some oil for the lock and chain but thinks better of it. He just wants to get home. With his wet clothes he just wants to find the warmth of his mama's flat.

The mountain is visible behind the hardware shop. With the mist cleared its shoulders shrug against the clouds. It rises strong against the grey sky and as he turns into its parkland Willem whistles. It is a shrill sound, it pierces the rain. He whistles every day when he looks at the mountain. He has done so nearly every day of his life. Ever since he could remember. Every time he looks at it he is amazed that something could grow so big. That anything so big could allow man to live in its shadow.

His legs slap together as he walks and within half a mile he can feel sores developing between his thighs. The skin rubs raw but he doesn't mind. He has felt worse, he has worked through worse. You don't spend over a decade labouring without your nerves numbing. Without knowing that cuts and bruises are momentary. When the sores heal he knows that his skin will be calloused. It will be harder than ever. It will always be able to take more the next day.

He passes a couple of people on his way through the park. The wet road sweeps past him on one side. It weaves like a snake, like his mama's snake. Long and thin and winding around something much bigger than itself. Older and stronger than itself. Cars periodically sweep up sheets of water as they skid through its bends. They splash his shoes but he doesn't mind. It is all momentary. It passes.

On the other side of the path the first grassy verge at the mountain's skirt lies slick in the twilight. Dogs roam through the long rushes and harsh bramble. They lay their scent, marking their territory. They run with their own kind. They run from their own kind, a game played out in cycles. Tired walkers swing leashes at their sides. They dutifully allow their pets to roam free for a half hour before dragging them back to the house, to the warm walls of home. Willem knows that Jap will be scrabbling at the door when he gets home. He has been stuck inside all day, he is sick of the warm walls. He will be bursting with energy by now, bursting to lay his scent and void himself.

The nubs, the crack

Willem leaves the park at its far end. He walks to London Road. He crosses over to Easter Road and his feet find their way back home. He tenses as he enters his neighbourhood. He loves his home, he loves the kebab shops and the old pubs. He loves walking past the footie grounds with their high floodlights and raucous shouts. But in this part of town he can barely walk five minutes without someone recognising him. Without someone hailing him to pass time in idle chatter.

'No thank you,' he mumbles. He prefers the nicer parts of town where he is a stranger, where he is left alone to think his own slow thoughts. People here always make him feel so small. They trap him in his sluggishness.

He thinks of the lock and chain rusting in the rain. It swings, the wind plays with it.

'No thank you.'

And then it begins. 'Hey, our Willie!' Old Jack is smoking a fag outside the Barrel. He squints in this life. He glares through the rain. He smiles, he cocks his head to one side. He breathes smoke. He breathes it through the drizzle. He obliges Willem to cross the street. Tidings must be given, the day's news needs to be exchanged.

'Hey Jack, what's up pal?'

'Nothing new brother. Same old, same old.' They say Old Jack is a hippie and a rocker. They say he smoked too much crack back in the day. That he smokes too much weed these days, that his mind is blown. Willem doesn't know too much about all that, but he knows Jack blew something along the way. His teeth are black. They are ground down to nubs and the grey wire hairs in his straggly beard are yellowing. They are yellow with tobacco stains and poor use.

His breath is rancid. It pools about his wiry jaw, it wraps around the two men. He cackles in a high pitched whistle which always scares Willem.

He cackles now, smiling through his nub teeth.

'And how's our Willie this fine day?' His cackle rises. It steams like a broken kettle, whining.

'Not good, buddy. Work stopped.'

'Stopped?'

'Aye. They told us to go home. Now the site's closed.'

'Typical shit. Stand us a drink and tell us all about it?'

'No, I'd better get back. Jap will need walking. He'll be wanting his supper.'

'Aye. Another time then. On with you, lad. Keep the peace, brother.'

'Aye.'

The face winks

The stadium is silent today. The walls are silent, they are strong. The lights are out. There was a match last weekend and the crowds soared. There is another coming up and the crowds will pour into town again.

Alleyways loom between the buildings. Inside the alleyways night has fallen deep.

Josef the Pole is sitting on a bench. He always tells them he is not a Pole, he is from somewhere else. But what does it matter to Willem? Celina's smile was warm and the Poles were always good to him. More so than the Albanians and Lithuanians. More so than the Scots. And Josef might as well be a Pole for the difference it makes.

Josef smiles and nods. He was sleeping a little while ago and his eyes are still blurred. They shine red through the damp air. He will be off to work soon, off to his labours. But for now he enjoys the cold night. He enjoys the rain dripping down his chin.

He has a dog at his feet, a bitch mastiff with black fur and a ragged jaw. Jap likes her, he likes to sniff around her when he has the chance, when they are both on heat and Willem and Josef have to drag them apart. She looks up at Willem and yawns, sleepy as her master. Her gums are red as Josef's eyes. They drip foam onto the pavement.

'Hey, bonny lad,' Josef smiles, imitating the Scots brogue. 'How's tricks, laddie?' Willem has taken his keys out of his pocket. He fumbles with them in the moonlight, trying to pick out the one for the front door. He tells Josef about work, about Charlie, about the chain and the lock left to rust.

'Yes, bad, bad times, my friend,' Josef agrees. He nods like a wise man. His chin bobs and his eyes scour Willem's boots. Willem sits down next to him on the bench. He carries on sorting his keys with one hand. With the other he scratches the bitch's damp ears. She rolls over, exposing teats and patchy fur. He tickles her belly and fancies that she smiles back up at him. His living room window is two stories above their heads. He can hear Jap scrabbling furiously at the pane. He wants his master's fingers, he wants them to tickle his belly.

'I just saw a rat running through bushes,' Josef tells him, looking over to the other side of the street. A low bush lines the bottom of a chain link fence.

'Sure it wasn't a squirrel?'

'No, I know squirrel. I know rat. This was rat, filthy beast. At home we kill them.'

'Let it be, Jo. It won't hurt nothing.'

'Pah. This land is soft. Make soft man.' He digs his boot into the bitch's stomach, prodding her into action. 'Come on girl. We have work to do. Enjoy yourself, brother. It's later than you think.' And he ambles away with his bitch plodding next to him. They both limp as their joints thaw.

Despite the rain the moon shines strong tonight. It is proud. He can feel its silver glow on his hands, resting on his thighs. He can feel its face watching him. 'Piss off,' he mumbles to the moon, to the winking stars. 'This is my time, lads.'

'Man is strong,' Josef told him once. 'Stronger than the wild beasts, strong as the anger in his heart.' He wants to be stronger. He wants to be strong in his heart.

A pretty girl walks past and he ducks his head down. He doesn't want to see her. He doesn't want her to see him. She has just locked up a deli on the corner. He remembers when she first came here. He remembers when the deli opened a few years ago. It used to be Jose's. It was a café and he bought his morning roll and cup of tea there. Now he doesn't recognise it, now the menu confuses him. Now he always waits until he gets into town to buy his breakfast.

The deli has a blue sign above the door. It has a foreign flag that his mama told him was French. They sell smelly cheeses and baguettes and expensive coffee to the students who moved in around here a few years back. They sell olives in jars and lots of vegetables in garlic and oil.

The students didn't like Jose's. They bought their food in town. Now Jose's is gone and a French flag flies and they must be happy, they can buy their food right here.

He can hear yelping from up above. Best see to Jap, he thinks. 'Poor wee bastard.'

The dog's breathe

Jap's breath smells like tuna and old tyres. It smells like mustard gas and it stings his nose. But it is warm and Willem is wet and the wee dog is a comfort in the dying day. His claws are out but they are blunt, they tap at the laminate flooring and they tap at Willem's jeans.

'Calm down boy, it's only me,' he says, putting his hand out. Jap grabs his palm between his gums, he drags him around a little and makes him laugh. 'Aye, you mad wee bastard. You daft beggar.

'And where's mam at, boy?'

The flat is empty. The full moon shines in through a window, lighting it grey through the rain. But all else is still and empty. 'Mam?' he calls out, but nobody answers. The house is quiet. The quiet is in the shadows.

He hooks the lead onto Jap's collar, snapping the buckle shut. The rope coils, red and lively. The coil ends with a black handle, bound tight for the city streets. Jap runs in circles, he shakes the buckle and the lead. He jumps, he paws. He yips as Willem opens the door.

As soon as they're outside Jap squats and takes a shit. The shit coils like a snake, steaming in the cold. He pisses into the corner of a low wall outside their block, marking it as his own. He sniffs around. He gauges who else has been about that day. He growls, he pees again and then he is happy.

His bowels are empty and his territory is marked. The two of them can carry on their journey.

The rain lets up after a few minutes. It leaves the evening smelling clean. The world smells like springtime. Willem's legs are sore and his jeans still cling to him, but with Jap dragging at the lead there is no chance to limp. There is no need. Too much energy is at work. Jap is manic like a child and he catches Willem in his laughter. They cannot stop to talk to anyone, Jap won't let them and Willem starts to laugh. 'Good boy. Good boy,' he says, throwing a dog chew from his pocket. Jap catches it mid-flight and Willem fancies he can see a smile flash through the dog's eyes.

'Good boy.'

The rising sun

He doesn't see his mama that evening. He eats a quick supper of beans heated in the microwave. He eats sausages and eggs and mushrooms fried in oil. The oil spits and slithers. It picks out white spots on his forearms. His arms smell like burnt hair but he pays them no mind. He butters some white bread. It is as soft as pillows and he mops up the grease and the sauce. He chews noisily and licks his fingers and his eyes start to close.

In the morning he wakes up on the sofa. He was so tired he fell asleep almost as soon as he finished eating his supper. Now the plastic leather is sticky, he peels his cheek from its glaze. His plate from last night is on the floor. It has been licked clean and Jap snoozes at his feet with tomato sauce on his nose. He snores and the red sauce rises and falls. His ribs are showing and they rise and fall.

Willem smokes a quiet cigarette. He stands at the kitchen window. They are on the third floor and he watches the world breathing below him. A loose cable from a neighbour's satellite is blowing in the wind. It slaps against the wall opposite his window, thump, thump, thump.

He sips at a hot cup of tea and wonders where his mama is. He didn't hear her come in last night and nobody answers when he knocks on her door. 'Might be she's at a friend's house,' he mumbles into his tea. Maybe she's off with one of her men. It's about that time, he thinks. She goes off with one every couple of months. A few days here and there. But she always comes back to him, she always comes home. She will be home soon enough.

He doesn't know what to do with his day. He threads his arms into his work jacket, zipping it up to the collar. He wraps a rain coat over it, wedges his boots on and leaves the flat. As he opens the door he thinks twice. He picks up Jap's lead and whistles. The wee dog's nails rattle across the floor and the red coil is rough in Willem's hand. He clips it to his collar, he tickles his ears.

'Come on, boy,' he says.

His feet take him back towards the construction site. His mama told him to speak to Charlie or whoever else was in charge of the build. That's what he will do, no matter how long it takes him. He has the time. He has little else but time.

He enjoys watching Jap run through the long grass. When he first came to them Jap had white fur. Now it has started to turn a dirty yellow. As he runs his belly along the verges and through gorse and brambles his underside darkens. Dew and mud cling to his coat. His pads cake with mud and other dogs' shit. But his face his exhilarated. His tongue lolls out. He is idiotic in his glee. He barks, he whinnies.

When he first came to them he had white fur and a round, orange-brown spot on one flank. One of his mama's men called him Jap. He said he looked like the rising sun. 'The Japanese flag, lad,' he told Willem. Somehow the name stuck, it lasted longer than the man's affections. Now his spot blends with the rest of his fur. It is only visible up close. But Willem still runs after him shouting 'Jap, Jap! Good boy! Who's a good boy?'

He is a fit man, he is strong. Half a lifetime of hard labour have thickened the muscles in his legs and arms. They are cords bound tight, coiling tight like his mama's scar. He drags himself through this world, he dragged himself into this world. Yet despite his strength he is out of breath by the time the two of them crest the hill at the top of the park. Man and dog swell with tiredness. Their breath swells and drops, swells and drops. His cheeks are pink and sweat is running down his back.

He puts Jap on the lead for the last quarter hour walk to the site. It's through town, through the residential streets of the city's south side. He doesn't want Jap to get spooked. He doesn't want Jap to spook anyone else. 'Heel, boy,' he barks and Jap obeys, trotting happily by Willem's left ankle. He is tired on his little legs, tired and happy with his master's voice rising by his side. He nuzzles at Willem's calf from time to time. He will curl up and sleep when they get to the bench.

Three setting suns

'What breed is he?' the one eyed man asks Willem.

'Jack Russel cross.'

'Crossed with what?'

'Don't know. We never knew his parents.'

'Where did you get him?'

'Found him on a site. Half starved, poor beggar. Mam said I could keep him if I trained him up, so I took him to my uncle Nick. He was one of her fellas. She saw him for a long while. He worked on the races out past Renfrew. We trained Jap up real good.'

He splits a sausage roll with Jap. The little dog wolfs it down. He licks himself. He licks the mud from his paws and he licks greasy saliva from his gums. He curls up on Willem's work boots. He rests his head on one steel toe cap and falls asleep, his ribs moving peacefully.

Willem eats a bag of cheese and onion crisps, flecking his chin and chest with crumbs as he talks to the one eyed man. He counts the crumbs as the seconds pass and all the time the one eyed man is talking.

'You back for more then?' the old man greeted him when he first arrived.

'Aye. Mam says come. She says talk to Charlie or whoever else. I guessed I'd better wait 'til someone shows up, ask them what's going on.'

'Nobody's showing up, you daft beggar. This place is shut up.'

'Maybe. We'll see.'

Old men carrying cans of lager and bottles of cheap whisky come and go. They carry supermarket sandwiches and bars of chocolate. They sit and chat with him for a few minutes, sometimes more. They pet Jap, throw him some crumbs and wish them both well.

The one eyed man turns up periodically throughout the morning.

'Where do you keep going?' Willem asks him. The seconds are growing longer as the sun rises high.

'Business to attend to.'

'Oh.'

The one eyed man is right, nobody comes that day. Nobody comes the following day either and Willem is starting to wonder whether his mama was wrong. How can he get his old job back like this? But he has nothing else to do.

Three days he comes, three days he waits. It doesn't rain again like the first day, but the wind is up and he huddles close to Jap to keep himself warm.

He hasn't seen his mama since he got laid off. He worries, he tries to call her a few times from his bench. He has her number set on speed dial on his mobile. But it rings through to her voicemail every time. If she's off with a fella then it's longer than usual.

The daisy's heads

The one eyed man brings a friend along on the third day. They both appear not long after midday, ambling down the street arm in arm. The one eyed man's friend is about the same age as him. She is wearing a long, faded dress and a raincoat over a patched up denim jacket. She is carrying a bottle of Irn Bru in one hand and her grey hair is plastered tight against her skull. A couple of plastic carrier bags hang on the crook of her elbow, crinkling in the wind.

The one eyed man is carrying a bottle of rum. The rum catches the afternoon sun, it winks at Willem.

'Hey fella. Hey lad, here's someone I want you to meet. A special friend of mine.' He tells Willem that her name is Rosa. Short for Rosamund. Willem nods to them both, he says hello. He says pleased to meet you. Jap leaps to his feet, he sniffs around under Rosa's skirt. She giggles at him. She is a woman of sixty years and yet she laughs like a little girl. Her voice is high and hollow and Willem frowns, trying to make sense of it.

'Our laddie here is waiting for his old bosses to turn up. How many days is it now, Willie?'

'Three.'

'Patience of a saint, like I told you!' Rosa giggles again as the one eyed man pokes her in the ribs, tickling her. 'Here, Rosa, show Willie your wee scrap,' he tells her. She dumps her carrier bags on the bench next to Willem. She rummages inside, moving aside cartons and packets until she finds a little story cut from the morning's paper.

'I've been showing it to all the boys and girls,' she tells him. The one eyed man has black teeth and his gums are as red as Jap's. Rosa has large teeth like a horse. The front two are missing. The holes yawn, they suck and blow as she speaks.

She hands him the piece of paper. He can read well, but not quickly. Not quickly by other people's standards. Black text crowds around a central picture. The picture is of three daisies, close up, standing in a clump of grass. The flowers are deformed, stretched and distorted. A violent yellow maw distends on each head. The centre of the one closest to the lens is split into two. The two seed heads meet at a seam and bright petals cascade away from them.

'Fucked up, no?' She takes it back before he has had a chance to follow the article, but the one eyed man steps in. He knows the lad is dim. He thinks that Willem is thick. He thinks he is this lad's translator, articulating the world around him into an idiot's brogue.

'It's from Fukushima. That wee nuclear plant that blew up way back. All the flowers around it are getting all monged up by the radiation. No doubt the wee animals around it are mutating too.

'And think. Them cunts down in London put nuclear missiles just off our shores. Next thing you know the whole of fucking Scotland's going to be looking like this. It's a travesty. Fuckers.'

'Mm.' Willem just nods. It's all too fast for him.

On the other side of the street a couple of teenagers are skating past. One has a dark blue skateboard with white stripes. The other has a red one and keeps trying to flip it over as he speeds along. He flips it just outside the construction site. He doesn't quite make the jump. He falls, skinning his knee. His mate laughs and then he laughs. Willem imagines the two boys with inverted heads. With two heads instead of one. With gums as bloody as Jap's and holes in their teeth and yellow petals spilling down.

'Aye. Fucking travesty,' Willem idly agrees.

The buzz

A couple of hours later the clouds shift and sunshine hits him. He unzips his jacket, he pulls his hood down and sits back. 'Feel that, boy,' he says to Jap. 'Heaven's smiling.' It was something his mama told him one time and he's never forgotten. 'Heaven's smiling on us,' he repeats, scratching behind Jap's ears.

His pocket begins to vibrate. He always keeps his phone on silent. If a ringtone goes off he panics. He doesn't like the interruption. He doesn't like the aggression, the loud, fast world. Someone somewhere is saying, look at me! listen to me! give me your attention!

He doesn't want any part in that.

He didn't really want a phone but Charlie said he needed one so they could get hold of him. His mama said he needed one so she could get hold of him. He hopes that it's Charlie now. He thinks, he wonders. Charlie would say 'hey pal. Sorry about the mix up. Turns out we didn't want to lay you off. You and all the lads have your old jobs back. What's that? You're at the site? Good man, very productive. Give me a mo' and I'll be down to let you in.'

Or he hopes it's his mama telling him she's home safe. She's got the kettle on and she knows a fella who knows a fella who can give him a job. As he feels it buzzing in his pocket he fantasises that he is on his way home. Back to her warmth after a long day's work.

As he is running the conversations through his head the phone rings off. He does this too often. Too caught up, too slow. He fishes it out and looks at the screen. Missed call, withheld number. As he stares at the screen it changes, it lights up and the phones starts to buzz again. Incoming call, withheld number. He lets it buzz three times. He breathes deeply, he prepares himself. He squares his shoulders and taps to answer.

'Mm,' he says.

'Hello. Is that Mr. Gyle?'

'Mm.'

'Hello Mr Gyle–'

'Willie.'

'I beg your pardon?'

'Willie. People call me Willie. Even my mama.'

'Well, yes. Then. Willie. Hello Willie.'

'Hello.'

It is the Royal Infirmary. They say they have his mother in. She was admitted two days ago, unconscious and half frozen. She had alcohol poisoning and hypothermia setting in. They are trying to keep her stable and she just woke up. She asked for her son, she gave them his number and asked them to call him.

'Mm. Good.'

'Could you come to the hospital?'

'Mm.'

'As soon as possible.'

'Mm.' He hangs up. He yanks on the lead. Jap wakes up, he growls, he squawks and then he is on his feet. He has his master's voice in his ears and his tail starts to wag. 'Come on boy.' The Infirmary is only a bus ride away, he'll make it within the hour.

The dewdrops

The bus is late. An old woman tells him that there are works on the route. She is short, not even five foot if he is any judge. He looks down on her. She has a bald medallion in her crown. She is wearing a knitted cardigan and an open mac. She thinks he is an idiot, she speaks slowly so he can understand her. He stoops to receive her words, he nods as she annunciates.

Across the street a young man with wiry hair and glasses and a Kinks t-shirt is playing an acoustic guitar. He has his case open at his feet. People throw coins into his case as they pass him by. The sun is still shining brightly and it flashes as the coins tumble through the air. The notes sparkle from his strings. They shine brightly.

As he watches the young man playing Willem imagines that tiny dewdrops cling to his strings. Every time he plucks one of them the dewdrops shimmer, they dance a little along the length of the wire. They refract the light and add their own cadence to the music. As he strums a chord Willem imagines they all shed a little of themselves to mix together. They are all refracting, all dancing.

He watches the man twinkling his music for nearly half an hour before the bus arrives. The seats are all full and the driver is grumpy. Behind his plastic screen he grunts at the passengers.

'Does this bus go to the Infirmary?' Willem asks him.

'Aye.'

'How long will it take?'

'In this traffic, who bloody knows?'

He has taken this bus before. He has done this exact journey before. But the world has taught him to be careful, to make sure. It has taught him to double check everything. Mistakes happen so often in his life when he doesn't follow this wisdom that all sorts can go wrong. Instead, he is tedious and thorough. He is careful.

'You bringing that fellow on board?' The driver looks down at Jap, frowning.

'Aye. But he's a good boy. I'll keep him quiet.'

'Be sure you do.'

'How much for a ticket?'

'One fifty sonny.'

He knows the price already. But before he digs his change out of his pocket he wants to hear those words from the driver's mouth. Behind him people are tutting. They have waited for long enough this day. They want to be on their way. 'Sorry, sorry,' he mumbles as he counts out his coins. He drops them into the little plastic box and tears off his ticket.

'Thank you, thanks, ta.' And he shuffles to the staircase, his face burning red. He swings himself upstairs to find somewhere to stand, gripping the bannister to lever himself upwards.

The wild horses

At the hospital a little boy is staring at him. He is three years old with dark curls and chubby cheeks and he is shaking a little rattle. The rattle is annoying the other people in the waiting room but the boy giggles and Willem smiles. The rattle is brightly coloured in yellow and red. He shakes in it threes, jangling and drawing glares.

Willem likes it. After a while the repetition soothes him, he nods his head and rests his chin against his chest. The room grows faint, his mother's eyes stare at him and he finds peace.

They told him to wait here. They told him a doctor would come to see him shortly. 'Where's my mam?' he wanted to know. But they just told him to take a seat. They repeated that a doctor would come, if only he could be patient.

'We're very busy today, I'm afraid,' they told him. He could see they were telling the truth. Everybody was rushing around in scrubs, pacing the corridors and wards with charts in their hands and tired frowns creasing their foreheads.

'When was the last time you slept?' he asked one of the nurses. She giggled and told him not to worry. She had been on for four days straight, twelve hour shifts each time. But she works fourteen hours, sometimes more. There is always work to be done.

'But I'm off the next two days, sweetie.'

'Will you sleep then?'

'Sleep? Wild horses won't be able to wake me!'

'Does that mean yes?'

She giggled again. 'Yes, it means yes.'

'Good. You look tired.'

'Hush, now! Are my bags that big? You'll make a girl paranoid.'

'I'm sorry.' She giggled some more and he left her to work. He found this spot opposite the child's rattle and began to drool on his chest.

The seagull

Twenty minutes later he awakes with a start. 'Welcome back to the land of the living,' an old man laughs. Willem smiles awkwardly and looks around the room. The television in the corner is flashing. It is on mute but the image shows a singer. He never follows music, all that noise is too much. But he likes the look of this one. She is standing at the prow of a ship. Her skirt is short, it rides up. Her legs are tanned and he thinks she looks pretty. A seagull flashes above the water, calling out. It flies close to the camera, the camera zooms in on its face. Its wings flash, it ducks and dives into the water. 'She's an American girl,' Willem mumbles to himself. He has heard that American girls are prettier than Scottish girls. He has heard that America is meant to be the land of freedom. That would be nice, he thinks.

He imagines the open prairies he used to watch in cowboy movies. Clint Eastwood riding across miles of empty grassland, driving cattle and horses. In his mind there are a thousand acres of freedom for every man. He closes his eyes and imagines Clint Eastwood swimming through the sea, climbing into the boat and kissing the American singer. The freedom of the fields calls to him. The emptiness soothes him.

'Mr Gyle?' A voice crackles, it belongs to a small woman with dark skin and friendly eyes.

'It's Willie. I told the woman who called me on the phone.'

'OK. Willie. I'm Doctor Kaur. Would you come with me, please?'

'Are you taking me to my mam?' His hands fidget and he stands up, towering over the doctor.

'In a little while, if that's what you would like. But first, if you could come with me I would very much like to have a chat.'

She leads him into a little office. She takes a chair behind a short, wooden desk and asks him to sit opposite her. When he is seated she leans forwards and tells him that his mama in dead. She died not long after the receptionist called him. The chairs in the office are brown veneer with stuffed green seat covers. The cover on his is split and yellow foam is poking out. He pulls at it, twisting a clump between his forefinger and thumb.

Dr Kaur says that an ambulance was called and his mama was admitted with alcohol poisoning. She had hypothermia from being outside in the cold. Does he remember all that rain the other day? She was soaked by it. She was paralytic. That means drunk, she tells him. Very drunk. They revived her this morning, but in the end she suffered a seizure. Dr Kaur wants to know if there is a history of epilepsy in the family.

He doesn't know. He doesn't know what it is.

She leads him out of the office. He feels sick. His eyes are hot and his stomach rumbles. It ties itself up. His eyes sting, his throat stings. Dr Kaur takes him through a corridor. She draws back a curtain and his mama stares up at him. Her blue eyes are tinged with red and yellow. Yellow around the edges, red blood vessels burst like a spider's web.

'I'm very sorry Willem. Just for our paperwork, could you confirm that this is your mother?'

'Aye. That's mam.' He turns around and walks out of the hospital. Jap is outside, tied to a bike rack. He will need feeding soon.

The starlings

For the past couple of weeks Willem has awoken every morning unsure what the day would bring. Sometimes the sun would remain wan and watery for hours, barely heating the ground, barely lighting the roads. Sometimes a chill would pervade, catching your throat. He has seen too much of the rain and the mist. The coughing on the pavements and in the shops summons them too often, soaking man and beast.

Other mornings Willem would wake to a rosy dawn, a dawn whose finger tips have beckoned him close, keeping him warm. On these days the scents of cut grass and new flowers on the breeze has been a balm. On these days his breath has grown thick with hay fever and the call to the wild.

But the uncertainty has been there, always. Will the long march to summer begin today, or is it yet another false start? This city will always know false starts.

And then the starlings came, as they do every year. As they have done since he was a child, before the world began to spin so fast. A week ago the first of them arrived. A week ago people's hearts were made light. Everybody knows that when the starlings pass by it is as sure a sign as god can give that springtime has come in earnest.

'What are you talking about, you div?' they asked him at work when he mentioned them. 'What the fuck's a starling? And who fucking cares?'

He pointed to the sky, mute. Overhead a hundred starlings swirled as one. They were graceful and lithe and their wings spoke of the summer to come. 'It's going to be a good one,' he said. 'Sunny and hot.'

'Aye, they're pretty enough. But you're still a fucking queer, Willie,' Charlie said.

Willem left for work earlier than usual the morning they arrived. The sun wasn't up yet, but the shadows above were weaving. 'They are here,' he said. He smiled and closed his eyes.

'What in god's name are you doing?' his mama shouted as he roused himself, as he clattered about in the kitchen. 'It's not yet five o'clock!' She was still sleepy. She was always sleepy. Her voice was thick when he went into her room. Her t-shirt pushed against her heavy breasts, bare underneath. Two angry red blotches stood out on her cheeks, bright against pale skin. Broken vessels spilling blood beneath, rosy as the starlings swirled.

'But look at them, mam!' he laughed. 'Look at them! Spring is here, the starlings have come. It's time to wake up!'

These are the thoughts which chase him as he leaves the hospital.

The birds have always been his friends. He likes to sit and throw crumbs for them. He likes to talk to them without them answering, free of confusion. 'Willem, you stupid wanker!' She laughs. Her laughter is a sigh of longest suffering. Huffing, she sinks back down and rolls over. She grunts as he puts a cup of tea by her bed. The thick duvet wraps her like a shroud. Only her hair is visible above her shroud, streaked with white and black and wiry like a grandmother's. But she smiles beneath her duvet, she is well cared for. 'You're a good lad,' she mumbles under her breath.

His head spins and he has to sit down on a low wall. Jap sniffs at his hand. He licks Willem's fingers. Willem feels old, like an old man with crumbling bones. The starlings turn with the breeze. They dance, first this way, then that, always in motion. Are they action or reaction? As he watches them dancing so far above he doesn't know the difference. He realises that he doesn't care. All he needs to know is that they are there. There is motion in the world today.

'Is that enough?' he asks. He asks his hands, clapped over his face. He asks Jap, sitting at his feet. The little dog looks up at him with doe eyes. He knows that something is wrong. He knows his master is hurting. But he can do nothing. He is nothing.

'Boy, you are everything,' Willem says, scratching Jap's ears. 'You and me now, pal.'

'It is a migration,' one of his mama's blokes told him when he was young.

'What does that mean?'

'These birds head south during the winter to where it's warmer. That way they won't freeze their wee arses off. But down south it's far too hot for them during the summer, so in the springtime they head back up north to mate and build nests.'

'What, every year?'

'Of course every year! The turning of the seasons doesn't change, does it? No, every winter as we turn up our radiators they fly south. Every summer while we sit in the shade they come back.'

'Which one is home?'

'What do you mean, lad?'

'Is the south home or is the north home? Are they on holiday in the summer or the winter?'

'Well I don't bloody know, do I?'

For a long time Willem didn't believe him. He thought it was one of his fairy stories. One of his jokes. He was around for a while and he always had his little jokes.

Willem asked his mother and she said that yes, it was true. But she must be in on it! He asked his pal, who also thought it was made up and teased. He laughed at Willem for even contemplating the truth of the idea. Finally he asked one of the teachers at school.

'Why yes indeed, by god's will they migrate every year.'

And now by god's will they dance the dance of life in the heavens above.

The long ride

He sits on the bus home for an age. The roads are quiet now. The rush hour came and went. One side of his face is glued to the window. The evening's cold moisture smears the bones of his cheek. Now the sky is turning dark and the street lights flash by outside the window. They glow orange and pale in the twilight. They march past his window. They march across his irises, blinking.

It is warm enough but it is not his bus. It does not go to his mother's house, but why would it? There is nothing there but two cold beds, two sets of cold memories. It will take him miles away, he doesn't know where. He doesn't know what route the bus takes, he doesn't know where it goes. But it started to rain while he sat on the wall watching the birds fly and he couldn't sit there all night.

Jap sits at his feet, eyeing him.

'Last stop pal!' the driver shouts up the stairs. Jap jumps to his feet with a yowl. The driver's voice is deep. It is a baritone, resonant with whisky after hours and a lifetime of fags. There is laughter and forgetting in his voice, and he uses it well. 'All change!' Willem's hands are shaking as he stands. His legs are weak. They clatter as he walks down the stairs, he crashes into the wall at the bottom. His elbow hurts, his shoulder hurts.

'Too much of a good thing, eh pal?' The driver is out of his cubicle, patting his jacket. He takes out a cigarette packet. He takes out a fag out and leaves the bus. He chuckles at his joke, his baritone hums in his throat. There is the laughter, there is the forgetting.

Trees line the street. There are no houses, no windows with their comforting lights. There is nothing but bushes and branches.

'Where am I?' he asks the driver.

'Wow, must have been one hell of a good day. Just outside Ratho.'

'How far to town?'

'Ten miles, I think. Maybe fifteen. Depends where you're going.'

'Leith.'

'Shit. The next bus to Princes' Street is in half an hour. Then you'll be wanting-'

'No.' He walks away from the driver. He can see the canal in the distance, glinting in the moonlight. He can see it snaking past the road. It will take him home. The water of Leith always runs true. An old man in the neighbourhood used to say that. It was one of his favourite things to say.

The dead man's wings

An owl glides over the water. The last owl in Leith died a long time ago. The same old man told him that as well. The owl's reflection swoops and dives, it dips its beak into the air. It catches a dark lump of meat. The meat wriggles in its mouth. There is a quiet crack and it lies still. It is dead with a whimper.

The last owl in Leith sat on the old man's shelf. His brother stuffed it. He was an animal stuffer by trade. 'A taxidermist, lad,' the old man told him. His brother gave it to the old man as a gift one Christmas. He said, 'here brother, the last fucker.' Since they were lads they both feared the owls, 'but only we, god and the devil know why.'

This owl is from a different world, he thinks. It disappears into the shadows, into the boughs. Where does it rest during the day? He wonders this, he wonders about the wriggling meat, he wonders how many fish swim through the canal. How many fish wriggle and crack every day.

One day two policemen came to the old man's house. Willem's mama was dusting the fireplace, she was dusting the owl's wings. She was dusting its beak and Willem was watching her from the corner when the pigs came in. They told his mama to get away from it, they said they had to take it with them. They took the owl and they took the old man.

'I'm not in any trouble, lad. They just want to chat,' the old man told Willem. He winked as they slipped the cuffs on his wrists. They put him in a white car, they drove off and left the house open. His mama watched with a cloth in her hand. These days the last owl in Leith is in a museum, it stands still and strong and rests its wings all day and all night.

'They busted him for trafficking,' they all said. 'That owl's arse was filled with brown.'

The old man died in prison, free from the birds.

Willem scuffs his heels. He kicks a pebble into the pond. He listens to its splash, he watches its ripples spreading outwards. They are faint in the dark and he has to squint to see the last of them. The wind starts to blow and bright lights are dive bombing overhead. They are planes from all over the world folding their wings, resting for the night in the city's airport way out on his left.

Bollocks, he thinks and quickens his pace. Jap trots along, panting.

'It's all bollocks, pal.'

The alley's siren

He can hear a low screeching from a back alley. The screech sounds inhuman. More than human, less than human. Jap perks his ears up. They have walked ten miles and his legs are tired. His front poor on his left side is limping, but the screech revives him. It brings him back to the world, he is a hunter once again.

Willem ducks into the alley to look for the screech's mouth as another hits the walls. A she-cat darts from the far end of the alleyway. She is rangy, her thick yellowing fur is plastered against wire. She is muscle without fat. Nothing more is needed, nothing more could be. A tom jumps down in front of her, cutting her off. Two more appear from the shadows, three more from the rear. These three have been chasing her and now she is cut off.

The cats circle as Willem watches. The noose tightens. He has to hold the leash tight in his fist. Jap's hackles are pricking, he is a hunter and he wants to join the game. They have walked ten miles and his legs are tired but his nose twitches as first blood is promised.

With his free hand Willem pulls out a cigarette, patting it between moist lips. His lighter flares, darting the walls with light. He uses his good lighter today. It is a special day, a day for sorrow. Its flame glows bright within these close walls. His smoke disappears quickly. The air is thicker than smoke, it is stronger. The smoke strips his tongue of moisture. It replaces it with sand. The sand is rough, acrid. The heat makes his nose sting, the tiny hairs inside his nostrils curl.

One of the toms pounces. Its claws extend. That screech lets loose again, wailing, but the air is thick enough to take it in. The two cats rut and the screech dies. The tom rises, the prowlers at the edge rise. The female is passive now. She knows when she is beaten.

A few of the toms climb the walls on either side of the alley. They use window ledges, bins, heaps of rubbish. They are all perching, watching, waiting their turn. One of the cats is slightly higher. He picks his way through the over-hanging cornices, delicately placing one foot in front of the other. His fur is brown, mangy. Brown as Jap's but with no beauty. His claws are white, his eyes are green. They flash, his claws and eyes.

A hollow in the damp of one ledge houses some bees. They crawl about, still young in the springtime. The tom's claws and eyes flash as he tears through the hive, falling now.

The first few bees are a low commotion, a low hum. They attach themselves to the fallen cat. They crawl over him. They sting. The pain makes the tom's eyes bulge. Green eyes grow red and his hair stands on end. They are swallowed in his hair, lost as they dig deep. His teeth flash. His head spins. He fastens his jaw over one spot, then another. He spits dead bees. He spits blood as his gums swell. They are raw and his skin is raw and he paints great, panicked circles in the dirty ground as he runs around. He tries to outrun them but their stings are already set.

The cat's claws dig deep and more bees flow through the rent in their hive. The lintel is rotten. It is crumbling and the wood is black. It is a good spot for them to have built and now they come rushing out to defend their home. Far overhead the starlings billow and down here the bees billow. Their dance chews the thick air.

Other cats start to grind their fur through their teeth. They spit bees, they spit blood. Willem backs away. The hair at the top of his spine is tingling. It stands on end. He imagines the bees turning on him, digging their stings in. He imagines his gums bloody, his lips swollen.

He turns to leave as the cats flee. Jap is going mad. He runs about Willem's ankles, whining at the commotion. Some of the cats rush past his ankles, brushing his boots with fur and dirt. Jap lashes out at them, biting chunks of fur before Willem heaves on the lead and pulls him away.

Some of the cats rush back the other way, hopping over walls. The lone female is limping badly. There is blood trickling under her tail from the tom's penetration. She cannot move fast enough and the cloud descends, the air is thick. She withers beneath them. As she opens her mouth to yelp it fills with bees. Her lips swell and she spits blood and screams into the night. As she lays her head in the dirt the blood trickles from her lips, from her gums and her eyes, from beneath her tail.

Willem rushes away. The night is too dark, the air too thick.

Part II:

Rough sleep and wakefulness

The spider's veins

He got to the top of Easter Road and couldn't go any further. He was tired. He had walked too many miles, too many hours. But he was tired in his heart as well, his chest was heavy and his belly dragged. He didn't have the strength in his heart to look at familiar faces. The streets his mama knew and walked so often were down that way and his feet couldn't take him there. So he looked elsewhere, he spent the night under a bench, freezing in the night's solitude.

Just now a watery sun has risen and he is coming around. It takes him a while, longer than usual. Usually he is up and about straight away. 'With the energy of a little boy,' he mama says.

Said.

But now his joints need time to revive. His belly needs time and his heart beats too faintly.

A spider has knitted its webs between the seat's slats. They puff above his head, in as he inhales, out as he exhales. A couple of bugs have been caught and the spider has wrapped them tightly in its net. It scuttles back and forth, excited by its captives. Jap is nuzzled against his chest. In his sleep his ears are twitching, his paws are groping. His warmth is Willem's warmth. They clung together last night in the damp. The cling together now in the damp.

The spider threads another silk cord between the slats. It is growing its little empire, spurred by its successes. The silk catches between the damp planks of wood and the spider works its way down. Down to Willem, to Jap. They are curled in a ball and the web works its way into Willem's body. Through the joints in his shoulders, through his numb fingertips. It criss-crosses his bones, striating them, splitting them. It holds together the cracks even as it forces them to grow wider.

He cannot move, he cannot stand. His muscles are dead with cold, his brain is dead with cold. And his heart isn't strong enough.

Mama, mama... Finally he rolls onto one side. He rocks himself to his left, he rolls over Jap and makes him whine. Jap leaps to his feet, frantic, under attack and on his guard. But he sees Willem and calms down. He starts to lick his face. He licks the spider's net away, his breath blows the cobwebs out. Willem's cold hands search out the wooden slats. He hauls himself out from under the bench, he hauls himself to his feet. He stands still, rocking slightly. Dizzy with the cold, with hunger.

A small café is open across the street. Light spills out. The smells and sounds of warm food spill out. He lets Jap take a shit under the bench, totters over and shoulders through the glass door. A small queue holds him back for a few minutes. He basks in the heat, he basks in the glow of the grills, of the coffee machines and the quiet chatter of breakfast. A girl behind the counter serves him when the queue dissipates. She asks him how she can help him and he orders two bacon rolls and a cup of tea.

'To eat in or take away?'

'In.'

'Sir?'

'In.'

'Could you wait one minute please, sir?' The girl is young, she is pretty. Her hair red, she has it tied back and her eyes shine. But she is frowning, she calls over her manager. He is a pot-bellied man with slicked hair and the two whisper for a second. His jowls wobble, his frown joins hers.

'I'm sorry, sir,' the manager says. His voice is slick. His hands and eyes are slick. 'We're only doing take out at the moment.'

But there are people sitting all around him. Students and professionals and mothers with their prams. There are a couple of tables free and he points these out. 'I'm sorry, sir. Take out only. But please allow me to give you the tea on the house.'

'Aye,' he nods. They saw him climbing out from under the bench. They can see the spider's webs in his joints. He takes a little brown bag with his rolls. He takes his tea in a paper cup. He whistles under his breath for Jap to follow and they both totter back to his bench. It smells from Jap's shit but Willem is hungry and he can't wait to find somewhere else to sit.

'Here, boy,' he mumbles, throwing half of one of the rolls on the floor. He tosses some extra bacon and tucks into the rest, warming himself from his belly outwards.

The lizard's tongue

He only has a little change in his pocket. The street is wide and lots of cars flash past. In the middle of the road and at either side sit islands of grass. At the far end a well-manicured roundabout displays a riot of flowers. As he walks along the sun climbs high and the change jingles in his pocket. That won't last me long, he thinks. He looks around, he looks out for a cash point. There is one close by, shielded in a deep hole in the wall of a bank.

Most of his money is at home. Charlie used to give him half of his wages as cash so the government wouldn't take too much of it. He stuffed all of the cash in a sock and hid it under his mattress. Nobody can take it, he thinks. Nobody knows it is there. But he still has a few hundred in the bank. He inserts his card and thinks for a minute to remember his PIN. He thinks too long and the machine spits his card back out.

It is a lizard poking its tongue, he thinks. He thinks some more until he remembers the number, inserts his card and takes a couple of hundred out. He can buy himself some lunch. He can buy a tin of dog food for Jap. He can get a sleeping bag so that he won't get so cold at night. He can buy himself a trashy newspaper and look at the naughty pictures.

'That'll keep us warm, Jap,' he says.

There is a McDonald's nearby. There are benches outside so he ties Jap to one. 'I'll be back in a moment, boy,' he says, fishing in his pocket. Five pounds come out in change as he pushes the door open.

'A meal deal. Large. Coke please.' A queue forms behind him as he waits. A father with two young children, an old couple in sweatshirts, a clutch of teenage girls.

'Excuse me, pal. Oi, move over.' He has been standing watching their reflections in a laminate poster. Now they are harassing him, pushing him out of the way so they can place their orders.

'Here you go love,' the woman behind the counter passes him a tray holding his order. He says 'ta,' his shoulders slump as he pushes his great bulk through the small crowd. He doesn't meet their eyes, he looks at his feet as they shuffle along. A sign by the door says that cleaning is in progress, he slips a little on the damp floor. But Jap is pleased to see him, he barks. He sniffs the tray. He runs in circles with his tongue and tail wagging.

The damp hole

The sun climbs and falls and he has been on the streets for a few days. The wide sky shelters him. He roams about, staying under different benches, in different dark corners. That first day he bought himself a sleeping bag from Argos for thirty nine ninety nine. He bought himself an extra hoody and some clean underwear.

He bought two dog bowls from the pound store, one plastic for food and one tin for water. He also bought some tins of dog food and a packet of treats. He has been living on sandwiches in plastic containers from supermarkets, fast food and fizzy drinks from kebab shops and cans of lager to help him sleep. He moves on to spirits, fighting the cold hours with a thick head and a warm belly.

The second morning he woke almost as cold as the first. He bought his breakfast from a garage. He bought a stack of the day's papers. He removed the pages with naughty pictures and used the rest as bedding.

Every time he closes his eyes he can see the owl's reflection diving for meat. He sees his mother's eyes yellow and red, staring into nothing. He sees the child's rattle shaking in threes. He takes a sip of vodka and the images lose their colour. The traffic loses its noise.

The other roamers try to talk to him. They try to share his drinks and his memories, but he evades them. He sits quietly with Jap. He sleeps long hours, rising to the site of people's ankles charging past his bedding. On the fifth day he finds himself on Easter Road, half a mile from his mama's flat. He beds down under a poplar. He wakes to the sound of Jap dancing with Josef the Pole's bitch. A young girl is walking her and she smiles at Willem before hurrying along.

That afternoon he wanders past his mama's flat. The lights are on and a couple of people are outlined in the windows. Their shadows curve and grimace and Willem panics. He runs, his feet moving faster than his heart. Jap jogs along next to him. He thinks it's all a game as Willem hides under his poplar, burrowing down. He swigs whiskey and smokes fags while his heart beats hard.

After a while his heart calms. After a while the whiskey swamps him and he manages to sleep a little. As he nods off he watches the eyes and the rattle and the owl diving down at him. They appear from behind the drink, from behind a thick curtain. 'The mist came back, boy,' he mutters as he dreams.

The dust sheets

As the sun sets a pair of policemen move him on. 'You can't sleep there, sir,' they tell him. They are wearing windcheaters and thick boots. One of them loiters in the back, the other approaches Willem.

'Where can I sleep?'

'Have you a home to go to?'

'I don't know.'

'Sorry, sir. You will have to move along, though.'

He gathers his things. He rolls his sleeping bag under one arm and stuffs his newspapers away. Jap's bowls are in another bag along with half a tin of food and his collar. The grass is damp, the street glimmers. 'That's it sir, have a good night now,' the policeman says, nodding as Willem retreats.

Willem stumbles a little as the pavement turns. It is slick with water and his feet are reflected in puddles. They stand upside down, his ankles facing the ground, the shadows cutting them off. The shadows chase him and he embraces them, he lurks in an alleyway. He watches the two policemen recede. It starts to rain again and they disappear into the drizzle. He watches his mama's flat. The moon rises high, the wind grows colder. Drunk old men and young students stagger along and he hides. He pulls out his sleeping bag and wraps himself up. He squats down onto his haunches and hugs Jap close.

The lights flicker out in his mama's flat and two men leave. Their outlines don't contort anymore, they stay close and small in the rain. They carry clipboards, sheltered under the fronts of their leather jackets. They have plastic pens in their shirt pockets and the looks of men who are pleased with their lives. They laugh as they climb into a car and disappear into the drizzle.

Willem stands up. He shakes his sleeping bag off, ties Jap's lead to a drainpipe and jogs across the road. His key lets him into the stairwell but his mama's locks have been changed. He pulls his own shadow in, he shrinks into himself and wonders what to do next.

There is a low wall around the back, a trellis and a window that his mama always leaves unlocked for him. She leaves it for when he forgets his keys and she's out at work or with one of her fellas. He has used it so many times in his life that his muscles instinctively carry him along. He jumps down the stairway, creeps around to the back, steps onto the wall and hauls himself through some ivy. He dragged himself into this world, he drags himself upwards, hand over hand over hand.

The window's lock has been replaced. It is sealed tight and he can't open it. There is a loose brick in the wall and he uses it to hack away at the top of the plastic frame. He prises the bolt off, he pulls the window open and falls inside.

The furniture has all been moved. The sofa and the armchairs are stacked against one wall. The television and the PC are gone, the dining room table has been taken apart. He walks into his bedroom and finds it empty. His bed is stripped, his wardrobe and chest of drawers are empty. He switches the light on. There is a new lampshade over the bulb, still in its plastic wrapping. His posters are gone, there are light patches on the walls where they used to be.

He switches on the lounge lights. There are new shades in here as well and in the light Willem can see that everything is covered in dust sheets. As he lifts the corner of one to look underneath footsteps hammer up the stairwell. A shaking hand manages to get a key in the lock and the door bursts open. He falls to the floor. The carpet grazes his cheek as he lands. It smells of industrial cleaner and it stings his raw face.

The two men in leather jackets rush into the room. They haul him back up to his feet. One of them holds his arms behind his back as the other punches him in the stomach.

His ribs crackle, he can taste iron as he spits blood and another couple of blows are landed.

'Who the fuck are you, skag head? What the fuck are you doing here? Cunt, fucking cunt!' Each word is a punch, each word hurts him and he starts to scream. It's a hoarse keening, whining through the blows. But he stays on his feet. He can hear Jap barking at him from far away. The punches lose their power, they stop. His attacker is blowing hard, gasping for breath. He is smaller than Willem, he is less fit. He tires of punching him before Willem's body breaks.

'Get this fucker out of here, call them pigs back,' he pants. They handle him, they push him out of his mama's flat and into the stairwell. The rubber floor squeaks under his boots as they drag him. They pull him down the stairs, bouncing him off the walls. He hits the back of his head as they turn, his stomach lurches. Cold air hits him, the door is open and they fling him to the grass. It is damp, it seeps behind his eyes, it stops his lungs and his throat burns hot.

'Not quite what I meant when I told you to move on, sir,' the policeman says when the world stops spinning. His colleague is writing in a small notebook. The walkie talkie on his lapel is buzzing and he is buzzing back. 'Easy boys, we've got him,' the policeman carries on and the pincer grips slacken. Willem is on his knees, looking up into the policeman's face.

'Reasonable force, guv. It's our prerogative.'

'Aye, but enough now. We've got him.' The policeman slips his arm around Willem's. He helps him to his feet, he holds him firm. Willem shifts his footing a little and it hurts his shoulder.

'Take a seat, sir,' the policeman says, putting Willem on the low wall in front of the block. 'Can you tell me what you were doing in that flat?'

'Looking.'

'What for?'

'My stuff. Money.'

'Why would your stuff be in there, sir?'

'It's mam's house. It's my house.'

One of the men in leather jackets chips in. 'That house is unoccupied. The previous tenant died last week and the owner has employed our company to clear it out. She was behind on rent, we've been brought in for remuneration. This man's got no business in there.'

'Where is you mother now, sir? Is this true?' the policeman asks Willem. The questions rattle, they made him sick.

'Don't know.' He doesn't. He hasn't spoken to anyone since he saw her body. They said they would call to make arrangements but he hasn't charged his phone in a week. The doctor with the dark skin and big eyes gave him the card for a funeral director but he threw it away.

'Do you have anyone else? Anywhere else to go?'

'Just me and Jap.'

'Jap?'

'My dog.' He nods at the alleyway and the other policeman walks over there. He comes back a few seconds later with Jap on his lead. The little dog is running in tight little circles, his eyes are wide with excitement. The policeman buzzes his walkie talkie again and ties Jap's lead to a lamppost.

'My money. It's in a sock, under my mattress.' The men in leather jackets look at their shoes. They say there is no way of knowing if this man is telling the truth. They say they cleared the place out and had it cleaned as per their instructions.

The policeman turns his back on the men. He looks down at Willem, sitting on his low wall. His mouth is moving but Willem isn't listening. Jap looks confused, his ears are flat against his skull and his eyes are showing white. Willem wants to pet him, to tell him it's OK, it'll just be them again soon enough. But the police are in the way, he can't get through.

Jap

'Sir. Sir, are you listening? Do you understand?' Willem nods as a van pulls up. Two more officers get out. They are wearing slightly different uniforms. One is a woman. She is pretty, with glasses and a round face and a blonde ponytail. Her navy jumper doesn't hide her breasts. They are large, they catch the street light and push upwards.

'This him?' she asks in a friendly voice. It is a sing song and she smiles at them all in turn.

'Aye,' the policeman with the walkie talkie says. 'He belongs to this gentleman. He was tied up in the alley over there.'

'Nay bother, we've got it.' She takes a biscuit from her pocket. She lets Jap eat it out of her hand. She unties his lead as the van driver opens the back doors. There are cages bolted to the walls of the van and she leads Jap into one. She turns a handle and a dull clunk sounds as the lock fastens.

'No,' Willem says.

'Sir?'

'No.' He is on his feet, he walks forwards. He is the largest man there and the policeman steps out of his way.

'Sir, you need to sit down.'

'No.'

'Just while we assess the situation-'

'No.'

He is moving towards the van and the walkie talkies are buzzing and everything around him is buzzing. The rattling is back, it hums through his feet and through his hands. A couple of voices glide through the dark street, angry in their tone. Footsteps clatter, car doors click and slam and the walkie talkies jabber away. A couple of pairs of hands grab him but he shrugs and people tumble to the ground. He can hear Jap whining, barking and he reaches the van doors. He pulls but nothing happens, they are locked tightly.

'Sir, come away from the van.'

'No.'

The handle bends slightly as two policemen flank him and grab him under his armpits. As their grips tighten on him he lets go of the handle and turns. He waves his arms. He is swatting at flies. One of the officers falls to the pavement, the other crashes into the van. The van rocks and Jap's barking grows louder. All along the street lights are flickering on, noses are being pressed to glass. The rain is still falling but it seems to Willem to part like a curtain. It parts and leaves him standing in a spotlight, with all these people watching him. People he knows, people he has always known are staring at him.

He pins one of the policemen to the van. He punches him with his other hand. Teeth crack and blood spurts from his mouth. The teeth fall, pearly white surrounded by the red blood. The rain washes them clean when they hit the floor. The rain washes Willem's fist clean as it falls to his side.

'Willem, lad!' An old man is shouting from high up. It's Old Jack, the hippie, the rocker with the dark spaces between his teeth. He's in his bedroom on the third floor, across the street. He is leaning out of his window, gesturing. Someone shouts from up above, the floor above his mama's flat. 'Willem, fucks sake!' It's Frankie, ginger bearded Frankie who used to give him shiny fifty pence pieces when he was a lad. Frankie who was always singing *Daisy, Daisy, give me your answer do, I'm half crazy...* 'Willem. Put that poor bastard down and run.'

'But they've got Jap.'

'Your dog will be fine, lad. Run.'

Willem drops the policeman. He brings his knee up twice, cracking into ribs and groin. He barges the two men in leather jackets out of his way and breaks into a run. He heads north along Easter Road. Behind him blue sirens wail into the night. They scream at him. Tyres screech. A door opens to his left.

'Willie! Get your arse in here.'

Charley is holding her door open, her bairn under one arm. Willem bowls through the door, he runs through her hallway with feet slapping hard and crashes into the kitchen. Cigarette smoke is pooling on the ceiling. Half a fag is smoking in the ashtray and the curtains are closed.

'Wait there, Willie.' But he won't wait. He can't wait. The world is spinning too fast. He kicks the kitchen door, splintering the lock.

'Oh, you bastard, that's-'

But he is gone, he flies through. Into her little garden, over the wall at the end and into the alley out back.

The night is dark. The shadows are wide and deep and long and as he runs into them he can feel himself becoming invisible. He weaves through the warren, he leaps and he crawls and at one point he even throws up. Chunks of half-digested burger swim in whiskey at his feet, strands sway from his mouth. But he

cannot rest, he cannot stay still. He runs and he runs and the
shadows grow deep, they drag him in.

The eyes at dawn

The orange tent covers a hole, it blocks Willem's view.
Steam escapes from behind it. Big engines with pistons and
gears are waking. The tent flap is open and a man is standing in it, blocking the hole. He is smoking a thinly rolled
cigarette. He is wearing black overalls with yellow flashes
and a hard hat as orange as the tent.

He holds his cigarette in one hand. In the other he
holds a coffee cup. His face sways in the vapours from both,
the smoke and the steam mixing. Only his eyes are visible
through the cloud. They watch Willem approach, they watch
his back as he passes.

The street has been stripped bare. It is contained behind
high wire fences. A wide patch has been rolled up, almost as
wide as the road itself. A two inch depression is left behind,
steaming. The steam sways through the site and a man in a
big machine is getting ready to sow tarmac, to sow his crops.
His eyes also follow Willem. They watch him stagger, they
watch his dirty coat and his ripped jeans.

They must be the last work crew left in Edinburgh, he
thinks.

Willem walks fifty yards and turns around. He glances
back furtively. The men have stopped watching him now,
they have begun their day's labours. Only the man in the
black overalls with the yellow flashes looks his way. He drags
on his cigarette and his face sways and his eyes gleam.

Willem puts his hands in his pockets. He left his sleeping bag in the alleyway. He left his bag of newspapers and

his half-drunk bottle of whiskey. He left his clean underwear and his extra hoody. He has a few greasy notes in his wallet, he has a few old coins in his pockets. He has his card and there is some money in his account.

There are allotments on the other side of the street. He leaps the fence and steals some tomatoes for his breakfast. He breaks into a greenhouse and steals some newspaper from a shelf. He takes a bottle of water and a cucumber growing with a glass jar around its length. The workman watches him hop the fence, he watches him come out again.

Willem walks quickly, even now. Even with no energy his feet continue to stomp. Even with his bones frozen his muscles carry on.

A few hundred yards later he hops a gate into a small park. He sits on the path and eats his cucumber, he eats his tomatoes and downs the water in one gulp. The gulp hurts, it bruises his throat. It bloats and knocks hard down his gullet. But his stomach feels better now, his mouth isn't dry anymore.

A bush rustles opposite him. It has pretty flowers. The flowers glisten, they are covered in dew. A pair of beetle black eyes stair out from the shadows. He jumps to his feet, his heart races and he runs away. The park is not large, houses surround it on all sides. He runs to the far end, stops and turns. A fox has emerged from the bushes, it watches him placidly.

The world is interrupting the city. Its animals and its bushes are cracking through the paving. The mountain rears in the distance, its shoulders push against the sky.

The ground rumbles. Far off the workmen have started. He can see the steam from their labours drifting above the houses. He can smell the melted tarmac, the chemicals clinging like a second skin to the earth. But here the world is green, the birds and the animals live on.

He takes out a fag. It is one of his last and he smokes it quietly. He watches the fox foraging. Its ears prick as a couple of squirrels dart across the lawn. They are up in the boughs of a tree before the fox can react. They are hidden, they are a small part of a big world.

The dawn chorus has begun and as he listens to the wood pigeons and the magpies calling to one another he sits down on a bench. His heart begins to beat more slowly as he sits, it beats as slow as his thoughts and he rests his chin against his chest.

Jap, he thinks. Jap.

The yellow broom handle

Nobody disturbs his rest until the park keeper shows up at ten. It is a warm and windy day, the elements are alive.

'Hey, you can't sleep there,' the park keeper says.

'Why not?'

'It's park property.'

'So?'

'So you can't sleep there. It's not what it's for.'

'What is it for?'

'For folks to sit and rest.'

'I'm resting.'

'For folks to enjoy.'

'I'm enjoying it.'

'Get the fuck out of here before I call the police.'

The mention of the police makes him angry. It makes him scared. His face flushes, it is hot against the chill wind.

He stands and the park keeper brandishes his broom. It has a yellow handle and stiff brushes. It is almost as tall as the park keeper. Its plastic length stays between them as Willem stands up. It stays between them as the park keeper shuffles him out of his domain. He hears the words, 'fucking tramps.' The words follow him as he walks.

A young couple are walking past as he leaves. The man is wearing a denim jacket and a baseball cap. The woman is wearing a leather jacket and a smart skirt. Her jacket is sleek with the damp in the air, her skirt is short and white. She has woollen tights underneath and the man places himself between her and Willem. He puts an arm around his girlfriend's shoulder. He is her buffer. She is his warmth on this cold day.

'I just wanted to rest,' Willem tries to tell them, but the yellow broom handle is there, the words are still there, chasing him.

In the street a few people are walking their dogs. He lets out a sob. It is a dirty sound. It makes him self-conscious. A few people look at him, they see his face and his clothes. He is unwashed, unclean. He turns on his heel and quickly walks away.

The porcelain bowl

Willem's beard is irritating him. He has never grown it out before. Now tiny bristles are poking out all over his chin. They catch food, they tickle his nose and the edges of his lips. His cheeks are blue, they chafe against his hood.

He stops at a chemist. It smells of bleach and air freshener. The woman at the counter is fat, she smiles at him and her cheeks bunch. He buys himself some soap, some deodorant and a pack of safety razors. He buys himself some cheap socks and a toothbrush. He buys a little bottle of mouthwash and while the fat lady's back is turned he slips a tube of toothpaste into his pocket. He slips a power bar into his pocket and thinks fuck you as he leaves.

There is a Starbucks on the corner. As he steps inside the smell of sweetly scalded milk washes over him. Loud Latino music is playing and a sign advertises a blend from Guatemala. A map of the world shows him where Guatemala is. 'Middle of nowhere,' he mumbles. 'Must be peaceful.'

'I'm sorry, sir?'

'Nothing.' He blushes. The girl behind the till smiles her fear at him, she asks him what he wants and he orders a cup of tea and a bacon roll. She eyes him suspiciously as she works the till. Her eyes are slits, her mouth is plastered on. It smiles her scorn but she doesn't make a fuss. She asks 'to eat in or take away?' He was scared of this. He was scared he would be asked to leave. But he wants to sit down in a comfortable chair for twenty minutes. He says 'in, please,' and she nods.

While he's waiting for his bacon roll to be heated he heads into the bathroom. He takes out his new purchases. His new acquisitions. He unwraps the power bar first. He stuffs it into his mouth in one go. He laughs as he chews. It's hard work and his jaw starts to ache, but he laughs anyway. It tastes like victory. It tastes like power. He changes his socks, he throws the old ones in the bin. They are stained black from the insides of his shoes and they leave his fingertips smelling like dog shit.

Next he brushes his teeth. He spits a little blood with the toothpaste, spattering the porcelain bowl. Red against white. He brushes hard and keeps his teeth white. He rinses them with mouthwash like his mama taught him when he was just a bairn. The green liquid washes the blood and the spittle down the plughole. Disinfecting it, anaesthetising it,.

Next he shaves. He runs the hot water tap to scalding, lathers his chin in soap and takes out a razor. He washes the razor in the hot water and takes a first pass. Over his left cheek, from bottom to top and back again. One of his mama's blokes taught him to shave when he was fourteen and his first downy hair was coming in. He gurns, he puffs out his cheeks and rounds his top lip. He makes a dozen flat surfaces out of his gravelly cheeks and jaw, shaving the hair close to the follicles.

Somebody starts to hammer on the door.

'Sir! Sir! Are you OK in there?'

'Aye.'

'There's a queue out here.'

'Mm.'

'Sir! Can I ask you to come out?'

'Mm.' He splashes cold water on his face, dries himself on a blue paper towel and unlocks the door. The other patrons' glares don't let him find a seat. The staffs' glares don't let him stay. They have made his tea in a paper cup even though he told them he wanted it for here. His roll is in a brown paper bag, not served on a plate. The young girl hands it to him. She tells him that there is plastic cutlery inside. There is ketchup and brown sauce. And have a nice day sir. And he leaves with their glares buzzing on his back.

He kicks over a little sign as he leaves. It stands on the pavement advertising their latest drinks. 'Fuck you. Cunts,' he mutters as it slaps the paving slabs. Its cheap wooden surface is dented, a chunk is pulled out. People tut and swear but he pays them no mind.

'Fuck you.'

The system

That evening he counts up all the money he has left. Six tens, a five and six fifty in change. He withdraws the last of his money from the bank. He has to go into a branch to withdraw it all. He has a special debit card his mama got him. He can't use it in shops. He can only get cash out. But if he goes into a bank he can get as much as he wants, 'for emergencies, not for going on the piss,' she told him. This is an emergency, mama, he thinks.

People keep their distance in here as well. He is as clean as he can make himself at the moment. Later he will buy new clothes and a sleeping bag. He will buy some more newspapers. But for now he must make do as he is.

An electronic voice tells him to please go to cashier number three. There is too much noise in here. People stare too much. As he steps up to the till he tells the man behind it that he would like to withdraw all his money. He doesn't want to have to come back here, he thinks. Too many eyes and ears and mouths. Best to be done with the place.

'Very well, sir. If you could just insert your card.' The man is wearing a cheap shirt in the bank's colours. He has a plastic badge on his chest which says his name is Daryl. He is very smart, very professional. He hides behind his professionalism. If he acts as he is trained he needn't meet this man's eyes, he needn't contemplate this man's misfortunes.

'Please enter your PIN number.'

'Charlie said you don't need to say number.'

'I'm sorry, sir?'

'PIN means Personal Identification Number. You don't need to say Personal Identification Number number. It's too many numbers. Just PIN.'

'OK, sir. If you could just enter your PIN please, sir.'

He taps the four numbers into the keypad and Daryl tells him he has seven hundred and forty pounds and fifteen pence. He taps a couple of keys on his computer and counts out the money. He licks his thumb before counting out the notes. His lips murmur the numbers as he counts, one two three four...

'There you go, sir. Is there anything else I can do for you?'

'No. Thanks. Ta.'

'Have a nice day then, sir.'

'Aye.'

The simple man

A simple man can live on little. Willem has always found this to be true. Of course, he likes to drink with the lads on a Friday night. Lads from school, from the site. The Polish builders once upon a time. And those rare occasions he took lasses out he would spend a lot on them, like he treated Celina. But day to day he requires little. Food, a little drink, cheap clothing. In this way he spins his money out for a long time.

He tries to look for a flat but few estate agents will let him in. Those who do tell him he'll need a reference and deposit and proof of income. His head spins and he says 'no, no, nothing like that,' and leaves with his eyes burning hot with tears. He tries to rent a room in a bed and breakfast when it rains but they all throw him out as well. He finds a bedsit but there are drug addicts in the stairwell and spiders hanging from the ceiling and he wants no part in any of that. So his money lasts and his back bends into the shape of the paving stones.

By the time his wad of notes runs thin the festival crowds are starting to arrive. They descend every year. First the starlings arrive and then the tourists come. He can see lots of yellow faces in the crowds. He can see lots of black men and women. Lots more whites. There are more people than Edinburgh usually sees. They double the size of the city, they are an organism, they breathe too quickly. The centre of Edinburgh manages to stand still and heave at the same time.

He has been begging for a few weeks. He is scared about having no money left. He is scared about not being able to feed himself. He has never felt this fear before. Before, when he laboured, he slept and he ate and his mama took care of him. There wasn't room for much of anything else. Now he has too much time. Now he has a lot to worry about. His life is a maze, he runs through it every day. Will he eat, will anybody be kind to him? Will he find somewhere to wash today? Most of the coffee chains know his face, most of the independent ones notice too much. The public toilets are an option but they are not clean. They are not safe. Just two days ago he bloodied his fists defending himself from an old pervert looking for satisfaction at his expense in a public toilet. The man had a gaping mouth, it opened like a hole. It sucked at the air, a giant fish gasping out of water. It sucked as he went down, it dribbled on the floor. Willem trod in the dribble and the blood as he made for the door. Answers took flight, they swirled far above in the starlings' dance.

He has been begging for a week and his bones are weary. Every day he has a choice to make. He can have peace and sit in a backstreet, allowing his own thoughts to keep him company. But his cap stays empty, his stomach stays empty. So he can sit on a main street, a royal street. A busy bridge or in front of a bustling department store. His cap fills up with tourists' change and locals' blank stares. But his thoughts are flattened out. They are pushed away and instead he has to deal with his benefactors' thoughts. Their chatter and their footsteps sound in his brain. They echo, they rattle about in there, they thunder. And the world spins too quickly and his temples start to throb.

The yellow and the black faces are kind, they drop lots of money. They have perhaps heard about the endless homeless of Edinburgh. They think they are buying tickets to a show. That he is on stage. They think they are participating in the local colour. Is his picture in a guide book, he wonders? Is he an attraction?

Who cares? They fill his cap with coins. He makes around one fifty an hour. Sometimes more, sometimes less, but he usually has enough for a couple of plastic wrapped sandwiches and a cup of tea. He is a simple man, he doesn't drink too much these days. The nights are warmer. He doesn't desire too much more.

The desires

He desires some things. He desires his health to return to what it was. He is a big man, a strong man used to taxing his body. But he is outside each night, huddled in alcoves or under benches. He never sleeps more than a few minutes at a time. He is scared. He knows the night is vicious.

The night is vicious and dealers and police officers come looking all too often. He can be hustled by a dealer, he can be taken in by the police. The faces of the men who took Jap have begun to loom in his dreams. They stand watching the owl as it dives out of the water, they watch his mother in her last moments. They tell the toddler with his rattle to stop disturbing their peace. Shake, shake, shake, the toddler's rattle sings as they clamp the handcuffs on and drive him off to their cage.

He is a big man but he fears becoming broken. He has developed a cough. The phlegm is in his throat. It sits in the tops of his lungs, raking at his breath and causing him to choke from time to time. He lies on the cold stone pavement with his ribs convulsing, with tears in his eyes. Even in the summer months the night time is no man's friend.

He went to a see doctor about his cough. He can't go to his old one. It is too close to his house and he worries that someone will grass on him. They will send the police to take him in, they'll cage him like they caged Jap. So he went to a new one. They asked if he was a patient of theirs. He said no and they asked where he was a patient. 'Wherever I am, I am a patient. I need a doctor,' he told them. They asked for his address and he said he slept under the stars, in the cold. He told them that it was breaking him, that he needed medicine to make him strong.

'Well, sir, I'm afraid we can't help you. We need an address for the database. I can give you the address of a walk-in centre. It's not too far from here.'

The walk-in centre scared him. It was a grey building riddled with cracks and dark shapes. It was square concrete with no plants growing near it. The men and women in the waiting room were cadavers. They were more than half dead and some of them looked like they would happily strangle him in his sleep. Their hands itched and made his own hands itch in return. If I show these people my weakness then I'll be a dead man, he thought. He fled the dark shapes, he fled the itchy hands.

Rather a cough than a death sentence, he thinks.

When he was a kid his mama gave him vitamin tablets. She bought them at the supermarket. They came in a little pot and she gave him one every morning. They were little red pills shaped like his favourite super heroes and she would place them on his spoon after she poured his cereal.

She told him 'eat this up Willie. And then you can have your breakfast.'

'Why, mama?'

'It'll make you big and strong. As strong as Superman. It'll stop you getting sick.'

She was right. He grew up big and strong, he never got sick before he hit the streets. In over a decade labouring he had only ever taken a couple of days off. He ploughed on even in the middle of winter when everyone else choked on the cold.

He went to a chemist after fleeing the walk-in centre. He picked up a bottle of multi-vitamins. He picked up a bottle of iron supplements. Iron was strong, these would make him strong. 'Iron in my blood. Good, good,' he muttered, shaking the pot a little. He picked up some vitamin C to get rid of his cold. They were two ninety nine a bottle. As he handed over the cash he sneaked himself another power bar from the counter. *Fuck you.* It has become his motto. It has become like a mantra to him. He sneaked another power bar and smiled and thought *fuck you, fuck you- Fuck You All.*

Now his pockets rattle as he turns over at night. They rattle as he walks. Sometimes he takes the little pots of colourful pills out and shakes them on purpose. They are his rattle and he shakes them in defiance. The little boy might get hauled off in handcuffs but Willem is a big man. He will fight or he will run, but he will keep himself free either way.

The three men

'Luck of the draw,' says one man. 'Schooling is nothing.' He looks at Willem and says 'my son's a mechanic. He's a little fellow but he's good with his hands. Learned everything under the hood of a car, now he makes his packet each month. School didn't do that.' Another man chips in, he says the first man is talking bollocks. 'You're son learned how to read and write at school,' he says. 'He couldn't work without his words, no garage would give him a chance.'

The two men pass a bottle back and forth. The bottle is dark with rum. It burns their lips and it burns their stomachs, but they keep drinking. They smile, they show the gaps in their teeth. The first man says that the burning reminds him how to feel. He says it reminds him of love, of the feel of a woman's body. The second man says the burning leads to numbness after a while. It helps him to forget love, to forget women. Festival goers march past them, they clutch leaflets and tickets and plastic bags and bottles of drink. They all swig, they all remember love. They all forget love.

They pass the bottle to Willem and he drinks his fill. 'Skoll,' the first man laughs. 'Salut, yamas,' the other chimes in, and Willem takes another swig. It burns. It burns and his head grows lighter.

'I got my education,' the first man says. 'And still I'm out here.'

'That's cos you're crazy,' says the second man. They both burst out laughing. A second later Willem laughs. He isn't sure what they're laughing about, but his head is light and the sunshine is warm and the laughter feels good in his mouth.

'Aye, we're a bunch of nutters all right.' The first man takes the bottle. He sips for a minute or two. He stares at the dark liquid. 'The whole family got it. My granny was locked up with it. My old man got struck by it and ran off to god knows where. Then I got it, stopped going to work, lost my house. Lost my girl last. She stuck around a bit. Until I went down. My boy sneers at me when he sees me in the street, but he'll be next. Mark my words, one day he'll be out here with nothing but the heavens and a bottle of the good stuff.'

The first man's name is Malkie. The second man's name is Thomas. They spend every day together, drinking under trees and telling jokes. They talk about their families. They have never met each other's families but they know them intimately. They know each other's stories and their backs are both broken, this is the bond they share.

Malkie's granny was called the ghost. She couldn't bear the sun and so she spent every day wrapped up. She stayed in when it was sunny and whenever she did go out she wore a wide brimmed hat to protect herself. So she stayed pale white all year round, deathly pale her whole life, and young children made up stories about her.

Her husband died after just three years of marriage. He left her with Malkie's aunt in her belly and his father in rags. Malkie's father was never sick a day in his life, 'but my granny's crazy struck him down as sure as any of us! Sucked the life right out of him.' His skin is dark, he looks like an Italian. He spends all his time under the sun and the wind and the rain. His face has been varnished by it all.

'Malkie's granny didn't leave the house for three years before the funeral,' Thomas says. 'From the day she got married to the day her old man died she stayed shut in, cooking and cleaning. She didn't even come to the wake.' But the day after the wake, when the town was getting back to business, she came out. She wandered down the high street.

She came into every shop, every café, every pub and asked if they had seen her husband. Thomas tells him all of this as Malkie nods, sipping from the bottle. He passes the bottle to Willem. The rum burns his mouth. It burns his throat.

Malkie takes up the story. 'She left my dad on his own in the flat. She wandered about the whole town, knocking on doors and asking for him. "You're old man's dead," they all told her. "We buried him, his plot is in the cemetery!" But she wouldn't have it, she didn't give up. Every day she left my dad to go looking and every day she came back tired and scared.

'Then one day the social picked her up. A neighbour reported her. Nobody ever spoke to the neighbour again, apparently- she had to move out of town in the end. You don't grass, not ever. But what else could she do? The social stuck my granny in a home, they watched her belly swell with my aunt. They kept her warm, well fed- she had it better than us fuckers, I'd say!

'They kept her locked up until she went into labour. They sent my dad some place else. He always said he didn't remember exactly where. A string of homes for orphans and rejects, he said. He wound up with a nice place for a while, though. A couple took him in to foster. They got on well and they adopted him. But then he ran off when he was sixteen. The crazy got him, it got his blood up. He ran for the hills, drank too much and knocked my old mam up. So I never knew his foster parents or his birth mam.

'I got these stories from him later, much later. I didn't have too much to do with him but we'd share a drink now and then.'

They kept the ghost locked up until she went into labour. Then when she gave birth they took the little girl.

They adopted her off to a well to do couple in England and turfed her mother out onto the streets. 'She spent the first half of her life never leaving her house. She spent the second without a house to go to. Took to drink and worse. Down in the Borders there's plenty of folk as knew my granny,' Malkie laughs.

'And then when I was nineteen the crazy caught me. It caught me from behind, unawares. I had a good job at a scaffolder's. I had money in my pocket and I was going to be apprenticed to a joiner soon enough. Had it all worked out. But I knocked my girl up and then the crazy got me. I quit my job when the boy was born and fucked everything I could find. My girl knew all this, she kept it from my son. She took him to her folk's when we were chucked out the flat.

'One girl I'd done it to rough went to the police. They sent me down for assault. They couldn't prove rape- but as I said at the time, she didn't say no to that bit- but they got me for assault. I had a vicious temper back then and I'll admit I was rough. There's nothing left for me now except my two mates, Tommy here and Captain Morgan.' He laughs. His laugh is a cold wheeze sipping at the rum.

'And what's your story, lad?' Thomas asks Willem.

'They took my job when the banks lost all the money.'

'Cunts.'

'They took my mam. They took my dog.'

'Fuckers,' Thomas spits.

Willem has had too much, he needs some air. He stands up, throws his rucksack over his shoulder and wanders off, swaying slightly. 'You OK lad?' one of them calls after him, but he just shrugs and keeps walking. He pops a couple of vitamins to keep his strength up, sips water from a public fountain and looks for somewhere to rest.

The strong force

He never liked getting too drunk, but it didn't matter. He can hold it alright. No man of his size gets drunk too quickly. He can throw it back with the best of them. He just gets depressed when he drinks. The sadness catches him and it makes his fists itch for a fight.

There is a little pub near his mama's flat. They sell lager at one forty a pint before nine. He used to take his mama there sometimes. On her birthday, on his birthday, sometimes on a Friday night just to let her know he loved her. And she loved him and she laughed as he downed pints. 'Look at my lad, got his mam's strength, this one!' she would shout and women would laugh and men would clap him on the back and offer to buy him another.

One time a bloke got too friendly with his mama. She liked it at first. She always liked the attention. She kept herself pretty as she got older. But she said no, 'not tonight, love, I'm here with another man! I've a mother's duties to perform tonight.' The bloke didn't like that, he got wide. He was raging and he slammed his pint glass on the table.

'You fucking slapper!' he shouted at Willem's mama. He grabbed her tits and laughed. He grabbed her hand and tried to stuff it down his pants. Willem put his own pint down, stood up, grasped the man by his shirt front and dragged him over their table. He swore under his breath and his mama shouted and stood back as glasses fell and smashed. Willem lifted the man, threw him against the wall and knocked the wind from him. His chest sagged, his face paled. He was done in, this was the last of him, but Willem wasn't finished. He had a lot of strength left. He threw the man into the pale moonlight. Into the street light, the star light. Their shadows danced as Willem let his strength out. Slowly at first and then with more force.

The man had a couple of pals in the pub who came out to rescue him. One of them punched Willem but he was in no state to feel it. It was a gnat's bite, it was a child's paw. He cuffed the man around the ear, sinking him to the ground. Their shadows merged and he loomed tall. He beat the third man as a flock of pigeons nearby took fright. They flapped their wings in their ascension, they flew free of the shadows' mess. They cried and cawed and Willem set to work. He was a labourer, he was labouring. He knocked them down and piled their limp bodies in one corner, groaning and bleeding and cradling each other. They were one shadow, he was another. And his shadow quickly disappeared as he joined his mama back in the bar.

'My hero, what a lad!' she laughed, holding his arm in the air like a champion boxer. The pub clapped. They had watched through the windows. They hadn't seen such a beating in months and their blood was up.

'He's a clarty old prick, that one. You did well seeing to him like that, pal,' the bartender said, replacing Willem's spilt lager.

'Mm.'

The shadow dancers

On the street drink is medicine, it is comfort. Its stinging warmth becomes his warmth. But back in the old life where his mama was alive and Jap was at his side and there was work to be done drink played with his brain. And too often it led to other things which played with his brain even worse.

He lives still, that Willem. He is convinced of it. Somewhere out there the old Willem is larking about, working hard and supping deep to calm his aching muscles. It may not be in this time. But what does that matter, anyway? One time is as good as any other, he thinks. The drink has made him think and his thinking is sodden. It has made him sleepy, as it always did.

And out there, who knows where, Willem is laughing along with everyone else. Maybe he missed the joke, maybe he didn't understand it. This happens all too often. But other people's laughter is infectious and it makes him happy enough to join in regardless. His mates are from work, from school, from his neighbourhood. They are not real mates, he can't turn to them when he is in trouble, but that problem doesn't belong to this Willem. This Willem has it just fine.

There are girls and he thinks one of them is flirting with him, though he never is too sure. She has long eyelashes which she flutters. She has a large belly and large breasts. There is a butterfly tattoo on one of her breasts, swan diving down her cleavage. It takes his gaze as it dives and she giggles when he speaks. Her breasts shake with her laughter, the butterfly quivers.

One of his mates knows of a rave by the shore. An old warehouse or factory or something just outside Portobello. Not one of these corporate gigs. Not sponsored, not pricey. The real deal. They should go, they will have a laugh. He has pills and there will be a killer DJ and they invite the girls and the girls say yes. Everybody is drunk and laughing so it's OK. It's all OK.

Willem doesn't want to go. He wants to stay here talking to the girl with the butterfly, but she was one of the first to say yes and so they jump on a bus. He follows her to the top deck. They take the back seats and one of his mates takes his cock out and pisses in a corner. He makes everyone laugh. Even the girls laugh at this, it's all OK. They are all handing around little pills. Blue pills and white pills, smaller than a fingertip. They make everyone laugh, they make everyone want to dance.

Willem takes one and he starts to laugh. The butterfly darts around, it dances in the electric light. They stop by a large industrial estate, abandoned since the eighties. The butterfly flies through the estate, bobbing along in the moonlight. On the far side it finds light and warmth and the rave has begun.

It flits away when they get to the warehouse, it is lost in the crowd. And Willem is lost in the crowd. The warehouse is excitement, it is dancing and sweating and popping pills and fingering and blowjobs in dark corners. He can see shapes moving in the shadows, shapes giving it and taking it and the butterfly is lost in the darkness. He can't see it any more.

He is bored now and so he drinks. There are bottles for sale and he slurps down one after another. He can barely stand and he starts to retch. One of his friends takes him outside for air. His friend laughs, he makes jokes about Willem. 'Big boy can't hold his drink down!' he laughs. People say he is a bad drunk. *I'm not, I'm not. I just need so much of the stuff on a night like tonight when the moon is out but the shadows stay so dark.*

That is how the other Willem spends his nights. That is how his past looks and he shies from it. That was shit and this is shit, he thinks.

So where else can he look? Where does the moon shine brightly enough to clear the dark?

The gods of man part II

The city's holy men and women come to see him from time to time. They circle the city at midnight, rotating, canvassing different areas. They are nocturnal hunters and some of the lads call them the vamps. 'They come down out of the night and try to pick you off,' they told Willem. He sits with the other wrecks, watching for them. They usually catch up with him when he is on his own.

He used to see the holy types on street corners. Jehovah's Witnesses, sipping from Thermos flasks. Mormons with shiny teeth and shiny hair, young lads sent from overseas to spread the good word. Godly folk with fire in their eyes and signs bearing names and numbers and passages from the bible. But he never paid much attention. Sometimes his lips would mumble little prayers, wish lists and pleas and questions half formed in the night. This was enough for him.

But now they descend from the darkness, from the black sky. Street lights shine at their backs, their haloes flicker dull. 'Hello, lad,' they say. They offer him cookies and advice. The cookies taste sweet enough but the advice leaves him hungry.

'Have you got anywhere to go tonight?' they ask him.

No, he tells them. Else why would he be out here?

'You have no family?'

He choked at first, now he just shakes his head.

'You have a family in Christ,' they say. 'The Lord our saviour is father to us all.'

He wants to know if he can stay with them.

'Well, no, that's not what–'

He wants to know if he can live in the church. It is god's house, he is god's child.

'No, no, that isn't the point... but we can pray for you. We will place our faith in god that he will look after you in your hour of need.'

'It's cold,' he tells them.

'I know, dear.'

'Mm.'

Some of them leave little books of prayers and psalms. Some leave bibles bound in plastic against the rain. The bibles have tiny lettering throughout, so small that an entire history of man can fit neatly into his pocket. He looks at their pages and thinks that every part of history is so small. He has been handed dozens of pamphlets bearing the legend 'THE WATCHTOWER.' He has even been given short biographies of Mother Teresa and of Joseph Smith. These are names he doesn't know and yet their faces loom large from glossy front covers.

He has never been given so many books in his life. But he throws them away fairly quickly. He has no shelves to keep them on.

The godly give him food as well. Proper food, not just cookies. He is grateful, he is hungry too often these days. His stomach growls low and makes the bones in his back ache long into the night. And then god's mission moves on, there are other bundles in the street. There are other souls to see tonight and the rain has started to fall lightly on their shoulders.

The empty pockets

He has little money left. He has a couple of scrunched up fivers and his back is aching from the street. His bones are aching. They grind as he moves. 'Why don't you get a job and work like the rest of us, prick?' a man asks him one day as he holds his cap out. He wants to. He knows now that things cannot return. He will not get his old job back. He will not get his old flat back. And mama and Jap are gone.

They won't come back. The future is his only refuge for the moment and he determines to get there in one piece.

Maybe the shadows aren't so deep in the future, he thinks.

The job centre is in town, a fifteen minute walk away. Through the crowds and the winding streets and the broad park lands. He arrives, warm through with the summer's heat. The sun is larger than the sky today. It is larger than life. It bakes him, it makes him sweat under his two hoodies and his raincoat.

'Have you got an appointment?' the guard on the door asks.

'No. But I need money. I need the dole. I need a job.'

'Can't come in without an appointment.'

'How do I get an appointment?'

'You call.'

'Call who?'

'Us. The job centre. Call Job Centre Plus. Here,' and he hands him a glossy leaflet with a number on it.

'I don't have a phone.'

'Use a payphone.'

'I don't have any money.'

'It's free from landlines. Now please move along sir, we're very busy these days.'

He calls from a payphone on the corner. He talks to a machine, he punches in numbers. He punches them slowly with a thick finger. Deliberate and slow, precise. He listens to violins playing as he is put on hold. Finally he speaks to an abrupt voice which makes him an appointment for a couple of days' time. The future starts to open up.

There are cards in the phone box for calls girls and exotic massages. There are spiders' webs and he is afraid they'll get into his bones again, lacing them with their cracks. He leaves, quickly, glancing back nervously. Come the future, come the refuge.

The kindness in absence

An evening comes in which a woman in Starbucks takes pity on him. It is cold outside, a summer storm has been blowing all day and the sign glows warmly as he passes. The cafe is upstairs, above a row of shops on Prince's Street. He cannot resist it, he cannot help but climb those stairs. He climbs and the warmth is in him, it runs through him.

'Can I help you?' the woman asks him. She is young and small and she reminds him of Celina. Her hair is cut short the same way, her accent is foreign. It cuts through her words like Celina's did. He nods, he mumbles. The counter and three glass shelves stand between them. The shelves are stacked with sandwiches and cakes. He pulls some change out of his pocket and asks for a coffee.

'What kind?'

'White. Two sugars, ta.'

'Filter or Americano?'

'Cheapest.'

'Filter. It's on for a pound at the moment.'

'Aye.'

'For here or to take away?' She is an angel, her face swims in the warmth. He starts to sweat a little. It has been so long since somebody invited him to stay, to eat in the comfort of warm walls and comfy chairs. It has been so long since he sat at a table that such memories belong to someone else, to his other, old self from before the streets broke his back.

'In. Yes, in. Ta.'

He passes her a two pound coin. Someone gave it to him earlier and it made him smile. He smiles at the girl behind the counter and her face shines. But she looks over his shoulder, she is bored. Her eyes are absent. This is no kindness, he thinks. She has served so many people today that I am lost. She passes him his coffee. It is in a mug of thick, plain china. The heat stings his hands as he holds it, it stings his callouses.

'Ta.' He stares down at the coffee. It is dark, it swims and the room fades.

'Milk and sugar are over there. Have a nice day,' she says. 'Next customer please,' she says, and he is gone even as she passes him his change. The change tinkles in his palm, a fifty, a ten and two twenties. One palm stings with heat as the other tinkles. The sounds and the sensations lead him, they walk him to a table in the corner.

Gentle music pumps in from corner speakers. The beats shimmer and he sips his coffee. It scalds his lips as he looks around the room. It burns his tongue and makes his mouth taste like metal. Oh, oh, oh, the singer croons. His heart is in pain, his soul is in pain and the bass hums and the drums keep on shimmering with the beat.

The cafe is in disarray. It is half past eight, the windows are growing dark and the staff are thinking of home. They are thinking of drinks with friends, of the arms of loved ones and the moments between moments in which they can take their breathes free of work. They are thinking of the comfort of their beds and their limbs move sluggishly with the dreaming. The day has taken its toll. Empty cups litter the tables. Empty muffin wrappers and sandwich crusts on white plates litter the tables.

Willem clears his own table before he sits down. He stacks the cups and the plates on top of one another. Too many stalls are clustered around and he moves these, he puts them back in their right places. He uses the arm of his hoody to wipe off the last of the crumbs and tea stains. And he sits and he sips and the singer croons through the windows' shade.

The men, the chants

His fingers and his toes grow warm as he sits. His nose is warm and his eyes are warm. He can hear crowds in the street below. Edinburgh Castle looms large against a bright pink sky and the crowds pump their fists and sing and hold on to one another.

'Watch out for the crowds,' Malkie told him one time. He sees the old man often enough. They swap stories and they swap wisdom. 'They're drunk and excited and their heads will come apart for the night. In a crowd like that every normal cunt is as crazy as me, maybe worse,' he said.

'Some will pass you by. Some will grow loving. They are in love with the world. They empty their pockets and their wallets into your cap. You can do well for yourself. But some are angry. They rage and they encourage each other's rage. They lost money betting or their team didn't make it through. Or their wives won't fuck them or their secretaries won't fuck them. Or sometimes life just got too big for them.

'They crack, they lash out at you.

'You and I,' he said, leaning close. 'We're hard as nails, but that doesn't stop us being soft targets, does it? No, not for a minute.

'So watch out for the crowds, lad. Things get loud real fast when folks get together like that.'

The crowd outside are wearing blue shirts and green shirts. The blues clump together, the greens clump together. They cheer together and make faces together. The ones in blue are wearing cheap felt berets plastered to their heads. Some are wearing tourist kilts, cheap cotton made in local colours. The ones in green are wearing big green top hats and have shamrocks painted on their faces. They shout the loudest, their fists pump the hardest.

'Ireland won,' an old woman tells him. 'Rugby was on tonight and now Murrayfield's emptying by the thousands.' She smiles at him from the next table. A few hairs cling to her scalp and her throat is wrinkled like a chicken's.

A barrista walks through the room. He says 'drink up now, please folks.' He is wearing a black shirt, black trousers and a green apron. He has a mop in one hand and the room has begun to smell of disinfectant. It suits the burn on Willem's tongue, it washes away the scent of roasted coffee and scalded milk. 'We close in five minutes,' he says and continues to mop.

'And so,' the old lady says. She creaks to her feet, slowly. She braces her hands on the table until she is upright. 'The night beckons.'

'Mm.'

The glass wall

He builds a glass wall around himself. His mama tried to show him how to do it when he was young. 'You can see through it,' she told him. 'But nobody can get to you. It can't crack but you can hear and see what you want, safe from the world.' He was never too good at it then and he isn't too good at it now. But he tries, he builds.

The wall is weak but his shoulders are strong. What can't be kept out can be pushed through. Angry drunks swear at him as he shoves through the crowd. A couple of them try to shove him back, a few try to punch him. But they bounce, they cannot match him. Others swear at him, they look angry until they see how high he towers. His bulk blocks out the evening, it blocks out moon and the stars and the castle beyond. 'Mam, maybe the wall is strong after all,' he mutters as the bodies bounce out of his way.

A piper squeals on the other side of the road. The crowd parts, one half flows away from the street and into the train station. The piper's wailing hurts his ears, it carves the crowd into pieces and his eyes can't follow them all. It shakes his wall, the shaking hurts him and he joins the path to the station. He turns with them, he descends and escapes.

He passes through the entrance and a hundred heads bob and weave around him. The concourse is wide, shops flank its edges and a hundred pairs of eyes search for trains and platforms and places to rest as they wait. He finds a bench and sits down. He leans forwards, hands braced against his knees, his chin high and his feet apart. My world, my space, he thinks. He watches the searching eyes and the coloured shirts. A fight breaks out as he watches and a couple of policemen rush in. A child sits on her father's shoulders, dancing to a tune that nobody else can hear. She is sleepy as the drunks are pulled away, her eyelids want to close around a softer dream.

Some pigeons land nearby. They take off, they land once more. And again and again. They flap and peck, searching for crumbs in the mass of bodies.

'The night beckons,' he mumbles, shoring up his wall.

The quiet roar

Later on and the fights have long since finished, and the little girl has been carried home to her bed, and the last of the drunks in the coloured shirts have faded away, and only he and the pigeons and a few more strays remain to remember this night. It is past eleven and the last trains are coming in. The security guards are eyeing him through his glass wall, their frowns are deep and their mouths curl downwards.

The last train arrives as he sits before their glares. The last people hurry from their carriages, they realise how cold the night has become.

A family emerges from the ticket barriers. They turn circles as the pigeons take off and land. Two girls and a little boy spin around their mother and father, giggling. They are excited by the lateness of the hour, their tiredness has made them giddy and they laugh and cry. Willem sits behind his glass wall like his mama told him. He holds his breath. The children's anxious laughter is too much, it flicks at his heart. He flinches and his shoulders tighten.

The pigeons land a few feet in front of his wall. There are four of them and they peck at an old sandwich packet. Their pecks are rhythmical, there is method to their search and they make him glad.

The children see the pigeons. They see them peck and flap and it is too much for their tired eyes. They pounce, squealing. They turn circles and they laugh. The boy runs straight for the middle of the pigeons, his sturdy little legs carry him far. The girls split and run around the edge, flapping their hands as the pigeons take flight, scared.

'No,' Willem mumbles. The children shriek in their excitement and his glass wall starts to crack. Thick splinters begin to drop, they shatter against the floor. He growls and the children look up. He is louder than the shattered glass and they see the scary big man with his bloodshot eyes. They smell the street on his clothes and it is their turn to take flight, scared. Their parents make shushing noises but it is late and they are tired and the glass wall has begun to crumble in earnest.

'Sir, the station's closing now,' a man tells him. He is wearing a bright vest and the shadow of a beard.

'Mm.' The night beckons. It calls for us all in the end. He leaves his wall behind, it doesn't work after all. He squares his shoulders.

'I tried, mam,' he whispers as he looks for somewhere to sleep.

The small man

The job centre will not help him in the end. They see him at his appointed time. They give him an application to sit and fill out, they give him a chair and a clipboard and a little blue pen. The chair is soft, it hugs him almost to sleep. His breathing grows heavy, his eyelids grow heavy and then a security guard prods him.

'Sir, I think you're being called.'

'Willem, Willem Gyle? Mr. Gyle!' There is a skinny man calling his name over and over. He is sitting at his desk, searching the crowd of faces for recognition of his words.

'Aye. Aye,' Willem says, coming to his feet, rushing over. The skinny man takes Willem's papers without looking him in the eye. 'Hello,' Willem says.

'Mm.' The skinny man continues to scan Willem's papers. Willem takes a seat, once more surprised by how soft a chair can be. How hard his body is becoming. As his papers are double checked Willem pats himself down. His paunch has gone. His stomach is hard now, he can feel his abdominal muscles. His trousers are loose, he can fit a couple of fingers in at the waistband. His shoulders are as broad and bunched as ever, but his chest doesn't strain the fabric of his t shirt.

'When did you lose your job?'

'I don't know. A few months ago. Five or six months, I think.'

'And you're only just coming in now?'

'Mm.'

'OK. You should really have come in straight away. They'll want to know how you've been living in the meantime. Savings?'

'What?'

'Do you have savings?'

'No. They were taken.'

'Taken?'

'Yeah.'

'By who?'

'I don't know their names.'

'OK. I'll just put down that you don't have savings. Would that be an accurate statement?'

'Yeah.'

'And what was the reason you left your last employment?'

'Laid off. All the lads got laid off.'

'Have you got your P45?'

'What?'

'Have you got your P45?'

'No.'

'Why not?'

'I don't know. I don't know what it is.'

'Your last employer should have given you one when you're employment was terminated.'

'No.'

'Didn't they give you anything?'

'No. Charlie said not to come in the next day. That's all.'

'Have you got a letter from them, an email? A contract? Anything saying that your position has been terminated?'

'Didn't have a contract.'

'Sir, did your employer complete PAYE for you?'

'They paid me.'

'No. Did they pay taxes? Income tax, national insurance?'

'Well I don't know anything about-'

'Well without any documents stating that you were employed where you say you were and that your employment has now come to an end, we can't put you onto job-seeker's allowance.'

'But I don't know if I can-'

'Also, you haven't put an address down,' the skinny man notes.

'Address?'

'For yourself. Where you are staying?'

'Why does that matter?'

'Without a current address we can't put you into the system.'

'But what if I don't have a current address?'

'Then there are shelters you can register yourself at. Then you can come back. Do that, get a correspondence from your previous employer and then we can put you on jobseeker's allowance.'

'But I need money now.'

'I'm sorry sir, we can't help you there.'

'But-'

'If you would like to make your way to the exit, sir, there are other people waiting.'

But he needs money. He needs some more food. He needs the security of a few quid in his pocket. He wants a job, he needs help finding himself a job. He is a hard worker but he has never found himself a job, his mama always sorted that kind of thing out for him. He tells the skinny man all of this. He grabs him by the collar to make him see. He throws him on the floor in frustration. The skinny man's jaw hits his desk on the way down and blood splatters his shirt. It splatters Willem's shoes. It is shiny and wet, it gathers in little pearls.

A security guard grabs him, but he shrugs him off and swipes at the next one who comes at him. He hits him in the cheek and his hand stings from the impact. As he tries to leave another couple of guards block him and they fly away. They spin away from him and his feet carry on. Where he walks jobseekers and staff are backing away. Their eyes are wide, they are showing white. They are scared. They are excited. This is the most excitement they will all get this day. Maybe for many days to come.

His mother's eyes flash. The little boy shakes his rattle. One, two, three and the guards are out of his way. He swoops through them, he cracks meat.

The rattle is painted in bright primary colours. His fists hurt, they are bruised. The skin is broken on a couple of knuckles. The breaks smile, they sing along with the rattle. The owl dives and he is out of the building, running along the tram tracks. Cars and buses add their horns to the melody and it is all too much and he starts to scream. His lungs burn, his legs burn and he runs and keeps on running.

The accordion

'They always dig,' he says.

'Aye, you're not wrong there lad,' Malkie replies. They are sitting in a stretch of parkland and a pale sun shines down on their heads. Paths cross the park at regular intervals, slashing the turf diagonally with potholed concrete. Willem is a little tipsy from white rum and coke and a yellow digger scoops and lifts in the foreground. Men wielding jack hammers are repairing one of the roads, they have fenced it off and they stride up and down, cracking the ground. They dig and pound and the digger keeps on scooping.

'Why?' he asks. 'Why do they dig so much?'

'Look,' Malkie points. They are sitting on one of many benches whose wooden legs line the paths. Bikes and passing feet and children's scooters churn the asphalt. They crack it and holes begin to grow. 'They can cover over the holes, but they'll only open up again eventually. So they dig the road up and replace it at its foundation.'

'Aye.' He nods. His memory opens up through the rum. He has done it himself, he has drilled and dug and replaced the ground beneath his feet many times. But he also knows how silly it all is. Even if it takes an age, eventually the paths will all be churned up again.

'I used to be like them,' he mumbles.

'What's that, lad?'

'I used to have hi-vis jackets. I went to wear in boots and make my way labouring.'

'What happened?'

'I honestly don't know.'

The workmen's tools ring every few minutes. When they are quiet distant notes waft through the park. It is a busy park and an accordionist stands at the intersection of two paths, ruddy in the afternoon's faint glow. He pipes, his fingers play merriment and he is a digger, he scoops coppers from the passers-by. Willem smiles, the music is good. It makes him feel better. It reminds him of the little French cafe opposite his mama's flat. After the students came and he stopped going in there. Every day he heard the music as he walked past. Every day the accordions sang and made his heart feel free.

'Slim pickings today, lad,' Malkie complains. He searches his pockets for change, his hands come out empty. They are nearly out of rum and coke and they have no food and the old man looks a little nervous. But it is OK, Willem is OK. He has a few greasy notes left in his wallet. He has company and the music is good and there are a few hours yet before the sun will die.

'Stay here,' he tells Malkie. 'I'll get us some tea.'

'There's a good lad. Aye, good lad.'

He groans to his feet. His knees have locked from sitting. There is a burger van on the other side of the park and he kicks his feet, he loosens up. He walks past the workmen. They are finishing up for the day. They are securing the site, finishing up the little jobs. They are coiling up some lengths of purple tubing. Tomorrow the last of the tubing will go underground, it will carry water and wires 'and everything else unnoticed beneath our feet,' he mumbles. And the accordion wheezes and the sun puts in one last show.

The gypos' wailing

'Bloody crowd of them here sometimes,' the burger man says. There was a queue and Willem waited. He breathed the smell of the burgers, his stomach drank it in. And now the queue is gone and his mouth waters and the burger man is nodding over at the accordionist. His bald head growls, his paunch growls. He is indignant and he glares.

'Gypos, from Eastern Europe,' he slurs. He is a weegie from out west. His accent is thick, it swamps his words. 'They come here and they beg, they take all the benefits they can get. They come here and they take jobs from honest men like us. I used to be a plumber, but then the EU sent us all those Poles and Albanians and what not. I couldn't hold on to any contracts. Now I'm stuck out here in all weather, cooking up food for the thieving bastards to buy on their way home from work.'

The queue stopped with Willem and now the two men stand together under the blue sky, talking. Willem talks, he says he says the accordionist doesn't look like any plumber he ever saw.

'Aye, aye. But you know what I mean, though. He's still a thieving fucking gypsy. All those Eastern Europeans are.

'Don't think this will last, either,' the burger man says. He spreads his hands around the van. Around the griddles and the bottles of sauce. It is his kingdom and it has fallen on hard times. 'Look,' he says, nodding at a stall on the other side of the street. It is selling Brazilian food, it smells of fried beef and chilli and boiled rice. A smiling fat man with tanned skin scoops it all into plastic tubs for his own line of customers to take.

'Between that bastard and all these chicken shops and Turkish kebab places I'll be lucky to have any customers left.'

'Aye,' Willem nods. The rum has made him giddy. He takes his order. He takes two burgers wrapped in plastic and a portion of chips in polystyrene. The chips are covered in vinegar and ketchup and they make his stomach grumble once more. 'Ta,' he says and walks back to Malkie. He walks past the accordionist as he begins a new tune.

The notes of home part I

Clouds gather. They are thin, they are muslin as they come together and they cast the lightest shadow over the parkland. The cafes around the park's edge begin to close, the mothers with their prams and the young couples day-dreaming have departed. And Malkie speaks, he has his own stories to tell of the gypsies.

'I knew a couple of them used to beg down the Grass Market. Brothers, as far as I could tell. From somewhere over East, Romania or Croatia or wherever the hell these people come from. They were travelling folk once upon a time. One of them had been about a bit. He had some English so we swapped stories sometimes.

'Back home their families settled in a village. They were fine, they worked the land. Got by alright I guess. The broth-ers were only short fellas but they both had shoulders as big as yours. Strong as anything, I thought.

'Both brothers had wives and kids back home. They said their kids were all strong as well. They said every man from that part of the world was born to work, born strong. But there was a bad harvest a few years back and the kids went hungry. And the next year and the next, three bad harvests in a row. And slowly those kids stopped looking so strong.

'"We went to loan man," they told me. The loan men were gangs, mafia type thing. They got some money, they squared their rent and filled their cupboards. But those sharks are nasty fuckers. They bleed you dry, I know the sort. It doesn't matter what country you're in, there are always sharks like them. Bastards, rotten through.'

The sun peeped its last rays over the western horizon and Malkie carried on. The sky burned orange, stronger by the minute as dusk fell and night chased its tail. Malkie told

Willem that the sharks sent the brothers over. Them and others, to Edinburgh, Manchester, London. 'They tell the poor lads "Go to Britain, the streets in UK are paved with gold, go scoop some up to pay your debts!"

'They load them into buses and pay off the border guards. They float them over in ships from Holland. They hide them in vans stacked with tins and boxes. The holes are there,' Malkie told him, 'and the sharks trickle them through.

'To beg and busk and sleep rough. They whore the women out, they make a mint peddling cunt to the natives.' The two brothers Malkie knew slept under a bridge with a dozen others from their part of the world. 'Albanians, Croats, Ukrainians, all fucking sorts, so I heard.' By day they hold out their caps and by night they give ninety percent of whatever they get to the sharks' enforcers over here.

'I saw them often enough. Fat pricks in leather jackets. Shaved heads, hard eyes. Patrolling up and down, taking money from every man. Fucking every man's daughters for free.'

But the brothers never made a dent in their debt. 'Every week they say transport costs are owed, and the exchange rate has changed, they have fines for late payments. This reason, that reason, and within two months they owed fives times what they did when they kissed their families goodbye.'

'This all true?' Willem asked.

'Oh, aye lad. Hand on my heart, it's the god's honest truth.' He chuckled, he wheezed. 'But I'm a crazy old bastard, didn't I tell you? And there's nobody as minds a crazy man these days!'

They finish their food as the accordionist packs up. He places his instrument into a battered old sports bag. It is too big and it sticks out the top. The wind is down, there is quiet in the park. There is no music, there is no sound until Malkie starts to snore.

Willem huddles in. He digs into his sleeping bag and throws a blanket around them both. He borrows Malkie's warmth. His eyes close as the rum drags him down. His breathing slows. In his dreams his mama sings along with the accordion. Home is sweet, she sings, but not as sweet as my bonny wee lad.

'Goodnight mam,' he mumbles as the song cycles true. The stars wink in the heavens, they are all that is left this evening.

The notes of home part II

The song dies in the night and in the morning he wakes up alone. Malkie has gone, he has left a shallow patch in the grass and a bed of damp newspaper pages. Headlines and horoscopes and the morning dew stare up at Willem as he shakes his head. It pounds, his mouth is dry and the first commuters have begun to tread the streets. The park is a shortcut between their homes and their offices. Their feet slap and their strides are long and fast.

He is half under a bench. He and Malkie both slept with their heads and torsos covered, with their legs sticking out into the wind and the rain. His sleeping bag is damp. He rolls out, he kicks off the cover of night. His joints are stiff, he braces his hands on the bench and levers himself upwards. He sits, he blinks and he breathes in.

Willem reaches around to his back pocket. He keeps his wallet here, he checks it every morning like his mama told him. Every morning he peels apart the greasy notes. Every morning he gathers all of his coins and he counts his worth.

But Malkie is gone and Willem's wallet is gone, his pockets are empty. Bastard, he thinks. He looks at his shoes. He holds his baseball cap in his hand, it is all he has now. His wallet had his money and his driver's licence. It had a picture of him and his mama with their cheeks together. The picture was taken three years ago, it shows the two of them laughing. And now Malkie is gone and the picture is gone.

The accordionist is back. He strikes a tune and Malkie is in the notes. 'Slim pickings, lad...' he sings. 'There's nobody as minds a crazy man these days,' he sings. His voice is rough and the notes are sweet. Those notes hover over his wheezy laughter, over his dirty jokes and his stories. And Willem clutches his baseball cap as the commuters pass him by.

The accordionist dances. He is an old man but he moves well. His knees are slow, his feet and his shoulders are slow. But they know the music, they know the stories in those notes and they sway in time. Only his hands and eyes are fast, they dart with the tune as he turns his slow circles. He grins and nods when people drop their change into his cap, the morning dew is fading and his song is spreading good cheer.

The castle and the bridge

Willem comes and goes as the day marches on. He has business to conduct. He has nothing left and he is hungry and he asks around. He asks after Malkie but nobody has seen him. He asks people when they saw him last and their eyes are blank. They ask to borrow some money and he tells them that he has nothing. He asks to borrow some money and they stare.

He sets himself up on a busy corner and his cap starts to fill. It fills with people's silver and bronze, it fills with enough to buy himself a roll and a coke. One young man bends down and gives him a fiver. The man has curly hair and says 'god bless you, brother,' as Willem's throat closes and his eyes start to sting.

He heads back to the park every few hours. He sits on his bench and listens to the accordion. In the late afternoon he hides. A few of the Poles from his old crew walk through the park. Bratomil and his wife are with them, Celina is with them. They smoke and drink, Willem ducks his head and they do not see him. They glare at the workmen repairing the paths, they want their jobs. Willem hides his eyes. The building trade is still down and he does not need their pity and they do not need his. Their stories are separate now and he waits for them to pass him by.

A church bell rings eight o'clock as he sits on his bench. The bell tolls and the day begins to die, the accordionist has seen enough. He has been on his feet enough. His slow knees are tired as he stoops to pack his things away. He fumbles, he stuffs his accordion into his bag. It squeaks and groans, it is as tired as all of us, Willem thinks.

The old man's songs are still in his heart as he follows him from the park land. He allows twenty feet to separate them, he matches the old man's speed so that the gap does not close. They walk for a mile and then turn left down a winding side street. The side street descends a hill, it's cobbles are slick. The moon is above, it is beginning to show its face. Down here its light dances on the cobblestones as Willem hums tunelessly. He hums the accordionist's songs and he hums the lullabies his mama used to sing. They are the same to him, they are sweet and he smiles under their charm.

They take some smaller alleyways, away from the crowds. The old man stoops with his heavy bag over his back. He glances over his shoulder at each turn. He can see Willem, they lock eyes a few times and the accordionist speeds up a little. Willem has to stride heavily to keep the music in sight.

Finally, breathing hard, the old man turns a corner and the chase is over. A low bridge cradles an alcove. Dirty shapes huddle within, they shiver in their blankets. Soiled and shadowy mattresses slump beneath groups of three or four. Young men sit just outside the alcove. They smoke and play cards, the smoke spirals far above the bridge.

The young men part and the alcove swallows the accordionist. The music stops and the night grows cold. 'Hey, shit head,' one of the young men calls to Willem. 'What do you want?'

Willem spreads his arms with his palms facing out as they all stand and walk forwards a few paces. Industrial wires hum behind grates at their backs and pockmarks swallow their eyes. 'Cunt, bastard, you want to rob old man? Huh?' His voice is thick, it is heavy with foreign cities far from Willem's own life. The foreignness weighs him down, it is too much for one voice to take and the young man slurs. 'Or what, you policeman? Come, police,' he offers his hands, he holds out his wrists. 'Cuffs, come on. Arrest me, come. Give me warm bed, give me food for the night.'

He sneers and he steps forwards and he spits on the ground between them.

'Or are you shitty Great Britain tramp, nothing in the world? Ha!' He turns his back. The songs has ended and Willem is dismissed. The streets swallow him. He lets them, he is tired tonight.

The laws of man as enemy

He breaks the laws of man repeatedly over the coming weeks. Summer fades and autumn browns the leaves on the trees. The smell of rot pervades as September dies. It invades. It is in his nostrils, it is in his skin.

And he breaks the laws of man.

He steals occasionally to satisfy his physical needs. He begs, but this isn't always enough. Some people pass him in the street and instead of giving him a few coppers they give him their words. They ask him why he doesn't work for his money like everybody else. He tells them he would like to work, but nobody is hiring.

'So volunteer. It's better than this.'

'I don't want to work for nothing. Why would I?'

When his outstretched hand cannot sate his hunger or his thirst his fingers must work their magic. They perform tricks and he thinks *fuck you* and he eats well enough. His fingers are subtle despite their size and training. They stick to bars of chocolate and to cakes. Necessity, he finds, is the greatest teacher he has ever known.

He steals sometimes to satisfy something else. He steals odd things. In an off licence he will pay for food and drink. He will pay for magazines when he can afford them. These magazines have pictures of cars and women he will never touch, but they give his dreams a richer flavour. He will take them to the counter and when the shop assistant's back is turned his fingers will set to work. They will lift from the pot of pens on the counter, they will lift cheap rubber bracelets, packets of children's stickers. These are things he doesn't need but he takes them anyway.

Theft is a small part. Deeper needs rumble in his bones.

A drunken couple walked past him one time as he slept in a backstreet. It was getting on for three, the coldest part of the night, and the man was yelling at his girlfriend. He was abusing her, she was in tears. He struck her. He punched her and she fell to the ground. He yanked her up by the hair and threw her against the wall. He pulled down her shirt and a couple of buttons popped. Her breasts bounced. Her nipples were pink and little and pointed at her attacker. They pointed at the cold, they pointed in their fear. He grabbed one of her breasts, squeezing hard and laughing. He called her a whore, a bitch and he head butted her. Her nose broke and blood poured and Willem stood up from his sleep. Willem broke the man's arm. The same arm that had struck the blow, the same that had squeezed the woman's tits.

Willem threw the man against the wall. He grunted hard and smacked the man's head into the wall three times until the man's eye lost their focus. He rattled. Bright primary colours burned through the gloom. A ribbon of blood trickled from the man's head. As the woman tried to push Willem away he unzipped his trousers. He took out his cock and pissed over the man's head, over his jacket and shirt.

'You dirty pig, you fucking cunt!' The woman was yelling at him. 'But I saved you,' he mumbled. I'm a good man and you were in trouble. Her nose was flattened, her shirt was torn and covered in blood. She spat on his shoe. She swung her hand bag, glancing it across his cheek. He pushed her, he loomed over her. He held her still with one hand and with the other ripped her shirt off. The last few buttons flew. They scattered like seeds at his feet. One of them landed on his shoe, it landed in her phlegm.

Her tits were warm, they were soft. The nipple was taught against his palm. He still had his cock out, but it was limp.

He didn't want it to go hard. He just wanted her to know. He wanted her to know he could play their game. He let her go, he put his cock away and zipped up his trousers. He picked up his bedding and slouched off, confused. The shadows confused him and the sounds of night confused him. The primary colours glared, he could see too much red and it confused him. It buzzed in his head more than the world's voices. It made him spin and he couldn't clear himself of it. It made him feel sick. It made him feel alive.

For weeks it keeps him warm at night. He lets it out in bursts, thieving and breaking as his will dictates and as autumn arrives and the leaves drop his heart grows strong.

The pockets and the holes

Last night he lost his temper. He smashed in a car window with his hands. As the alarm sounded he threw his final punch and the glass splintered outwards like spider's webs, like veins crackling. He cut his wrist, he cut his knuckles. The blood ran down the glass' veins, it ran along his wrist and dripped from his fingers.

Now his cuts are itching, he scratched them through the night. As dawn rises he looks at his hands. The injured one is puffy and covered in thin blood. The other has blood caked under the nails. The nails are jagged, broken in places. His arm is stinging and his joints are bruised from the repeated impact.

He has seven pounds left in the world. He heads to a supermarket and picks up a can of coke and a chocolate bar. He heads to the pharmacy section and pockets a bottle of disinfectant. He slips a packet of plasters up one sleeve. He takes a power bar, tucking it into his waistband.

He knows how to go unnoticed, and in the silence he works.

Fuck you.

He would like it if he were seen. Then he could let them know what he was doing. He could release some of the noise built up behind his eyes. *Fuck you, fuck you.* But he needs the plasters and the food. His body needs them more than it needs satisfaction right now.

He walks to the counter with his pockets rattling. He has replaced his jeans with a pair of jogging bottoms. They have deeper pockets. Deeper holes in which to hide his treasures. His vitamins, nearly finished, are in those holes. The last of his money is in those holes. His injured hand is thrust deep into one of those holes, his blood spills into the emptiness.

'That all, mate?' the cashier asks.

'Mm.'

'Thank you. Have a nice day.'

'Mm.'

Outside he downs the coke. He eats the chocolate. He walks to the car park behind the shop as the sugar hits his eyes. He sits in one corner and spits on his hand. He spits on the gash up his forearm. He rubs the blood away. It is brown and runs like rust. Like the rust in a beaten up old motor. It pools on his wrist, caking him in rust.

The antiseptic stings his cuts and it stings his nose. He has no cotton wool or gauze. He has to pour it straight on. Too much flows and it washes the rust away but leaves a chemical stink. He sits still as the day passes. Every few hours he pours more antiseptic, he stretches fresh plasters over his wounds.

'You alright there mate?'

'Mm.'

The sun is falling and the one eyed man has arrived. His face glows purple as he re-enters Willem's story. He burps, he farts and a garlicy waft encloses them both. He slumps down onto the pavement next to Willem, groaning the last few inches until his backside finds its seat.

'What happened? You been in the wars?'

'Aye.'

'What did you do?'

'Just punching.'

'Looks like you punched your way through plate glass with those cuts.'

'Yeah.'

'Yeah? Shit, kid! What's your mam say about all this?'

'She died.'

'Shit.'

They both sit in silence for a few minutes. Their shoulders are touching, they lean in and support each other. The garlicy aroma is still there, it burns deep in Willem's nose. It mixes with the antiseptic. Across the street a squirrel chases the wind. The wind whips up and the squirrel runs full into it, its tail bushy. Its ears fold flat against its skull. The wind dies down and it waits. It stands still, nothing moving. Its hair is bristly, grey across its back, a dirty yellow on its front. Its paws wait, its nose waits and then the wind blows again. It chases forwards. A bag from the supermarket swirls in the gust. It chases the squirrel and the wind chases it.

'You got a fag?' the one eyed man wants to know.

'No.'

'You used to have fags all the time.'

'I used to have a lot of things.'

They lapse into silence once more. Willem opens a couple of plasters. He sticks one end of the first over a cut on his palm. He stretches it out a little and lays the rest down. He does it again and again, one more on his palm, three on the back of his hand and two on his wrist. They cover the worst of his cuts. He tears a strip from the bandage. He puts a couple of plasters on his arm and wraps the bandage around them.

'You should get stitches.'

'No. I'm not a patient anymore.'

'Well I don't know about that, son.'

'Mm.'

'So what you been up to?'

'Nothing much.'

'You look like you've been sleeping rough.'

'Aye. Mam died and I didn't want to go home. Home was too full of people. So I stayed away for a couple of days. Me and Jap wandered about, slept where we lay.'

'And now?'

'When I went home some men had come. They changed the locks. They took all the money out of my room. They took the computer and the TV and my PlayStation. They said it's not my home anymore. The landlord wanted it back.'

'Cunts.'

'Aye.'

'Where's the dog now?'

'Jap?'

'Aye, Jap. Where's Jap?'

'They took him too.'

'Cunts.'

The Dutchman

'You don't get too many Willems. I don't know I've ever met one.'

'It's the name my mam gave me.'

'It's Dutch. You know that?'

'No. It's not Dutch. I've never been to Dutch country.'

'Holland.'

'Mm.'

'But the name's Dutch. Anyone in your family Dutch?'

'No. Mam's from Glasgow. Was. Her family's all from there and Edinburgh.'

'You don't see them?'

'No. Never had much to do with them. Most of them died when I was a kid anyway.'

'And your pa?'

'Don't have no pa. Mam had her fancy men but I never had no pa.'

'You didn't know him? Maybe he was a Dutchman.'

'Mm.'

'You look like maybe you're Dutch.'

'Mm.'

'You ever consider it?'

'No. Mam said the nurse was a Paki. Said she didn't understand the Queen's English. She said she told them William and they put down Willem. Mam liked it so she kept it.'

'Oh.'

They lapse back into silence for a while. The one eyed man burps again. He farts twice and the smell mixes once more with the antiseptic. He brings out a bottle of whiskey and offers some to Willem. It is dark brown. The one eyed man's hand is barely visible on the other side of the bottle. The liquid sloshes around and the glass winks at Willem. It glimmers and he says 'aye, give it here.'

It stings his throat. It tastes like antiseptic. He killed the germs on his skin. Now he's killing the germs inside. He is burning them out. His mouth burns and his eyes burn. His stomach burns. It rumbles, churning the chocolate bar. Someone told him once that chocolate releases the same chemicals as a hug. His mama hugs him, her hug burns as he drinks more whiskey. Jap licks his face and his tongue burns his cheeks with its slavering foam.

He unwraps his power bar. He splits it in half. He gives the one eyed man a piece. He chews the other himself, working it around. It is chewy, it makes his jaw ache. Finally he swallows. He washes it down with another swig, then another.

'Good to see you, lad. But I'll be on my way.' The one eyed man puts a hand on Willem's shoulder to lever himself up. He grunts as he stands. He bends over, bracing his hands on his knees. 'The old joints aren't what they were,' he puffs. After a minute he straightens, grunting again. Willem takes one more swig from the whiskey and hands it back.

'Ta. Take care, lad.'

'Mm.'

Willem watches the one eyed man totter away. He staggers to the right and the left. He takes a half step forwards and then a lunge. He totters once more before steadying himself. His old puffer jacket has mud stains down the back. His corduroys are discoloured. Maybe they were navy or black once but now they are yellowing, grey green in places. They are the same colour as the squirrel's mangy front. They are ragged at the hems, they fade into the puddles at his feet and the wind chases him, whipping at his back.

The naughty pictures

He is in one corner, between two walls. The sun is dying and the street lights are glowing and his cuts itch as they heal. To his left there stands a pair of big, round industrial bins on squeaky wheels. They are so big that they block out the setting sun. Without standing he shifts his weight. He puts pressure on one hand, on his good hand. He cradles his damaged hand to his chest. He takes the rest of his weight on his heels and crab walks, shuffling against the wall. He shuffles along until he is behind the farthest bin, out of sight. He pulls his sleeping bag out of his rucksack, rolls to one side, takes his cock out and sprays the wall with his piss, relieving himself for the night. The piss splashes off the wall. It forms into a little puddle. My ripples, he thinks. It forms a little stream as his cock flops, empty. The stream smells. It runs towards the bin, it gathers under its squeaky wheels.

Good. The foxes will be out soon and he wants them to know he's there. This is his bed tonight, his nest. This is his territory.

He shifts further over to the left, shuffling on his arse. He takes his wad of newspaper out of his rucksack. He saves a couple of naughty pictures. He spreads the rest out, patting them down in thick sheets to make a bed. He opens the hood of his sleeping bag and digs his feet in. He leans his weight onto his shoulders and shimmies the bag upwards. Before it reaches his waist he stops. His cock is still out, flopping against his jeans. He takes it in one hand. With his injured hand he opens the naughty pages and arranges them next to his bed.

The girls' breasts are big, big as his head. He thinks they look soft, they look warm and comforting. His injured hand flexes unconsciously, he is trying to squeeze their tits and in his head they are supple. One of the girls lets her fondle him. The other lays his head against her bare chest. It is warm and smells of springtime. He closes his eyes and another girl puts her mouth over his cock. She is naked, she has her legs spread. She sits on his cock, moving up and down. He can smell her sex, it mixes with the smell of his piss. It ripples, it forms puddles in his head. She rests her breasts against his cheek as his cock releases. The two girls curl up around him. They curl around him like Jap used to. Like his mama did when he was a bairn.

He wipes his hand on one of the naughty pictures. The ink smears with the goo. His fingers are dry but they have toner on them. They are purple as he gives his cock one last squeeze. One last drop comes out of its end. He shakes it off, puts it away and zips up his jeans. He pulls the sleeping bag up and shuts his eyes again. He is asleep quickly, dreaming of warmth.

The sandwich packets

He sleeps for an hour in his nest. The wind is cold but the bins interrupt the worst of it. They rattle and squeak and after an hour he is woken. The foxes haven't come, he made sure of that. But there is noise, there are footfalls. Lights are flashing behind his bin and people are talking, loud and rowdy. The sound of heavy bags being half carried reaches his ears. They are half carried, half dragged and the men dragging them swear loudly.

He is alert straight away. The streets have taught him this. As soon as he wakes his heart rate soars, his muscles tense. His breathing is ragged but he keeps it quiet.

Who are these people come to disturb him?

There are about twelve inches of nothingness from the ground to the bottoms of the bins. The wheels and their legs raise them high. Through this gap he can see four pairs of shoes. They are cheap leather, made to look smart. They are not as good as his own boots, but they are designed for less stress than his are. Blue trouser hems sit on their shoes, moving closer to the bin's edge. Green plastic sacks swing next to their legs.

As they get close the legs tense. They lunge forwards in pairs, two by two, two by two. As each pair lunges a sack is lifted up and a second later Willem hears a thud. A metallic clangour. The bins rock slightly on their wheels. It is like thunder in his nest. All this noise is unwelcome.

One by one the bags are thrown. They clang and finish and then the legs leave.

Just as he allows himself to breathe again he hears more footsteps, more half dragged bags scraping the floor. The legs are back for a second drop. Four times they come. Four times the bin peels like thunder, interrupting his thoughts. He can hardly breathe, his lungs are tight. Bands hold them in and his throat is ragged.

They leave and he waits. He waits ten minutes and they don't come back. He waits another ten minutes and pokes his head around one bin. There is nobody. There are a few cars and a lorry in the car park, but not another soul.

He stands, shaking himself out of his sleeping bag. He hooks his fingers over the top of the bin closest to his nest. It is taller even than he is. There is a small sill halfway up and he jumps, levering himself up. He lands the toes of his boots on the sill and peers into the darkness. Thirty or so thick green plastic bags are in the bin. A couple of them are half open and baguettes and fruit in nets and unopened yoghurt pots spill out.

He hooks one leg over and allows himself to fall into the bin. He splits the bags. Inside are tins of beans and packets of crisps. He throws a couple of packets of crisps behind the bin. He tears another open. It is a large pack, a party pack and he is hungry. These days he is always hungry. He stuff the crisps into his mouth a handful at a time. His fingers turn orange with cheesy powder. His tongue feels like it is dancing. The salt and the spices are a delight, they sing.

He rips open another bag and a hundred meals fall out. They are packets of sandwiches, one or two to a carton. Cardboard slick with the supermarket's artwork, plastic film slick with spilled egg and tuna and cheese. He picks up a BLT, he rips the packet in two and wolfs it all down. He licks his fingers. He licks the bacon grease, the tomato juice and mayonnaise, the cheesy powder from the crisps. His stomach gurgles, it ties itself in two. It is working harder than it has in a long time.

He pulls the wrapping off a tuna sandwich and eats it, slower now. The initial panic is over. The initial excitement is fading. Now mechanics are setting in. His teeth grind, up and down, side to side. His tongue works the fish and bread into a paste, his gullet opens and sucks it down in great gobbets. He takes another bite, swallows and takes another. Afterwards he licks his fingers, he sucks off the remains of the food. He sucks off the purple toner and his fingers are slick with saliva.

He is thirsty. Cartons of orange and apple juice sit bound side by side on a little palette. Little waxed cardboard boxes with straws. They are built for a child's picnic and he drinks each one down in a single swallow. The sugar hits his brain quickly, firing it up. The liquid soothes his stomach, it unties the knot and washes away the last of his hunger.

He falls back, he smiles. He is properly happy for the first time since Jap was taken. His cheeks ache at first. From chewing, from smiling. The bags are comfortable. He sits for a while, suspended on green plastic and disposable food. There are spiders in here. They spin their webs as he watches, catching dew drops and flies. They don't come near him. He is too big, their nets won't work on him.

After a while the sugar wears off. The food makes him sleepy. As his eyes grow heavy he hauls himself to his hands and knees. He climbs out of the bin, dropping down onto his newspaper mattress. He climbs into his sleeping bag, enjoying the ammonia smell of his own piss inches from his head. His stomach is heavy. The food is swelling inside, growing with each breath he takes until it weighs more than he does. It weighs him down, it drags him into a deep sleep with no waking for hours.

He dreams vividly that night. His mother's eyes and the owl ascending flash through his brain. Jap chases the boy, the boy runs along laughing, shaking his rattle. And Willem sits in the middle of it all, eating bacon and tuna and drowning in a child's juice box.

The rain dance

He sleeps late. The sun is high when he comes around. He needs to piss straight away. He drank too much last night. He rolls his sleeping bag down to his feet. He unzips, takes his cock out and marks his territory once more.

When he is done he opens a packet of crisps and eats them, savouring the salty tang. He finishes them and opens another, working them with his teeth and tongue. With his tongue he crushes them against the roof of his mouth. With his molars he grinds the broken shards into paste. He breathes heavily. He closes his eyes to block out everything else.

The car park is busy but he is hidden from its eyes. He is in his own world. The undersides of cars flash by beneath the bin. Shoes and trolleys glide along, burdened with their week's groceries. Every pair of shoes he sees is shiny and clean on top, muddied underneath. He gazes at them, he enjoys the contrast.

He spends his whole day watching people's shoes. He watches two hundred pairs before losing count. It rains a couple of times and he huddles back into the wall, he flattens himself against the brickwork. The water pings against the bin's steel walls, rattling. It makes the ground slick. The floor becomes a mirror with an upside down bin, with Willem's face staring back out of it.

His memories swim, they grind and he is dancing in the rain. He was wet and it kept flicking his shoulders and the crown of his head.

He didn't want to dance, he was shy, he was uncoordinated. But the girl insisted. She drove him. They were in a pub car park and loud music was playing. Inside was creamy and warm, but out here in the rain the two could smoke and talk and listen to each other. He didn't have too much to say for himself but she talked unendingly. She barely breathed, she only paused to drag on her fag.

She had thin bones. As they danced he held on to her thin bones carefully, afraid that he might crush her. She had pale skin and a warm mouth. Her lips were coloured with lipstick, they burned a bright red. They moved, they squirmed and smiled and he listened to every word she said. He laughed when he was meant to, he smiled when he was meant to. He shook his head and tutted when he was meant to.

Her wet hair was sticking to her face. He could feel water running down his neck. He wanted to kiss the rain off her nose, to kiss her eyelids dry. He wanted to fold her up and keep her thin bones warm.

A bassline started on the jukebox and she held his hands to her hips. When she knew they wouldn't go anywhere she put her arms around his neck, reaching up almost on tiptoes. He loomed over her but she held him in place. She led him through the steps. They turned in circles. The circles were a dance, they made him dizzy. But he kept smiling, he kept laughing when he was meant to.

A spider walked across his shirt collar. It climbed out of his bones, out of his heavy cracked bones. He didn't see it, he didn't feel it. He was working too hard on the circles, on the girl's words. On holding her without crushing her. He didn't know it was there until she jumped. She screamed and she jumped out of his hands. If only he had held her more firmly, if only his own bones weren't so big.

She pointed to his collar, she backed away, laughing, screaming. 'Oh, I hate them, I hate them, I hate-!' she said and then she left. She turned on her heel, laughing. She was carefree. She ran back into the creamy warm pub, she went to find other dance partners. He squeezed the spider between his thumb and forefinger. It popped and he wiped the blood and flesh on his jeans.

He lit another cigarette and walked home. Now he sits behind his bins and lights a cigarette, careless. Now night is falling and he doesn't mind the rain. He looks at his hand, at the bloody plasters. He peels them off and sees that they have begun to heal, a layer of gooey skin has started to grow. He pours more antiseptic, he puts on more plasters and sits back, dragging on his cigarette.

That evening the shoes approach once more with their sacks. Their legs tense, their bags swing and disappear. The bin rocks slightly as the bags land and then the world is at peace. He eats well that night. He eats a mozzarella sub and a salmon panini. He drinks a coke and a bottle of blackcurrant squash. He finds a quiet corner and takes a shit. He wipes himself with newspaper. He cleans his teeth, he rinses under his arms with rain water. He returns to his nest behind the bin, sleeps well and stays in place the following day.

He eats well the following night. He thinks it cannot end. His hand begins to heal and his stomach grows warm and he doesn't mind the rain.

The torch

'Hey, what the fuck?' The voice demands too much of him. It is harsh, gravelly. It is from up north somewhere. It comes from the highlands, it comes from above. 'Fucking tramp, get to fuck with you.' It demands from nowhere. He can see nothing. He can see a bright beam of light, it glances at his eyes. It pierces the shadows of his nest.

A hand as rough as the voice slaps his face. It grabs his collar. It yanks him sideways. His legs are tangled in his sleeping bag and he rolls. He tries to stand and trips. 'Fucking drunk. And hey!' the voice squeals, its roughness lost as it soars through the high notes. He looks at the litter, the empty sandwich boxes and juice cartons. 'That's our property. You thief, you fucking thieving drunk.'

A shoe rustles through the litter of empty sandwich cartons and bottles. 'It was in the bins,' Willem stammers, shielding his eyes with his hands.

'Still our property. You're still a thief. Wait there, bastard. I'm calling the police.'

'No, no.'

'Shut the fuck up. Hey, Jimmy, shut this wee bastard up.'

Something hard hits him across the head. It is metallic and it bludgeons his skin. It opens his skin and one eye blinks blood.

'Hey, yeah, police,' the rough voice says. It's gone back to its gruff low notes. It rumbles. A shadow is forming behind the beam of light. A small man holding a big torch glares down at him as he speaks to the phone. 'Hi, yes, I've got a trespasser and a thief here. Looks like he's a homeless man, looks like he's messed himself on the car park floor...'

Another shadow has formed to Willem's right. Jimmy stands tall. Almost as tall as Willem, but he is rangy with small bones where Willem is a solid block.

Willem manages to get his feet out of his sleeping bag as the rough voice gives the supermarket's name and address to the phone. He puts one hand on the wall behind him. As he tries to stand Jimmy kicks him, but it doesn't do much. Jimmy tries to raise the heavy metallic object again, but as he brings it over his head Willem stands.

Both men's eyes pop. They are shadows and staring eyes and one bright light cutting through them all. This is all Willem can see of them, but it's enough. He lashes out at Jimmy, sending him reeling. He grabs the rough voice by the collar, head butts him and lifts him above his head. He throws him in the bin where he crashes into the rubbish pile.

He falls on Jimmy. He sits on his hollow chest. He breathes heavily as his arms work. His knuckles bruise once more, they are bruises on top of bruises. They are purple blisters in the shadows. His own eyes stand out. They are three pairs of white eyes, three shadows, three voices dancing in the dark. The metallic object is near at hand. He picks it up. It's another torch, heavy and industrial. It is cold to touch, it soothes his fingers. He raises it above his head.

His shadow is part of Jimmy's now. Jimmy's has enclosed his own. Jimmy's face cracks, concave as the torch descends, one, two three. One, two, three. The torch's glass shatters, its rim dents.

Jimmy isn't breathing. His face is inside out.

Willem peels his shadow away from the dead man. He wraps it about himself. He wraps his sleeping bag about his shoulders. He leaves his newspapers littered on the ground. They are spattered with blood. With shadow and blood. He breaks into a run, he hops a fence and runs down an embankment. His shadow runs alongside him, stark against the moonlight.

The cold miles

'Hey, laddie, what the fuck are you doing?'

The one eyed man has chased him down the embankment. He might be an old man, his joints stiff with his years and his legs and shoulders bowed, but he is nimble nonetheless. He is a man made hard by the hardness of his world and he scrambles down after Willem with little effort.

'What's all the shouting, what's all this blood?'

'I killed a man.'

'Jesus fucking Christ, lad. Come on with you, follow me.'

'Where?'

'Where the fucking pigs can't find you, lad. Where they don't look.'

The embankment is an old railway track. Thick sleepers withered with age cross its breadth. Old tracks are sunk into the remains of the sleepers. They are pitted with rust and circled with deep, wet mud. There are rocks everywhere. The rocks are covered with ivy and grass and the two men slip and stumble as they run. Willem staggers often, scattering the rocks, tearing the plant life. He makes a racket and the one eyed man hisses at him to be quiet. The one eyed man is silent as he slips and slides. 'I've been at this game a long time, lad. I know how to disappear. Stick with me and I'll see you right.'

They jog for a mile or so. Willem is breathing hard but the one eyed man barely seems affected. His face is swollen and purple on one side, but the other side is serene and calm.

'This is our stop, Willie,' he says as they reach a fork in the tracks. On one side it carries on into pitch darkness. The other is stopped up with rubbish. Large blocks of concrete are wedged into place. Hundreds of battered old bottles, cans and wrappers litter the blocks. Old toasters and shopping trolleys and sofas and microwaves are shattered against it all, dropped from the backs of vans at the top of the verge.

The one eyed man leads him into the middle of the two tracks. 'Every path and every shadow has its secrets, lad. You've just got to learn how to look. My good eye never misses a beat, I've told you that before and I'll tell you that now.'

They follow a small trail for another mile or so. It runs through woodland. It takes them down ditches and over streams. After a mile they come to a rise. The two men scramble up, scratching and stinging their hands on brambles and nettles. At the top a stretch of bare road reaches to the north and south. A couple of lamp posts line the road, revealing nothing but barren scrub land. On the horizon the silhouettes of tenement flats and terraced houses loom black.

'Pigs won't think to look out here for a couple of hours. We've got the jump on them.'

They turn left, they leave Edinburgh's streets behind them. For a couple of miles they hike through the suburbs. They hike through council estates and abandoned retail parks. 'These are the invisible places, lad. The police don't come this far out if they can help it. The tourists don't come here. Nobody even calls this Edinburgh. They say the tram will come out this far if they ever get the bloody thing built, but I'll believe it when I see it.'

The bridge

Trolls live under bridges. One of his mama's blokes told him this one time. They live under them and they lay in wait for travellers. They waylay them, stripping them of their gold and making feasts of them. They grind their bones into jelly and churn their blood for soup. He used to look for them whenever he walked underneath a bridge. He would look for them in the open spaces and in the shadows, always scared that they would jump out and gobble him up.

This bridge is no different. He looks into its open spaces and finds strange shapes lying about in rags. He looks into the shadows and sees the whites of eyes tracking him. The bridge rises over them all, shielding them, trapping them. It is about twenty feet wide and it spans a river. Struts thrust out of the river to hold up its bulk and on the banks beneath a makeshift campsite houses a community who call the land their home.

'There's usually fifteen or so of us at any one time. Folks come and go, that's their nature. But you can always count on a good crowd.'

'They're all homeless?'

'Aye. You meet a lot of folks begging on the streets. They usually have homes to go to of some kind or another. Maybe a room in a bedsit. Maybe a friend's sofa. Maybe they share a two bed flat with ten other people. One way or another, though, they've all got somewhere to go.

'Everybody needs somewhere to go, lad. Well, for us that place is here.'

They trudge down a muddy bank. The mud sucks their feet. Willem's legs are tired, they feel like lead. His bones feel like lead. The man's life evaporated in his hands, his blood became Willem's blood. That blood drags him, clogging him. The adrenaline of the fight and the chase has worn off and now his head has grown thick. His thoughts have slowed, soon they will stop altogether and his eyes will shut tight.

As the one eyed man announces himself and introduces Willem to a couple of people his ears buzz. He is stuck in the mud, he is become the earth. People take his hand, they squeeze it but he doesn't feel. They speak to him but he can only stare into the darkness of the river. 'Come on lad, let's get your head down,' the one eyed man says at last, breaking his reverie.

The crowd of people disperses and Willem is led through their ranks. The floor is filth but there are concrete platforms lining the point at which the bridge meets the bank. Blankets and cardboard boxes and sleeping bags and steel bins filled with burning flotsam cover the platforms. The one eyed man guides Willem to a bare spot on one of the middle platforms.

'Here you go, lad,' he says, stopping before an old mattress covered in grey blankets. 'You can sleep here 'til you get yourself settled. There's room enough for both of us.'

Willem collapses, his eyelids shut immediately. He is too tired to notice the stench of mildew. He is too tired to be bothered by the fleas. He is too tired even to notice the old man climb in an hour later.

He wakes up in the morning with heavy limbs. The old man is curled in tight, snoring peacefully in the pale dawn.

The stories part I

He stays in the community under the bridge for a week. On the first day he is convinced that he will stay there forever. He can think of no more perfect place. They are outside the law, above the law. They live huddled closer to nature's true purposes.

He accumulates stories over the week. They are stories he never wanted to acquire. Yet they pile themselves on top of him anyway as one by one their narrators run through their lives at his side.

The first morning he eats a tuna sub. He squashed a couple into his coat pockets when he was staying in the car park. They are out of date and the bread is starting to go hard, but they fill his stomach nicely. As he licks the tuna mayonnaise from his fingers a young man sidles up to him. He is a little younger than Willem. He is in his early twenties and his voice breaks slightly as he says hello.

'My name is Nicky. My mother had me on Christmas day, so she named me Nicholas after St. Nick.'

'Mm.'

Nicky has fought hard. He has tough skin and tough eyes. His voice quavers. The quaver says that the fight has taken its toll.

'When you're a kid you never think you'll end up out here, do you pal?' he asks. He sweeps his hand around the encampment. Willem shakes his head, staring down at his shoes. They are sitting at the edge of one of the concrete plinths, swinging their legs and skimming the muddy puddles.

'As a kid I got on with my folks. My dad died early on and my mam found another bloke. He was alright at first. But when I grew up a bit we fell out. We took to rowing and they chucked me out. I moved in with a mate for a few weeks. Next time I heard anything about my folks they'd upped and left. Dundee. So I had to stay with my mate.'

He glares out over the water. His eyes are hard, they flit from side to side. They are like stones, they offer no reflection. 'But my mate's mam was hard up. She couldn't keep me too long. I went to my teachers and one of them gave me the number of a hostel for kids like me. I had a bed in a dormitory. The other kids were rough, I got beat up. But I soon learned how to take of myself. The government gave me benefits so I had some money.

'But then the hostel ran out of money. Cuts, they said. That was last year. My benefits stopped, we all got chucked out of the hostel. Some of us wound up here. That girl there, Jessie. She's my girlfriend. She's from the hostel. And that boy, Pete. He was there. He was the first bastard to beat on me, but we get on alright now.'

The one eyed man scooped them up. He found them begging on the street. The two boys looked after Jessie. She used her mouth and hands to make money in Edinburgh's back alleys. For some clients she used her cunt. The boys always made sure she got paid, that she got treated right. But she grew sick from all the men, she gave too much of herself. That's when the one eyed man stepped in and brought them here.

'It's paradise,' the one eyed man often laughs. 'A place where the invisible folks can be free.' Nicky's eyes are shifty, they point in slightly different directions so that Willem doesn't know which way he's looking. People get confused, they tell Willem that Nicky looks at places nobody else can see.

Around midday his friend Rosa arrives. She rides a little moped. It's a dirty old thing, faded blue with broken wing mirrors. Her boots are covered in mud. Wet mud clings to dry mud and she cackles when she sees the one eyed man. She grabs his crotch and they embrace, kissing.

'Clear off for a while, lad,' the one eyed man tells Willem. 'We'll be needing the mattress for a bit.'

The rest of the encampment trudges up the river bank with him. They sit by the side of the road, huddled in blankets as Rosa's laughter chases the wind. 'They'll be a few minutes together. When she stops laughing it's usually OK to go back down,' Nicky tells him.

The warm miles

Nicky tells him there is a bus service from down the road. Sometimes Rosa brings a van with supplies, but this is rare. For the rest they either go to a small village nearby or get the bus into town to beg. The village is a half hour in the other direction, but the city calls to him. The fight yesterday got his blood up, he wants to taste Edinburgh's air once more. He eats his other sub and is out of food. He has a few coins and he uses them to buy his bus ticket.

'You're new,' the driver remarks.

'No. I've been about for a while.'

The driver laughs. His laughter is a series of short barks. 'Ha. Ha. Ha. Aye. But you're one of them mud flappers. You must be new. I haven't seen you around here.'

Willem takes his ticket and takes a seat. There is only one deck and he sits at the back. The bus is warm, the heating tickles him. He dozes as the countryside skitters passed his window. The fields sprout estates, they tangle in a mess of wire fences. Concrete blocks loom large in their midst. They are dirty, they are covered in filth and graffiti. There is large balloon writing and there are cartoons of angry looking men. They are enclosed behind chain link fences, staring out at the world as Willem sleeps. His head bumps the window as the bus jumps over potholes, the graffiti sings loud and his mouth hangs open.

After a while the new builds grow less frequent and old town houses grow in their place. They are in the city now and city dwellers keep their houses tidy. They grow ivy on trellises and keep their fences and doors freshly painted. The tarmac beneath the bus's wheels gives way to cobblestones and the bus rattles, it judders at each red light. Willem is fully awake now. He is shaken awake. The noise of the city invades as fully as the graffiti's song.

He unties his tracksuit bottoms and takes out his cock. There are only three other people on the bus. They are old ladies in bonnets and plastic hoods and they sit at the front of the bus, chattering. He releases a slow stream of yellow piss. It is thick, it stinks of ammonia. He is dehydrated and the piss dribbles, but it is enough. It pools on the floor, it runs down to the aisle. It forms a little trickle, working its way to the front. It snakes and the snake's head rears, laughing, smelling. He smiles, he is pleased. He is satisfied.

He presses for the bell. It rings once, twice. He rings it a third and fourth time as little orange letters appear on an electronic display behind the driver's cabin. They say BUS STOPPING, they flicker lazy and dull.

'Give my regards to Rosa,' the driver says as Willem gets off.

'Mm.'

The crow's eyes

The first thing he does is steal a drink. He goes into a small supermarket and slips a bottle of Lucozade into his pocket. He shakes up all the other bottles. He shakes up some cans of fizzy drinks. He puts his hands down his pants and fondles the wet tip of his penis. He rubs his finger around the lips of all the cans. *Fuck you,* his mantra runs. *Fuck you, fuck you.*

He slips a chocolate bar and uses the last of his change to buy a sandwich. Outside he downs the Lucozade. The bubbles gurgle in his stomach, they tickle his throat as they slide down. He eats the chocolate bar in three bites. He enjoys the sugar, the creamy sweetness. With his stomach crooning he saves the sandwich for later.

There is a cash machine around a corner. It is opposite a pleasant garden with leafy trees and neatly bordered flower beds. It is on an empty street with slick cobblestones and neat pavements. He sits in the garden for an hour and nobody bothers him. Nobody comes, nobody looks and he thinks *fuck you*. After an hour a crow lands a few feet from where he is crouched. It squawks, barking at him. Another lands on the other side of the small garden. Its eyes glitter, they are dead and hard as any man's. The two birds circle each other, each with its head turned to one side. Each eyeing the other.

Finally they launch at one another. They squawk, their beaks dart. Their calls are shrill, they whistle in his ears. A few feathers fly and one is chased off. It flaps its wings, it drags itself upwards. The other clucks, it turns a beady eye on Willem and waits, watching him.

'Fuck you,' he tells the birds.

Willem watches the street, waiting. A heavy set man is the first to come. He takes his time as he withdraws some money. He is too big. Willem would be able to take him down. He could tear him apart, but not quietly enough. Not quickly enough. Then a teenager comes to use the machine. No, he won't have enough money in his account. It's not worth it.

Finally a small woman in an expensive business suit clacks down the street on her heels. Her suit is grey and her hair is golden. It flashes in the pale sunlight and the crow flaps, it cries out but she doesn't notice. She is speaking on a phone, laughing down the line. She is obviously flirting, her eyes flash and she smiles. She turns red, she is flushed with excitement.

She stops at the cash point. One hand fumbles in her little bag as she roots for her purse. The other collects the debris she uncovers. A hairbrush, a bundle of receipts and letters, a compact mirror. All this time she is chatting on the phone, breathless. She has wedged it between her cheek and her shoulder. She arranges a meeting for later, for eight pm at a nice restaurant. She laughs, she giggles, her eyes keep flashing.

She finds her purse and one hand takes out a debit card. She slots it into the machine, she leans in close and enters her PIN number. Charlie told him that the extra 'number' is unnecessary, but Charlie is a long way away. He is far from Willem's life. He is from the past and Willem doesn't want to look backwards anymore.

Instead he looks forwards, he looks at the woman in her tight skirt. He looks at her arse straining at the fabric. He emerges from the bushes, he calls out 'excuse me, love,' as the crow takes fright and swoops to the far end of the garden.

The woman jumps, she is surprised and her giggling stops. She drops her phone and swears. She stoops to pick it up and Willem has crossed the street with long strides. She is bent over, that arse is facing him. He bends his knees a little and puts his waist against her arse. He leans over her body and locks his arms around her chest. He folds her up, he picks her up and throws her against the wall. He slaps her head against the wall, opening a gash. The red blood seeps out, colouring her golden hair. It is a dark spot. It mouths obscenities as she slides down the wall, unconscious.

He bends in to the cash machine. He presses a button to show her balance. The little screen tells him that she has three thousand one hundred and eight pounds, eighty six pence. He presses a button to withdraw cash and takes out three hundred pounds. The machine spits the card out. It shuffles the money and then ejects it, a tight wad of twenty pound notes.

Willem picks up her purse. There is another sixty pounds in notes. There is about three pounds in change, jangling as he searches. He takes it all, he folds it tight and puts it in his pocket.

He sits her upright against the wall. He undoes a couple of buttons on her shirt. He reaches in and slips his hand into her bra. Her tits are big and soft and he rubs her nipple between his finger and thumb. He cups and squeezes and then withdraws his hand. He opens her shirt fully and pulls down her bra. Her tits bob as they fall out of their cups, her nipples are small and pink and he kisses them softly. He sucks them a little and pulls her bra back up. He rights her shirt, kisses her on the top of her head and folds her hands in her lap. He puts her debit card back in her purse. He puts her purse and mobile into her bag and places it on her lap. And then he walks away, hoping that nobody heard them.

The warm spot

He has been told that there is a pub on Edinburgh's south side in which homelessness is not prohibitive to patronage. He never went, he was careful with his money. But now his pockets are full, they are burning with the blonde woman's money. He stands in the rain, he stares at its front doors as customers sit at the bar. They are chatting with the staff, offloading their worries. They slouch over tables, they sit in corners brooding. They grow rowdy with drink and sing songs and football chants. They vent, they rage. They laugh and cry and the air is soaked with the emotions of the street.

There are flats above the pub and people often complain. They have alarm clocks set for the early morning and eyes made heavy from long office hours. They cannot afford to lose precious hours of sleep, they cannot afford interruptions. The police are called to the pub a couple of times each week. Their station is around the corner and all their officers know the landlord well. They haunt it as often as many of its patrons, but no laws are broken, no reasons exist to tempt them to bring people in.

The police are leaving as Willem watches from across the street. He watches their shoulders hunch against the

patrons' taunts, he watches them climb into their car. One
of them speaks into his radio. It is beeping and whistling at
his shoulder and his eyes are wide.

Willem is half cut already. He has spent nearly ten
pounds on cans of lager and the day died as he swigged their
foam. He has been sitting on park benches and wandering
through alleyways, pissing in the shadows, belching, burp-
ing, swigging. But winter is early this year and the nights are
cold. His bones are cold and his blood is cold so he weaves
his way in search of warmth. He listens to the policeman
revving the engine. He watches their tyres start to turn. The
street is turned away below them and the officers are carried
into the darkness.

Willem is turned away, he is spinning away from them,
he spins towards the pub's warm light. The heat hits him as
he swings the door open. The air is soaked, his cheeks break
out in a sweat. He removes his layers and the pub absorbs
his unwashed body.

The naval

Midnight looms. Last orders will soon be called and they
will all have to leave. The air will release them back into the
cold. They will slink away, they will be absorbed by the darkness. They are the shadows of their shadows and the world
will spin on as they find their beds for the night, each to his
own in their forgotten corners.

Nat is standing in front of a mirror with scrollwork
around its edge. The scrollwork is wood painted gold, matt
in the steamy room. The glass is inlaid with the images of
race horses at the corners. It steams up with the room's
humid scent, the horses spring out of the mist. The horses'

eyes follow her, they gleam through everything. They follow her as her hips turn. She wears skinny jeans and boots up to her knees. She wears a hoody which is too small, it only covers her breasts. It is half unzipped and the tops of her bra cups poke out. Her breasts are small but they are tight. Her stomach muscles stretch and writhe through the pub's half-light. Her collar bone stands out, casting a shadow of its own. There is nothing spare for the horses to watch. There is no excess, just the dance and the thin bones and her muscles' tautness.

Her hoodie is pink and her bra is white. Her hair is dark, dyed too many times to have a distinct colour. The jeans are threadbare and the fraying cotton binds. They are artful, they came that way. It is the fashion and Willem can see flesh and pale down through the rips. He can see the bright white of her skin through the holes above her knees.

Her jeans are low slung and the tops of her buttocks are round against their seam. Her hips turn in time with the music. She has a piercing in her naval. A crystal pokes through her belly button, it pokes through the horses' eyes. Her naval flashes in time with the music. Her stomach makes the music dance and Willem's eyes are in the mirror. He is at an uncomfortable angle. His face is red and it shines between the horses' heads.

He is at the bar, watching Nat dance. He has been told her name is Nat. He has been looking at her all evening. Most of the men have. She has noticed, she dances, she turns her hips and flashes her naval. There is no excess, nothing is wasted in this room.

His heart is beating fast. His voice is slow, it is sodden. He has drunk too much lager, he has drunk too much vodka. He leaves for the toilet every half hour or so as his body struggles with such a volume of liquid. The front of his boxers are damp, he has nearly not made it a couple of times.

His piss runs clear, it has no smell now. The tip of his cock is purple. A blue vein snakes up its length. It is a snake. It has grown and shrunk a few times tonight as desire for Nat fights with a need to empty his bladder. He is nearly empty now as the landlord rings a bell. A jangling signals last orders and the bar is suddenly swamped with bodies. They haggle, they plead. Most have drunk their money away and the landlord ignores them, he knows he has dried them out. He has emptied them.

He has eyes only for Willem. Kat has eyes only for Willem. They have seen how he spends, how he drinks. Most of the men have nursed their pints. They have been sneaking sips from bottles of spirits secreted in their pockets. But Willem spends like a rich man. He spends like a man made desperate, drinking quickly and ordering quickly. As the jangling dies he orders a pint of lager and another vodka. The landlord pours them out. He pours a double shot of gin and tops it with lemonade and ice.

'What's this?' Willem frowns as the drinks blur. The landlord nods at Nat and takes the money from Willem's hand. He smiles. There is fear and satisfaction in his face. And then Nat is at Willem's side, her dance is nearing its finale.

Her lipstick lingers on the edge of her glass. It is sticky, it glistens. It lingers in his eyes. Even when he sips his beer he can't pull his gaze away from the lipstick stain. Even as she whispers and men shout and plead at the bar the glistening red patch looms, too large for this life.

Her lips are burning his ears. She is murmuring words to him that he doesn't hear. Her teeth brush his ear, her breath steams his neck. She nibbles his ear lobe, she kisses his cheek and he wonders if her kiss leaves a red stain. He looks for the mirror to check but finds only her eyes, swimming in the half light. They are shining in the thick air, they are shining with gin and the horses are still. Her dance is ending and they have finished their race. Her fingers are white sticks, they are toying on his thighs. They toy with the bulge in his pocket and he thinks of Celina, he hears rapid Polish as she climaxes on top of him. He watches her little tits quivering, he stares down at Nat's little tits leaning close. His mind races and his trousers bulge and she plays, she toys.

One pocket bulges with his purple cock. The other bulges with the blonde woman's notes. Nat plays with both, exciting both. She reaches into both. She pulls more blood into his cock. It is hot, it strains against his jeans. She pulls a few notes from the wad. She tucks them into her own pocket and motions for him to drink up. The foam tickles his throat as he downs his pint. The vodka is fire, it tastes like Celina's hot kisses. It warms his belly and it burns his nose and he says something to her. He tells her that she looks nice, that he likes her. But he is talking to the walls. The air in here is too thick for words. She puts a finger to his lips. It smells of cigarette smoke, it smells of his pockets. It leaves his lips and beckons him outside. The wolves whistle all around them both as they climb into their coats. The whistling is the only sound that parts the air.

The warm spot part II

'Wait,' he grunts. She has pulled him into the alley. The cold air hit them hard when they left the pub's warmth. It slapped Willem's cheeks, it dried his mouth.

'What's wrong, hun?' It is the first time he has heard her voice. It is low, her lips dance as she speaks. She has unzipped her coat, she has unzipped her hoodie. Her bra is as bright as her eyes. Her eyes are as bright as the moon. They swim in the darkness.

'Need a minute,' he murmurs and turns his back to her. He unzips his trousers and his balls shrink as the cold air whips them. The cold has shrunk his bladder and he splashes the wall, he splashes the floor. His piss lets off a cloud of cold steam. It floats on the breeze, it is without weight or scent and she laughs behind him. Her laughter tinkles, it is good natured. She has dealt with men at night too many times to mind their needs.

'All done, big man?' she asks, and he nods. He is ready, he is cold. She walks to his side and looks down at his cock. She raises her eyebrows and smiles. 'Aye, big man,' and she holds onto it. Her white fingers are warm, they are the only warm thing out here. She holds on with one hand, she places her other to his waist. She squeezes and he grows hard as she pulls his body into her arms. She puts her back to the wall and pulls her bra down. Her nipples are hard but she is used to the cold. She is used to comforting men through the cold.

Her hands stroke him. She kneels down and uses her mouth. She refreshed her lipstick when his back was turned. Her lips glow, they leave their mark on him. He is mesmerised once more. All he can see is the red smear and she turns her back to him. She drops her jeans to her mid thigh. She pulls him close, she places his hands on her chest. Her heart beats through his hands. The moon above swims as Willem holds on to her. They can both be a comfort, they can both be warm. She opens her legs and pulls him in and a few seconds later he releases and she laughs again. He gives her another note before he leaves. She tucks it away and kisses him on the cheek.

The red mark burns. It burns his cheek and it burns below. It keeps him warm as he walks to the bus stop. 'I've got two hundred and thirty five left,' he mumbles, fingering notes. 'Two hundred and thirty five, mam. I'm doing OK. I swear, I promise.'

<u>The stories part II</u>

'People call me a gypsy. I'm a traveller. I was a traveller. And so living in a camp's OK, I guess,' Shaun tells him. He is eighteen years old and his face is blurred. His breath is rancid with cigarettes and alcohol. It plumes, he spits steam. 'Home was anywhere, it was everywhere. And so we were close knit. When the garden's always changing the house has to be firm, my mam used to say.

'But mam wasn't too stable in herself. She had mood swings. Manic depression. The others didn't like her trashing the place when she was high and she slowed everyone down when she was low. They didn't chuck us out, but after my old man died they didn't make us as welcome as we used to be.' When he was nine his mama moved them into a council flat in Edinburgh. They sold their caravan and bought furniture. Beds, a television, a dining table.

'The world was inside out, mate. Fucked.

'Without my pa and the rest of them she got worse. Nobody to tell her what to do, how to behave. And I was nine, I had no idea how to sort it all out. Of course she drank. And she'd beat the living shite out of me. I didn't know where to look.

'The school gave me the chuck. I punched a teacher when I was fourteen. Knocked the cunt's teeth down his throat. But why not. Being punched ain't no big deal. I had it every day.

'I got no certificates, no qualifications. The year after the school chucked me my mam ran away, god only knows where she went. The social came and put me in with a foster family. But they were a bunch of gobshites. Coloureds folk from some shit hole town in Africa, they only took kids in for the money.'

Shaun leans back and takes a swig. Willem brought some bottles back with him. He gave everyone a drink and the rest of the kids are out cold. The older ones are sitting in a corner, whispering around a half bottle of bourbon. Their eyes are bright in the shadows. They dart, they skip. Shaun's eyes dart and skip and the moon swims in his breath.

'I got out of there quick as I fucking could. Three days I stayed shut up with them darkies, then one night I shinned out the window. I stole all their money, stole some of their flashy bling and ran for my fucking life.

'I looked for my old camp. They were all I had, but once they leave ain't no one can track down a traveller. Not if they don't want you to. They make their homes in the hills far away from them nosey cunts in the government.' He drank, he got hooked on cannabis, later on crack. He slept rough, he stole. Finally, the police caught up with him. He robbed an old couple's house, he took everything he could carry and they found his fingerprints everywhere.

'They put me away for eight months. When I come out there weren't nowhere to go. I wandered about for a bit, I lifted things from shops. I stayed in a hostel when I could, but they're dark places. They'll have your soul quick enough and there's no weed strong enough to make you forget that. So I wound up here. The tithes are steep and the work rots your insides and old one eye doesn't take shit. He'll give you a hiding straight up and he's a tough old cunt. But,' he spreads his hands. 'What else is there in this life?'

The sunrise umbrella

'Son,' the one eyed man says to him as the sun rises the following morning. 'Son, I told you once: my good eye doesn't miss a thing.'

The encampment is bigger than the sky and Willem's eyes ache with the day. The day is bigger than life, bigger than the lives lived inside it and those lived outside it. It folds them up and Willem cannot see straight. His head is as thick as the mud on which he is lying. It pounds and the smell of stale water forms cold puddles in his nose and mouth. He is dizzy and the world is tilting. It tilts one way and then another. Last night he got home covered in piss. He pissed himself on the bus ride home. He pissed over the back seats and over the floor. The driver and the other passengers were too scared of his hulking, tilting presence to say or do anything. But they watched him stumble, they watched his big purple cock as it marked out his territory, they listened to him as he shouted 'the torch, the fucking torch, fuck you, fuck you!'

Now he is lying in the mud. He tried to climb onto his plinth last night. He wanted to sleep on the mattress. But every time he tried to climb up old one eye kicked him off, he kicked him in the ribs and the face and sent him sprawling in the mud. Willem gave up, he shared his booze with everyone around the fire pit and then passed out where he sat.

His bones ache now. They are crystal, delicate as glass. Brittle and cracked. Winter is rolling in and its cold climbs out of the mud. It has frozen him to the marrow.

'Son, you're a daft prick. No denying it, you stupid cunt. Our invisibility is well earned. We work hard for it. I work hard for it,' the one eyed man tells him. He is sitting serenely above Willem. He is sitting cross legged on the plinth, looking down at the giant with the messed trousers and the blue bones and the eyes trying so hard to see, blinded by the morning. 'And last night you tried to shatter it with your antics.

'Do you know that they have CCTV watching every cash machine? And do you know that I have eyes other than my own watching the streets?

'And do you know how fucking hard it is to make the bus drivers look the other way? Do you honestly think Freddie won't talk after you messed up his bus? It will cost me, it will cost us all. Subtlety is key to invisibility. We are only allowed to shrink into the shadows so long as we stay quiet when we're in the light.

'You shined a light on all of us last night, lad. And nobody wants that. You will have to pay dear for it.'

Willem looks for his money. His pockets are empty, his socks are empty. Mud is frozen over his legs, brown and yellow, and his cash is gone. He stashed the notes on his way home last night. They are his refuge, his hope. And now they are gone.

'I have it. I hid it. It's time for you to earn it, Willie.'

Willem tries to spring to his feet. He lurches, his frozen knees buckle and he vomits into the mud. His sick steams, it is the warmest thing in miles.

'The tithes are due me, lad,' the one eyed man growls. 'The fees I get from the girls are handsome enough. Eighty percent of whatever their cunts make. It's only fair for the safety I give them. And the lads too, they earn, they pay up. Lots of my customers like the lads, they like them young and old. This world takes all sorts and my good eye doesn't miss any of it. When I saw a man of your size so close to joining us under the stars, well, I thought, this one will do nicely. Men will pay well for a chunk of flesh your size, Willie. And you'll get your money from them and you'll get your money from yesterday. Just you wait, lad. But for now, sit down and mind yourself, don't try any shit with me. I've dealt with harder men than you in my time.'

The one eyed man rises on his plinth. He stares down at Willem. He spits in the puddle of sick at Willem's feet. 'This,' he says, gesturing above at the underside of the bridge, at the concrete plinths and the roads beyond. 'This is my operation, lad. My word is law around here.'

The fall

A few days have passed in the cold. They wink at him as they breathe and die. Overhead the seagulls are swirling. They call out from the water's depths. Their caws ricochet from the river's surface. Above, the river responds, an unstoppable tide. It barely pauses at it sweeps past the bridge's struts.

Rosa is here and so the others have dispersed. A couple have gone into town, a couple are walking through the fields. A couple are at work in dark rooms or alleyways. Edinburgh is always busy, there is always money to be made. The one eyed man cut Jessie this morning. She said no to work, she said she was tired and he slapped her. He slapped her to the ground, she sank in the mud and he brought out a little knife. He cut the skin on her collar bone, he said the next one would be her face. 'And then you'll never work again. You'll have no place here, you'll have no place anywhere. That pretty face is all you've got, my love, and don't think I can't take it from you.' The boys looked at their feet, they can't help her. They are invisible, the world is too large and they stay quiet.

The old ones are at the end of the bridge. They watch Willem as he climbs. They glare anxiously, they breathe anxiously. It is all so new.

When Rosa arrived they fled but Willem waited back. 'Can we help you with anything, lad?' the one eyed man sneered. He was wiping his knife clean as the boys carried Jessie away. Willem lashed out. He caught the old man on the temple with one great sweep. He kicked Rosa's legs out and then stomped on her ribs. His foot was fast. The air was brittle with the cold and he shattered it with his boot, unstoppable as the river's song. His footfalls have caught them all in their current and now the old men and women, the young boys and Jessie watch to see in which direction the river will fork.

He tucked one under each arm. He carried them up the bank. He dragged them along the road. Their shirts tore as he dragged them along. Rosa's shrivelled breasts fell out. The one eyed man's wrinkled, shrunken back and shoulders beaded with blood as Willem pulled him along. And now he trembles, he is too small.

'Listen lad, I'll give you your money back,' he pants as they come to a stop. They are in the middle of the bridge. Overhead the sun is watery, the clouds are thick. A mist is rolling over the horizon, blowing in before a northern wind.

It will be here by nightfall, Willem thinks. It will chew us all up in the end.

'Did you hear me, boy? You'll get your cash.'

'I know,' Willem grunts. He is watching Rosa's chest. It is heaving, it is panicked. Her breasts are crossed with blue veins. Their wrinkles fold deeply, her nipples point to the earth. Her ribs are red, they are turning purple. He broke a couple of them. He felt them snap as he crunched his foot down. It was like stepping on ants, he thinks. It was like crunching through fresh snow, leaving his mark. But there's nothing fresh out here, he thinks. There is the old and the wasted, and soon enough the end will come.

'Just leave us be, lad. You can go on your way, no hard feelings.'

'No.' The old men and women are watching. There are two men and three women, all wrapped in blankets and sleeping bags. They have worked hard for the one eyed man, they have sold themselves a hundred times over. They stare, impassive. One is eating a baguette. His old jaws work it slowly. His gums bleed. The blood mixes with saliva and pools on his chin as he takes another bite. Jessie is shivering, her eyes swim and the two boys hold her up, their eyes are great circles taking in the day. Willem laces his fingers through Rosa's hair as they watch. He understands now. The owl doesn't haunt his dreams any more. It doesn't dive out of the water with meat in its beak. He is the owl, he has ascended. His is the meat and his wings carry him.

'Give me your keys, Rosa.' Her moped keys have a little plastic skull attached to the ring. They have a cheap toy ninja and a saltire. He pockets them with one hand as he tightens the fist holding her hair.

He hits her head against the concrete wall. She moans and her eyes glaze. The one eyed man tries to stand. He braces his shoulder against Willem and pushes. They are stone, they stay rooted until Willem slaps him and the old man falls. He whimpers, he reaches out a bony hand to Rosa. He begs, he says 'no, lad, no, please no.' But Willem pays him no mind. He is a labourer and there is work to be done.

He smiles. He says 'fuck you' and he grins. It feels good to be using his hands. It feels good to work his callouses. His fingers in his tramp's gloves feel every hair, every motion. He knocks her head into the wall in threes, shaking her like the child's rattle. One, two, three. One, two, three. She is limp but he carries on. He is breathing hard, his lungs are tired. His bones are tired and each breath comes raggedly. He can taste metal, he can smell the water below. She is dead and her head is coming apart but still he shakes her, still he smacks her head as the old man sobs. One, two, three, she rattles. Finally, when he is done, he throws her over the side. There is a splash from below and then all is quiet.

'Now,' he says to the one eyed man. He knows the old bastard is not stupid. He knows he wouldn't leave money lying around for any of them to take. He is right. The old man reaches a shaking hand into his jacket. The sleeves are coming away at the shoulders where Willem dragged him. His hands are bloody. They quiver as he holds out the wad of notes.

'More.' The old man reaches into another pocket and then another, pulling out wads. Finally, Willem is satisfied. 'Good,' he says, nodding. 'You did good, old man.'

'Thank you, Willie, thank you lad.'

Willem picks him up. A buses' engine rumbles through the hills. Its wheels churn the road and bring it to the bridge. Willem looks into the driver's cabin as it passes them. The driver has bright eyes. They are white and wide and she looks shocked, scared. Her passengers press their noses against the window as Willem twists the old man's head, snapping his neck.

It is all so much easier than he thought it would be and his smile grows wider as the bus disappears around a bend. He throws the one eyed man over the wall. The river yawns and swallows and carries on. The one eyed man is lost in the current.

Willem walks to the end of the bridge, counting up the money. He counts slowly, his mind works at a happy crawl.

There are seven hundred and thirty pounds in the wad. He gives Jessie a hundred. He hands some out amongst the old men and women. He walks down the verge and distributes the rest amongst the others' bedrolls and blankets. He takes sandwiches in packets from various beds. He takes the old man's sleeping bag and water proof coat. He changes his clothes. He takes newspapers with naughty pictures for bedding. He takes the last of his own supplies and packs it all in his rucksack.

Rosa parked her moped at the side of the road. The ignition flares as the key vibrates his hand. The toy ninja wobbles as the engine bursts into life. The saltire flashes metallic at the waning sun. He pulls off the plastic skull. He tosses it down the verge, revs the engine and drives over the bridge. There is blood on the pavement but the rain will wash it off in no time.

The first time

It is the first time he has driven a moped properly. One of his mates had a dirt bike and they used to ride it around the shuttered warehouses. One of his mother's fancy men owned a Vesper and he let Willem drive sometimes. But this is different. There is no traffic. There is nobody watching him. There are no conditions, there are no boundaries. Without a helmet he can enjoy the wind whipping into his face. He can enjoy the stinging in his eyes and the rush of air past his ears.

The fog on the horizon grows closer. The world obscures his view as it thickens. He accelerates, welcoming the oblivion. The world around him has never been a priority of his and in the fog he can paint his own. He can paint it with his own colours, in his likeness if he chooses. It can run as slow as he wants, he just needs to get there first.

He doesn't know how to switch the lights on. As the fog folds him up he cannot see. He slows to be safe. But this is good, he slows to his natural speed. Slowness is his birth right and he can feel the world around him start to crawl. The wind rushing past him dies down, he breathes deeply of the still, shrouded air and smiles.

But even this cannot last, he discovers. He has travelled for maybe three hours. He has stayed on smaller, twisting roads where the moped's small engine won't make him fall behind the rest of the traffic. He has stayed in the quiet back lanes. A few times he has even driven through fields, chuckling at the cows and sheep startled by the noise. Chuckling as he emerged from the mist. But the engine sputters now, it slows down. It dies with a whimper.

He takes his rucksack off the back and slings it over his shoulder. He loops his other arm through and picks up the moped, swinging slightly at the waist. He twirls in a circle, he chucks the moped behind a bush and says goodbye to Rosa and the one eyed man. Hitching the rucksack higher across his back he sets out. He opens his arms wide as the mist swallows him whole.

PART III:

THE CLUCK-HENS AND
THE MOO-COWS

The days

He has been walking for days. He has passed out of time. He has passed out of space. Sometimes the fog comes to shroud him, sometimes the rain soaks him through. Sometimes the sun shines and he breathes deeply. Sometimes he closes his eyes and Jap runs alongside, laughing with him, barking. His tail wags, his head wags. He is happy and the world is at peace.

Willem is no judge of distance. He doesn't know how far he has travelled, how far he travels each day. He doesn't know if he walks in circles or cuts through the world in straight lines. But from sunrise to sunset he doesn't stop. His work boots are barely recognisable. He used to polish them every Sunday evening as he watched the football. As the players ran through the mud he wiped the grime from his soles, from his steel toes, from his lace holes and tongue. His mama would be on the sofa, reading a magazine or texting friends. He would sit at her feet with newspaper spread out around him. No naughty pictures, not with his mama there. This bed was clean and the boot polish was thick and dark. Jet black. It smelled of chemicals, it smelled of cleanliness and he rubbed for a solid hour. His hands smelled of chemicals and they rubbed concentric circles, buffering with a rag until the boots shone. Until he could see his own reflection looking back from inside the leather.

Now his hands are dirty and his boots are rags. The steel is visible. The leather has worn away. It has left nothing but rusting, pitted plates hanging over the fronts of his feet. The heels leak. Winter is strong in this country and every night he beds down further north. Snow litters the foothills on the horizon. It threatens the ground through which he trudges. It piles high on the peaks surrounding his odyssey. Icy water seeps into his socks, it marks his heels with the cold. It spreads around to the sides of his feet, freezing. His toes have started to itch. They smell like they are rotting inside his boots.

But he closes his eyes and Jap's paws fall into step with his ragged boot prints and he smiles. The cold is strong but it cannot take everything.

The twin peaks

His body shrinks with the passing days. He is a small man in a valley. Or a ravine. He doesn't know the difference. He didn't want to come this way. There is flatter ground to the west, but in the early morning darkness he could see myriad lights. There is a town over that way and he doesn't want to get mixed up with other people. Their voices will clatter, they will mute the world.

On either side of his path steep hills sweep to the heavens. They disappear into mist. Before the mist takes them they give way to snow drifts. It is smooth and clean and makes the ground shimmer as the sun rises mid-morning. The mist clears from time to time and the peaks grow dizzy in his head. They are vast, they are taller by far than anything he has ever seen. Taller than the sky and the clouds, they touch the rising sun.

They are peaceful and he nearly weeps. Serenity stares down from their heights. They are not malevolent, they are not kind. They offer no words. Their vast silence is so old that it has become a language of its own. It speaks to him of the deep purity of snow, it speaks to him of years he missed and years he will miss. Years in which he will be forgotten faster than he lived, in which the peaks will still be standing.

'Bollocks, Jap,' he says. 'Will you look at that, boy?'

They are dizzying in their scale. They are vast in this life. Countless lives loom large on their flanks. They loom large and they die and the mountains don't blink. Their breadth spans time and it spans the miles. Both are meaningless to these giants. He shrinks, he is shrunken. His broad shoulders belong to children. His deep chest is nothing. His heavy legs, breaking up the miles with ease, tread with the steps of an insect.

He is dizzied by his own body, so small and empty. His heart is empty, his stomach is empty. His food ran out three days ago and he hasn't eaten since. He stops every hour or so, he stoops down and gathers up snow. His tramp's gloves have given way. They grew mouldy, they fell to bits. He scoops snow with his bare hands and chews it. His stomach gurgles and the cold hurts in the front of his head. He braces himself with his hands on his thighs while the weakness passes and then he carries on. The small miles and the big miles sweep below his long legs, weaving forgotten pathways through the mountains.

The path to heaven

He ascends. His ascent has barely stopped. For an age his thighs have burned, his stomach has grown hollower as he lives on snow. He has no clear direction. He does not know the countryside, he does not know where he wants to end up. He does not want to end up anywhere, the journey itself is enough.

But the gypsy boy's words echo from the mountains. *They make their homes in the hills far away from them nosey cunts in the government.* Nobody finds a man travelling up here if that man doesn't want to be found. And as long as he doesn't care where he is going the paths take him upwards. Solitude knows his face up here. It is just him and Jap and nobody else noses in, nobody else mutes the peace with their chatter and their rules and their silly little puzzles.

Night falls early up here. By three the sun is disappearing behind the peaks. By five total darkness claims the ground. The clouds above are obscured by starlight. They glow, hollow and silver. The moon rarely manages to peep out from behind their shadows.

On the tenth day since he set out from under the bridge a hollow in a rock face passes him on his path. There are gorse bushes around its entrance. He hasn't eaten in four days and the bushes swirl, but it is adequate shelter for the night and he pushes his way through the brush. He tears some of it out of the ground. He tears the ground from its roots. His palms are hard and calloused, only a few beads of blood break the skin as he tugs. He has stolen fallen sticks and twigs from the daylight hours. He has a few sheets of newspaper left, the last of his naughty pictures. It makes good kindling, it burns quickly.

He looks at the pictures for a minute. His heart shakes as the blood in his hands beats hard. The sun is dying and the light is faint but he can make out a slim girl with improbably large breasts. She has blonde eyes and blue hair and they curl as he lights the paper. And she is smiling at the camera and she is smiling at him... Her hip juts. It curves and thrusts her body to one side. Her hands are on her hips, her elbows pointed back so that her chest opens fully... Her breasts are as exposed as she can make them. The mountain's cold is hard in her nipples. They invite him and his heart shakes some more.

He closes his eyes and imagines laying those peaks beside his head.

He opens his eyes and screws the paper into a loose ball. It smokes, flames lick its edges. He places it on the ground and takes the smaller twigs he has collected. He makes them into a tepee around the ball. He arranges the other twigs and sticks in piles nearby and keeps his lighter in his hand. It is the good lighter his mama gave him and as the flame bursts it clicks into life. The flame is bright, it is the brightest thing for miles around. He torches the paper in a couple more places, licking those scrunched up breasts with yellow flame. The smoke blazes into the ball. The twigs catch at the fire. They are a little damp and smoke for a few seconds before burning true.

He places some slightly larger twigs on the little fire. They catch and he moves to bigger sticks. He places one of the bushes he has uprooted in front of the fire to protect it from the wind. To protect its light from prying eyes. After ten minutes or so he puts the other bush on the fire. It is the smaller of the two and it burns brightly. Finally, as the bush breaks apart, he puts the biggest sticks on the fire. He used to light fires in metal incinerators to burn site refuse, all the materials not needed to make homes and offices. He built teepees, he burned and he watched the smoke rise over the city.

And now this fire burns bright, it dies down. It turns into red dust and silver-black coals, its fingers warm the fissure. It warms his empty body. He rolls out his sleeping bag, he climbs in and shuts his eyes. One side of his face grows hot as the heat licks him. In peace he begins to snore, breathing deeply of the warm air and wood smoke.

The cold shakes

He wakes up in the night. The fire has burned out, it is white ash. It burns cold in his brain and the darkness closes in. The cold wraps him up. His bones climb deep inside the cold, they rattle in its hoar. His brain rattles and his eyelids shut around the chill wind. Celina is gone and the mountain shakes, it holds him against the hard ground, pinned down under its vast weight. It is relentless with its impossible years.

The cold is in his bones and his skin is on fire. He smokes, he smoulders, he rises above the city, drifting on the midnight breeze... he drifted here, against the current... He is damp, his sleeping bag is wet through with his sweat. His sweat freezes to its fleece lining. It cocoons him and burns him with its touch. He lies in his fever for days. The hours are long, the night never leaves him and his mama's voice comes to him from so close at hand that he can hardly make out her words. 'My boy, my good boy, my strong lad...' and all else is gibberish, garbled by the strong mountain winds. Echoing in the fissure's shadow.

The icy white is large. It is larger than the sky, than the world, than his life. It covers him, it is his blanket. It is his death and his comfort. His jaw rattles and his ears clatter and in his teeth the wind roars, chasing his mama away. Jap licks his face but his breath is cold, his tongue is cold and his saliva freezes to Willem's cheeks.

I am dead, he thinks. The world has killed me. He smiles. There is perfection in death, there is death in perfection.

The one eyed man asks him why he committed his crimes. I needed to so I could eat, he says. But his jaw is shaking too violently. His words won't come, his teeth hurt and his tongue is a useless lump. 'Bollocks,' the one eyed man says. 'You stole money and food to eat. But you pissed on the world. You lashed out at the world. You wasted your strength raging against all those little people. Why, why waste so much on so little?'

Because they made me a sinner.

What?

They made a guilty man out of me, so how else could I behave?

He was punished for something he did not do. His home and his life were taken from him for an offence of which he was innocent. He doesn't know what the offence was. 'I only know what the punishment was. They took mam, they took my home. They took Jap.' And so he purged himself. He freed himself from impotence by making himself guilty. 'An innocent man can't take what they threw at me. An innocent man can't take any of it. So I had to be guilty to keep my head screwed on.

'We are too big to be so small,' he chatters. The society of man swallows you. The laws of man hold you tight. Your arms can't move to work and yet your legs can't stop running.

'We are too big to be so small…' he sighs.

'Aye, you keep talking lad, keep yourself awake. There's a good lad, good boy.'

'We are too small to be so big…'

'That's right, you're right lad.'

'Jap, Jap is that you?'

'No, lad. But I'm a friend.' Jap is gone and Celina is gone. His mama is gone and his ears are roaring. The roar comes from far below in the valley. And strong fingers are here and a voice that smells of pork fat wafts over him. 'Come on now lad. Let's get you some help.'

The kindness and the strangers

Strangers have found him, this night belongs to them. The roar was real. It was from a truck and it called through the pale starlight. A rough voice calls out. Rough voices and rough fingers drag him down from his crevice. They pack up his things and throw them in the back of a truck.

They load him in the front. They strip off his wet clothes. They strip him down to his underwear and pat him down with a towel. The towel smells of dogs, their breath licks at his blue goose flesh. His bones burn in the wind and his heart starts to shake again.

The strangers wrap him in blankets, they place a cap on his head and a jacket around his shoulders. The jacket smells of fish and smoke and the hat is too small, it pinches his head. The strangers slam the door shut and start the truck. Hot air fills the cabin. It is musty, it is blowing dust from an ancient engine. Dust and dogs' breath warm him against the wintry sun and crack his knuckles and toes. His bones come apart in his arms and legs. They unwind. They take the spiders web veins with them and leave nothing but hot and cold fighting over the remains.

His chest is tight. He can't fill his lungs properly. The dust is in his throat. His eyes droop. They are the only parts not burning and they feel good as their lids close.

The world is shut out. He is shut out of the world. He is boneless and half dead and the warm, ancient air licks his broken body. It rocks him to sleep. And the days begin, the days of waiting through the cold.

The roof, the walls, the bed

His cheek is greasy. It is overgrown, it has been overgrown for a few weeks now. It has been scratching his face, the growth has crept down his throat. But now a soft pillow holds onto him. He has been sweating, he has sweated so much over the last few days that his head is light. It glides over the damp pillow. His throat is on fire and it is swollen and warm.

There is a ceiling above his head. It keeps the rain outside, it keeps the cold outside. There is a radiator hanging on the wall and the warmth eddies upwards. The ceiling catches it, it holds it in. It holds Willem in and keeps his body sweating.

'Welcome back to the land of the living.' A thickset man with a short beard is standing in the door, leaning against the frame. He is old, in his sixties at least. But he looks strong, he looks like his hands have made his living. 'I'm Gregor. Nice to meet you.' His face is ruddy, his arms are crossed and he is frowning slightly. His crossed arms push his biceps up. As he speaks his chest swells. As Willem watches him the room swells and his stomach turns. There is a lead weight pushing his chest.

'You take it easy there lad. The doctor came, he says you had pneumonia. When I found you he said you had hypothermia setting in. He said I found you just in time. A few more hours and your core would have got too cold. You wouldn't have come back from it.'

'What-?' he rasps. His throat catches and he begins to cough.

'There are no hospitals for miles so we kept you here. He warmed you up. We've kept you warm since then. The doctor gave us some antibiotics for you to take. A month's worth, so I guess you'd better stay put lad. We'll keep you here if you've nowhere else to go. Plenty of rest, plenty of fluid. That's what he said.

'Here,' and he walks forwards, uncrossing his arms. He has a white pot folded up in his hand. 'Take a couple of these, choke them down.' He shakes a couple of pills into his hands. His strong hands feed them into Willem's mouth and pass him a glass of water from his dressing table. Willem takes a sip. His throat swells and bruises as he swallows.

'Ta,' he rasps. He can feel the fluid on his lungs, he can feel the mucus clogging his windpipe. Such a weight as to keep a man down for weeks.

'The doctor said not to give you cough medicine. And he put you on this,' the old man says, nodding over Willem's shoulder. A tall metal stand holds a bag of clear fluid. A line runs from the bottom of the bag into his arm. A needle pricks his skin, it opens him up and keeps his life flowing freely.

'We give it back in a few days, but for the moment we've got to keep you hydrated. Now get some rest. Sally will have dinner ready at seven, you look like you could do with a decent meal inside you. Sleep now, lad.'

He backs out of the room. The door closes gently as he leaves. It clicks softly and Willem's eyes grow heavy. His chest pulls downwards. The room is a tunnel, his vision shutters it from the sides as he drops. His head is fuzzy, it is warm. He sleeps.

The gammon joint

'Come on lad. Steady as she goes.' Gregor is half carrying him. Willem is shrunken. He can only stand with Gregor's help. Together they manage to get downstairs. Willem sways, bumping into walls in a crooked corridor. His legs are cramping, his feet curl upwards and he staggers. He reels as Gregor guides him through a low door and sets him down at a scrubbed wooden table.

'This is my Sally, lad,' Gregor tells him. Sally is bringing in food. She is holding a steaming platter on which roasted pink meat and boiled potatoes are piled high. 'Welcome back to the land of the living,' she says. Her hair is curled. It is cut short and rinsed a pale blue. She has no eyebrows or lashes so that she looks shocked to see him sitting at her table. Her lips are plum red and her mouth is crooked. She smiles and her smile is crooked. Wrinkles pan out from her lips, from her eyes and across her forehead.

'I hope the bed's comfortable. It belonged to our youngest. But even he's long since gone. It's just us and the animals these days, I'm afraid.' She chatters as she lays the food down. She chatters as she and Gregor take their seats. She chatters as she carves slices from the pink meat and places them onto their plates, as she loads potatoes and spoons greens from a silver dish. 'The gammon's from one of our own pigs,' she says.

'We never did catch your name, dear.' She passes him the gravy. He pours some over his meal. It is thick, it glops into greasy pools. He hasn't smelled food like this in a long time. His eyes sting, his stomach growls and he begins to shovel forkfuls into his mouth. He cries as he chews. He can barely get it in quick enough.

He nods when she offers him seconds and ploughs through some more. He doesn't breathe, he doesn't chew. He inhales the graceful steam. He inhales the thick gravy and the salty meat. Finally he sits back and sighs. Tears stream down his cheeks, they mix with his dirty beard. They run into his mouth, adding their own salt to the aftertaste of the meat.

'Your name, lad?' Gregor rumbles.

'Aye. I'm Willem.' He struggles to look Sally in the eye. She is a mother born. He thinks of his own mother and her face blurs behind his tears. 'Pleased to meet you folks. And thanks. Thanks for everything. I don't know-'

'Enough of that, dear,' Sally says. She is curt, she is crisp. She is not used to hearing such emotion from the men at this table. 'It's what any Christian would do for their fellow man.'

'Mm.' He isn't so sure. He can still feel the one eyed man's bones under his fingers. He can still feel the mud clinging to his jeans. He can still see the line of the invisible tenants at the encampment. They trail away as Rosa's moped cuts its engine and the mist takes him from that life.

'Would you like some desert?' Sally asks him. 'We have rhubarb crumble and custard.'

'Aye, ta. Yes please.' Again he eats a double helping. The sugar courses through his blood and his stomach bloats. It is all too much but he could go on like this forever.

'You should get back to bed now, lad,' Gregor says to him when they are all finished. 'Come on, you need your rest.' He helps Gregor to his feet. He slips his arm under Willem's and lifts him half off his feet. He floats, his head floats and his eyes droop. He can barely make it back to bed before falling asleep. Gregor throws a blanket over him as he descends. His mama's face looms. She smiles at him with plum red lips. She pulls him close and holds him tight. Jap licks his fingers and curls up at his feet.

The house and the hands

He is on a farm. He can see their fields from his window. Every morning the cock crows and Sally swings through the garden gate and into their coup. She comes back with a basket piled high with eggs and a few minutes later the taste of frying fat wafts up to his bedroom. She brings him bacon, sausages and omelette every day. 'To put some meat back on those bones,' she laughs. Her laughter tinkles, it makes him feel young.

Every morning after breakfast Gregor meets a few men in the front garden. Willem watches from his room. The men have a quick chat, Gregor points to distant pastures, he gives them their jobs for the day. They jump into tractors, onto quadbikes. Engines rev and they leave Willem's story for the moment. They are labourers, they have their own callouses to work.

Willem still hasn't been outside. For a full week he has stayed in bed, sleeping through the days and nights. He gets up only to use the bathroom, to wash and shave and to eat his evening meal. He eats with Gregor and Sally, he makes them feel young. He shaves with an old cut throat and a bar of soap that Gregor gave him. He cuts close, skimming a little skin from his cheeks and jaw. The water scalds him and he lathes it from his face. His face is newly born, it is raw and strong. It is a young man's face once more.

'My great-grandpa built this house with his own two hands,' Gregor tells him. Sally laughs, smiling and frowning at once. She shakes her head and rolls her eyes. 'What?' Gregor asks. He is amused. His eyes twinkle.

'He built this house with his own two hands and the deepest pockets for a hundred miles in any direction! Oh,' she sighs, looking over to Willem. He is chewing a chicken leg, he has grease on his fingers. He has grease on his lips and tongue. 'My husband does like to romanticise. The fact is that his family helped to build the railways in India and America. They made a fortune. Don't let the English fool you- the Scots kept the empire running, and Gregor's family did well for themselves. His great-grandfather used his inheritance to buy up this land. Walk any direction for an hour and you'll be on our land. He hired a team of builders, surveyors, an architect... so many men. So many hands, not just his own, you daft old beggar!' And she laughs again, looking at her husband.

Gregor is sheepish. He grins foolishly, his cheeks turn rosy. 'Well, yes. But he was very involved. And we've kept this farm going for coming up to a hundred years. A hundred years of sweat and toil. That's enough for any family, don't you think Willem?'

'Mm.' He licks his fingers. He stabs a fork into a roasted potato. It is hot, it burns his mouth. He blows hot air as the fluffy potato sticks to his tongue, to his cheeks. He takes a sip of beer, swilling his mouth out. The suds bubble, they tickle his throat.

'You're a bad man, giving poor Willem that beer,' Sally scolds her husband. Again he looks sheepish, again he grins like a fool.

'I just wanted the lad to try it. I thought it might cheer him up a little-'

'Pah! It was vanity made you pour that glass! My husband has a brewery in one of the crofts,' she says, leaning in a little. 'It's his pride and joy. Sod the chickens, sod the cows and pigs! All he wants to do all day is tinker with hops and barely, with that damned still.

'And he wants us to think he's being kind giving you a draught. Pah! He just wants you to say it's nice so he can pat himself on the back.' She winks at her husband and they both burst out laughing. Gregor slaps his thigh, he wipes his eyes.

'It's very nice,' Willem says and takes another sip.

The red coals

'You're in the country now, lad,' Gregor tells him. 'We need thicker waists than those fairies in the cities!' He laughs and slaps his thigh. He spills a little beer. His jeans are dirty. They are covered in soil, they are damp with beer suds. In the city people avoid men with dirty jeans and beer on their breath. They avoid people who laugh and spill their drinks.

Dinner is over. Desert is gone. They had some boozy left-over trifle with whipped cream stacked high on top. It wobbled and he had to scoop it with a spoon. It was too sweet for him, it made his teeth ache. The booze in the pudding and the strong beer in his glass have made him wobbly. The sugar has made his hands shake.

But now he is sitting in the lounge with Gregor. Sally is bustling in the kitchen. She clacks the dirty plates together. She jingles cutlery into the dishwasher. She scrubs the table, she mops the floor. The lads' boot prints come in from the cold every day. They mark her floor with their labours. The dogs' paw prints fight them, they dance, they weave in and out over wooden boards. And so she always has a mop and bucket to hand. She scrubs after every meal. She makes it shine for a couple of hours before the next feast of muddy prints descends.

Sally and Gregor have two wing backed chairs in front of a little fire. The fire pops, logs chant in the light. Gregor sits in one. He motions for Willem to take the other. The fire warms his toes, it is a balm. The smoke reminds him of some of his mama's blokes. They smelled of smoke and they breathed as heavy as the chimney flu. Willem remembers that he used to smoke, back in the city. But that disappeared along the way. There is fresher air to breathe out here. He doesn't want to suck at ragged ashes any more.

'What do you say to a couple of toasted muffins?' Gregor asks him, winking. 'Bring you back down to earth a bit after all that drink.'

'Mm.'

'I know I could use an extra lining! And besides, you're in the country now, lad. We need thicker waist lines…' and he cackles. The flu cackles. Sparks fly as he laughs and slaps his thigh and spills beer on his messed trousers.

'Aye,' Willem says. Sally brings a tray over. She brings a plate of muffins, two knives, butter, jam. 'Fatten you up, lad,' she says to him. She winks as she leaves them to it. Gregor winks as well. Theirs are separate winks, both meant only for Willem. He is their conspirator, their secret.

'Mm.'

They sit and they chew. Sally's television burbles away in the kitchen. She is watching the news. She calls out, she asks if they have seen this? 'There's a serial killer down in Edinburgh. Killed three people, same DNA on each victim. Pah, these cities. Never know what you'll get.'

'Aye, crazy business,' Gregor says. 'Every mother's son down there's got muck they don't want folks to see. And they call the countryside dirty!'

'Mm.'

'Do they know who he is?' Gregor calls out. His laughter still rumbles in his throat. It's still ready, still waiting.

'No, not yet. They say they're looking.'

'My arse they are.'

'Gregor! Language.' And Gregor winks at Willem again. The wink tells him that they are men. They are in on a man's game. They both play, they both know.

'Policemen and politicians. Can't stand any of them. Both lots full of lies, taking honest money and pissing it away.'

'Mm.'

As Gregor talks Willem stares into the flames. The coals burn bright. They stand out from the gloom and hurt his eyes a little. They are red and orange and yellow. The smoke is gone, the moisture has burned away. The flu has fallen quiet. All he can hear now is the gentle crackle of the fire taking hold. Gregor takes a knife and opens two muffins. He spears them on a couple of long forks. The forks were hanging by the fire. They are black iron with wooden handles.

They are heavy in Willem's hand and the iron weight and the fiery crackle soothe him.

The sweet butter

'You going to vote when the referendum comes?'

'What?'

'I said, will you vote in the referendum?'

'What's that?'

'Jesus, lad. You been living in a cave or what?' He catches himself, he laughs nervously. He laughs again, more heartily this time and with a great, sharp slap to his thigh. 'Of course you have! I didn't find you anywhere else, did I?

'The vote on UK membership. Time to ditch the English I say.'

'Mm.'

'Don't be daft,' Sally says. She whisks through the lounge. She has a basket of washing pressed against her stomach. Her tights are ripped at one ankle and her white slippers are dusty with soot. 'They've not even announced it yet.'

'Aye, but they will. And lad, how do you think you'll be voting?'

Willem shrugs his shoulders. He has no attachment to the English. He has no love for their government or their queen. But he has no attachment to Edinburgh, to his birthplace and the kinship of his old town. These days he knows only the hills and the farm and the open spaces. As long as they don't take them away like they took his mama and Jap he doesn't mind. Rulers can rule, always will. It makes no odds to him.

His muffin is browning. He takes it off the fork. His fingertips burn slightly and he blows on them. He blows on the muffin and spreads it with butter. Sally said the butter is from a neighbouring dairy. Gregor's cows are good for beef but their milk doesn't churn so well. Something to do with the grass in their valley. The soil on the other side of the hills make the grass sweeter. The butter is sweet and warm and a little dribbles on his lip.

'Well, I want to separate. England doesn't matter. It hasn't mattered for a long time. It never really mattered to begin with.'

'What does Scotland matter?' Willem asks him.

'What?'

'What do we matter?'

'Well, that's god's own decision.'

'Maybe god thinks the English matter. Maybe he thinks none of us matter.'

'Aye, well. If that's his will. But Scotland is a proud nation.'

'I'm not proud.'

'Well you bloody should be.'

'Why?'

'Oh, to hell with you lad! You don't speak more than three words for days and then you come out with this rubbish! Here, cut up some more muffins, I've a hunger.'

'Mm.'

The burning

They are walking through the garden. A low, shabby wall surrounds them. It cuts the house off from the rest of Gregor and Sally's land. It is made of large, grey stones roughly hewn and mortared into place. Moss grows over it. Ivy clings to its stones, it trails over the mortar.

'Honeysuckle and roses grow over it in the spring and summer,' Gregor tells him.

'How did you find me?' Willem asks. He was in the middle of nowhere. He was blind to the world and the cold held him firm.

'Everywhere is the middle of nowhere up here, lad,' Gregor tells him. 'The idea of *nowhere* shrinks right down when it's all you know.'

'But still.'

'I have the lads drive my sheep up in those hills in the spring. I was checking the roads and paths around there. When the snow melts I need to know we'll get up there OK. And I saw your fire blinking away around eleven. Far off in the distance.

'I called the police to let them know what was up. I thought you were poachers. It wouldn't be the first time. The police told me they'd come the next day, it's a three hour drive for them. More like five in snow like that. I didn't want to wait so I took my shotgun, loaded it up and drove my truck up the ravine. It took me hours and all the time your light was winking. As I got closer it got smaller. When I found you curled up there was nothing but ashes. I thought there'd be more of you. I poked you with my shotgun, I wanted to ask you what was what. But you never woke.

'I looked over your clothes. I thought this is no poacher. This is some poor wanderer down on his luck. I felt your pulse, I felt your skin. Half dead and more than half frozen, poor bugger, I thought. So I dragged you down to my truck, got those wet clothes off you. Got a warm blanket around you and switched the heating right up.

'I called the doc on my way home and he was waiting for us when we got back here. He helped me get you up to the bed and then shut me out of the room. Half an hour later he came out, he gave me those pills. He told me how to keep you warm. How to get your strength back up.

'A couple of hours later he came back with that drip and told me you'd need plenty of fluids. And then we left you to it, said a prayer and kept our fingers crossed.'

'No,' Willem says. 'There were loads of people. I felt them.'

'Just me, I'm afraid. Not too many people out here.'

'Mm.'

'You get used to the solitude though.'

'Mm.'

The cemetery

Crosses stick out of the earth in one corner of their garden. One stick stands proud from the ground, another lies across two thirds up. Brown twine has been used to lash them together. Six of these structures are evenly spaced and at the foot of each there are clumps of green hibernating through the cold.

'That's out pet cemetery. But don't worry, none of them have ever come back to life!'

'Mm.'

'We've got a couple of border collies in there. Mary and Joseph. And a boxer, big old Conor.' He points to graves with each name. 'And there's Thump. He was a mix, a real bastard dog. But he had a heart of gold and he could get anything out of Sally. His real name was Noah, but we called him Thump because of his tail. Wherever he went it wagged so hard and so fast that it thumped along everything. Knocked Sally's good crockery off the coffee table, it shattered and went everywhere. But she couldn't scold him. She didn't have the heart, daft thing.'

'And them?' Willem nods to the last two.

'They were our cats. Jezebel and Twitch. Mousers, lived for eighteen and twenty years. Twitch was almost as old as our marriage when she went.'

'We want to be buried in this plot. Buried in the land we sowed, buried next to the beasts who helped us. But the council won't let us. We have to be disposed of in a correct and safe manner, apparently.'

'Mm.'

'So they say, anyway.'

A cold wind is blowing. Mountains loom at the four corners of the farm. They cast such long shadows that in the farthest fields it can feel like night time in the middle of the afternoon. The rest of the farm sweeps outwards and upwards. The house is in a valley, sheltered from most sides. A river runs passed it, bisecting the land. All the rainwater in the basin runs into this river and the river in turn feeds the crops. A brook slithers away from the main river to trickle through the garden.

'Sally had me dig that,' Gregor says as they walk over it. There is a slab of stone acting as a bridge and fronds swirl at the water's edge. 'Completely artificial, but it waters her herbs. Rosemary and thyme, mint and nasturtiums, tomatoes in wee hot boxes, bulbs, sticks of celery, rhubarb...' he lists them, nodding to dead patches in the soil. They are dead with the cold, hard as iron.

'We have a vegetable patch and chickens for eggs,' Gregor tells him. 'We use our own milk and cream. Everything you need, more or less. We rarely go to the supermarkets.'

'Mm.'

They leave the cemetery behind them. The living have a home here alongside the dead. The garden houses two dogs. They have a little kennel each. The kennels are wood covered in tar to weather proof them. They lean against the house, they borrow heat from the house. They have fur linings to keep the heat in.

The dogs are called Jacob and Marley. Jacob is a Jack Russel. He is a pure breed, not like Jap. 'They make the best watch dogs, surprising enough,' Gregor says. He whistles and the dogs come bounding out. Jacob is white with brown patches. Marley is a border collie with a white streak running from her muzzle to her tail. It spreads into her black coat, a white flame in dark coal.

'You make any noise near a Jack Russel and their ears prick up. They start to yap and its god himself can get them to hush.' Gregor squats down, laughing. He tickles Jacob behind the ears. Jacob rolls over, slumping down and exposing his belly. He has a little penis and no balls. He was neutered at infancy. Now all he likes is to be tickled. Gregor tickles his belly and motions for Willem to do the same.

'Aye,' Willem says. His eyes are hot, his throat is tight.

Marley is less forthcoming. 'She's great with the animals,' Gregor says. 'But she never took to humans too much. She'll let you pet her for a while, but only as a duty. She'll soon grow bored and wander off.'

The smells

Willem likes the smells on the farm. He likes mucking the pigs out with Gregor and his workers. He likes slopping out the shit as he grows stronger. He likes feeling the earth beneath his feet, he likes to walk through the fields. They are dead now, the soil is iron hard with the cold. Snow lies about, it coats the fir trees on each field's border. The world up here smells like cold, it is piercing and fresh. The snow is clean, the puddles are deep crystals.

He likes the cows most of all. When he was a bairn his mother would read him story books about farms. They were amongst his favourite stories. She would ask him if he wanted to read about the moo-cows. She would ask him what noises the cows made and he would start mooing. She would ask him what noises the hens made and he would start clucking. He would giggle as she tickled him, she would call him a cluck-cluck-hen and tickle him until he crowed. And now the fairy tales are coming to life.

The cows stare ahead, they stare at nothing. He is sorry their milk is not good. He is sorry they are good only for breeding and eating. But they don't seem to mind too much of anything. Their eyes are impassive. They do not flinch, they barely blink and Willem spends hours at a time sitting with them. 'Come in from the cold, you daft sod,' Sally scolds him. 'You're still recovering and we need to keep your strength up.'

'Why?' he asks. She doesn't know how to answer him. She doesn't know what he is asking. She doesn't like the way he stares at her, impassive. She flaps away, there are chores to do.

His mama's stories were only ever stories. They lay on glossy paper, narrated by jolly authors. They were pleasant but they have never before been real. They were not real until now. Now the smells and the sounds and the feel of the animal's fur bring the stories to life. They bring him into the stories. He is one of their characters, his boots carry the earth's muck on their soles.

He squats on his heels, he stares at the cows. At first they start, but very soon they are used to him. They don't take any notice. They chew cud, they huddle together when the cold wind blows. In the barns they mooch about the hay on the floor. It is warm in here and they waddle about, disconnected.

In the fields they connect, they stay in a herd and warm each other. If one strays away the others low. They scold it, or so it seems to Willem. They do not like it when one of them strays. When they grow used to his presence they scold him each time he is called in to dinner. They low and moo until he is some distance away. Then they huddle together once more, they know they have lost him.

The warm work

The rain falls in thick sheets every night. There is hail and snow mixed in with it, more and more as the days grow shorter. The lowlands don't see too much of it, Gregor tells him. But up here the air is thin, it is cold. And as winter advances the snow covers everything.

Everything freezes by morning. Willem's paunch has started to grow out. His shoulders are broadening again. The meat and the vegetables are filling him up. The farm is giving him his old strength back.

Every morning before breakfast, before the first cock calls and the lights start to flicker on in the house he takes a shovel and a pick from the tool shed. He swings the pick in large arcs like Gregor showed him. When Gregor does it the ice cracks. One, two, three swings and it gives way. He is a big man but his bones are too old. They have forgotten most of his strength, whereas Willem's are just starting to remember his. When Willem swings the pick the ice explodes in one blow. It scatters everywhere. Little shards like diamonds catch the starlight and flicker around his feet.

He shovels ice tirelessly. Gregor rests every few minutes, catching his breath and mopping his brow. The sweat runs down his cheeks, it runs across the deep lines of his forehead. Willem never rests. He scrapes the ice, he flings it to the side of the path. He creates his own mountains in the drifts. Only when the path is clear and the smell of frying eggs and bacon from the kitchen catch up with him will he set his tools down and mop his brow.

'We always need help around the place,' they tell him. 'We always need lads like you, good with your hands, strong and fit. Stay, help us get the place ready for spring. Get yourself strong again, work out what you're going to do with yourself.'

The bacon smells strong this morning. 'Our own stock, we had some ham smoked a while back,' they tell him. He puts his tools down. He has cut a wide swathe in the ice. When the lads arrive in the trucks they will have free reign of the place. They will be ready to work.

He clumps inside. Gregor is drinking tea at the kitchen table, Sally is unloading eggs from her punnet. Her smile crinkles her mouth, it crinkles her eyes. Gregor's eyes are dull with sleep, bags lie deep under his eyes as he inhales each sip of his tea.

'Good morning, lad,' they say as he sits.

'Aye. Good morning.'

The stories part III

Ravens settle in the garden. He chases them away each morning. Each morning they remind him of his mama and her stories. He asks Gregor and Sally why they haven't flown south like the starlings, but they don't know. They don't know the answers and they don't know the stories.

There was an ancient civilization, his mama told him. They were Greeks, but not the Greeks we know today. Willem has been to Kos and Corfu and there is nothing there that he recognised from the stories. There he got drunk and jumped up and down to music. He watched girls jump up and down. He watched their breasts bob and sometimes fall out of their bikinis. The stars above shone brightly, lighting their breasts on the beaches and in the streets. He got hard and bought the girls drinks and they felt his hardness.

They played with it and drank some more. He came home pink from the heat and lonely for those girls. In Edinburgh girls were wrapped up against the cold. Even in summer they usually went about in sweatshirts and jackets. Nobody jumped up and down, nobody slipped out. Nobody let him buy them drinks and touch them under the stars.

Ancient Greece was different, his mama said to him. She had a big book of stories and she read them to him when he was a bairn. There are some he remembers better than the others. He remembers the raven.

There was an ancient civilization, his mama told him. A woman in that civilization consulted the seers about her baby son. The seers predicted that her boy would be killed by a raven. Their word for raven was *korax*.

The woman was scared by their prediction. She had a large chest built and she locked the boy inside to keep him safe. She put a big padlock on the chest to make extra sure. Willem remembers the picture of the boy locked up in the chest. He has blonde curly hair and the padlock is big and bronze and there is a hooked handle on the chest's lid. The raven is dark with black eyes and it watches over their house, menacing.

Every day at the same time the woman chased away any birds near the house. She unlocked the chest and gave her son as much food as he needed. But then one day when she had opened the chest and was giving him his food, her son stuck his head out. He was tired of the dark, cramped space and he wanted one look at the sunshine outside.

As he stuck his head out the hooked handle on the chest fell and split his head open. It killed him immediately.

The book said that the name for a hooked handle in ancient Greece was *korax*, the same as their word for raven.

The storyteller's lot

He knows these stories from his mother. He learned them at her lap. He enjoyed her voice, he found it soothing. When everybody else's chatter came too fast for his peace of mind her voice shut them out. When their words grew too fast and unpredictable the words read from unchanging pages were a pleasant constant.

One of his schoolteachers once brought a copy of these stories out. He called them fables. He read a couple of them and Willem mimed along. He knew each story by heart and his lips spoke the words in silence. After he had read them the schoolteacher asked the class what they thought they meant. People started to chatter immediately. They had opinions. Some of them scorned the writing, they called it boring and shit and wanted something more up to date. This was their opinion.

Some of the others liked them. They got different things from the words. The words formed whole worlds in their busy heads.

Why can't you just enjoy the words, he wondered? Why can't you be soothed? Why can't you just *be?*

They saw the teacher again a couple of days later. Again, he brought out his copy of the fables. But this time he kept the covers closed. This time he kept the stories shut away. Willem thought about the boy in the trunk. Willem thought about the raven's black eyes and the boy's blonde curls and the big bronze lock.

Instead of reading to them, the schoolteacher spoke about the author. He was a Greek slave named Aesop, he told them. He was bought and sold. He was tied to his masters. But his words lived on, the schoolteacher said. Long after his masters' yokes had diminished and their names faded to dust this slave's words were still being used. What did they all think of this? Was it better to live free and be forgotten or to attain immortality? 'Well, he's dead. What the fuck does he care if we read his stories?' one of Willem's classmates asked. Everybody laughed, the schoolteacher went red and began to shout. He gave the lad a detention, he phoned the boy's parents and told them about the language their son had used.

But he is right, Willem thought. He is more right than the schoolteacher.

Willem realised that he wanted to play the master. To live free and then fade into the dust, forgotten. He does not want to be remembered, he does not want to be known. He does not want people to look at him or talk about him or think about him. He just wants to be free. He just wants to wander without restraint and be caught up in the end of it all when he is finished.

The wooden spoon

'Man is a jack rabbit.' Gregor is out at market and Willem is sitting at the kitchen table. Gregor sells Sally's preserves and their own cured meats. He got a licence two years ago and now he sells his own beer. Willem is drinking tea and watching Sally fuss over a rabbit stew. 'My old ma used to say that. She was American, from the south. She had all sorts of funny sayings,' she says.

Jacob is sitting at his feet. He has taken a special liking to Willem. With Gregor out Sally has let the dogs in. 'It's so cold out there, I don't see the harm in keeping them in here. But Gregor's adamant. They're worker dogs, they need to know their place, he says. Men!'

Jacob is his friend. Marley is not. Every morning after he finishes breaking ice Willem has taken to stooping outside the kennels. He takes off one glove and holds his hand out. Marley comes out sometimes and gives his hand a tentative sniff. She licks. Her tongue is rough as sandpaper and drags at Willem's skin.

But Jacob bounds out every time. He yips, loud and clear through the morning cold. He crunches frozen blades of grass as he leaps. He pirouettes in mid-air. His back spasms in his attempts to get higher. To get closer to Willem.

He runs figures of eight around Willem's ankles. He is a white and brown blur. He giggles, Willem is sure he hears it. Amongst those excited barks and yips and barks there is the breathless pant of a child's laughter.

Only when he has tired himself out will Jacob come up to Willem's hand. He will have smelled Willem's crotch and his shoes. He will have leapt high enough to paw at his belly and to place his mitts on Willem's lower back, pushing in excitement. Only when these rituals are over will he stand still long enough to sniff the proffered hand. To lick those fingers and allow them to tickle his ears, his belly.

'You'll spoil that one if you're not careful,' Gregor laughs at him each time Willem comes in for breakfast, his hand wet with the dog's laughter.

'Aye, he might,' Sally bustles over. 'But what harm will come of it?'

And so when Gregor is gone Sally lets Willem sit with Jacob at his feet. The little dog is resting his head on Willem's shoes. He is snoring and every so often his back feet kick. He whines, grunts and carries on snoring.

'Why a jack rabbit?' Willem asks. Sally throws some rosemary and a pinch of salt into the stew. She stirs the pot with a wooden spoon and breathes in deeply. The spoon swims, it glides and releases the stew's steam, the stew's deep smell. She inhales the vapours blowing from its surface. Willem inhales the vapours and he wants the smell to live with him until his dying days.

'He runs,' she says at last. 'He always runs. His ears prick up and he's off.'

'What do you run from?' he asks her. She laughs. Her voice is musical, it is a tinkling bell.

'I never run from anything, Willie. I don't think it's right to run.'

'Have you ever been in danger?' She looks puzzled. Her eyes are deep. They swim in the stew as she checks it. They swim in his eyes as she looks back, frowning.

'What on earth would have put me in danger?'

Willem shrugs and tickles Jacob behind the ears, waking him up. Jacob leaps to his feet and immediately starts to nuzzle his hands.

The roof

He wakes up one early one morning and staggers across to the bathroom and his toes sink into the cold. The carpet is soaked. It smells of damp, of mould. It holds him for a second, it freezes the blood in his bare feet. He looks up, he peers into the darkness. The ceiling is also damp. It is white plaster and around one spot it is discoloured. The discolouring is about a foot wide, round and yellowish white. A slim crack runs along its length. Another slightly wider crack branches off from the middle for a few centimetres. He knocks on Gregor and Sally's door.

'What is it, lad?' Gregor asks him. He is wearing shorts and his chest is bare. His chest is thick and hollow wrinkles carve his sternum. Grey wires run from his throat to his belly button, curling in the morning half-light. Stubble covers his jaw and his mouth opens wide with a yawn. Willem nods to the damp patch on the floor, he points to the ceiling.

'Leak,' he says and Gregor swears.

'That's all I fucking need.'

'What is it?' Sally calls. She isn't yet used to having another man in the house. She is wearing a translucent night gown with nothing underneath. Willem can see her large nipples pointing downwards. He can see her belly. She has a scar like his mama had. One of her boys must have been carved out of her, the same as he was. He wonders if it still hurts her, he wonders if it haunts her dreams.

'Leaky roof,' Gregor tells her. 'Go back to bed for a bit. It's early yet. Me and the lad will see to it.'

With the last light of the dying stars shining against his back, Gregor roots about in one of the sheds. He brings out some dark grey nails, a couple of hammers, a selection of chisels and a saw. He puts them all in a bucket and passes them to Willem. A light snow is falling, it gathers on Willem's shoulders. A couple of flakes tickle his nose, they make him sneeze. The nails in the bucket rattle as he sneezes.

'God bless you,' Gregor says. He has a couple of lengths of timber under one arm and some tarpaulin draped over the other.

'Grab that ladder for us, will you lad?' he asks, nodding at a collapsible step ladder leaning against the shed wall. It is icy cold to the touch and the hinges are showing spots of rust.

Gregor places the ladder against the house. He opens it up and digs two of the legs a little way into the earth. 'The damned earth is like rock today. Damn the cold,' he curses. He is muttering under his breath. They are both wearing scarves and gloves, thick sweaters and raincoats, but their jaws still chatter.

Gregor holds the ladder still while Willem climbs. The roof tiles are slippery with ice and he loses his footing a couple of times. 'Careful there, lad,' Gregor rumbles as he passes up the tools. His fingers cling to the ladder, to the guttering. He climbs up to join Willem, the cold steams in his lungs. It steams between them.

But the old man's footing is sure, his legs are firm.

'There's the problem,' he growls, pointing a torch at a gap in the tiles. 'Bats, I reckon. They make their nests in the rafters if we're not careful. Looks like we weren't too careful this year.'

A wooden beam is exposed. It has started to decay. The underside of the roof tiles is covered in mesh to insulate the house. A ragged hole gapes through the mesh where the bats have opened it up. Gregor and Willem use the saws to cut into the rotten wood. They use the chisels to chip it away. They work for a half hour in silence until it is cleared.

They work by torchlight. The sun peeps over the horizon as the last piece is dug out. It is watery today. 'The days are only going to get colder as the new year comes in,' Gregor says. 'Shorter and colder and my old bones will start to ache worse every morning.'

They cut a length of timber and nail it along the old beam, strengthening it. They pull out the damaged tiles and cover the hole in the mesh with tarpaulin. They lay new tiles, hammering pegs in to hold them in place. 'That'll do her for the moment. I'll have to get a roofer in the spring to do a proper job of it. I'll have pest control in to clear out the nest,' Gregor says.

'The first of December's nearly on us. A week away. The first day of advent,' he tells Willem when they're back on solid ground. 'You know that?'

'Nope. I guess I lost track of the days. Never had much to do with it anyway.'

'Aye. Me neither. It's for children and women and gift shops' profit, I always say. Nobody's god fearing these days, nobody looks to the real meaning of the holidays. But in this house we'll light candles, we'll say our prayers like good folk.'

'Mm.'

'But it will be a month to the day since you woke up here.'

'Mm.'

'The lads are all shocked at how fast you've recovered. The doctor said it's strange. Good, mind you, but strange. Anyway, me and Sally thought we might put on a bit of a dinner, mull some wine. Maybe even crack out my good whiskey for a toast. Just to mark the day.'

'Aye,' he says. His throat has closed. He doesn't know what more to say so he nods. His eyes sting, Gregor looks away. He concentrates on folding up the ladder and storing the tools as the smell of bacon and eggs wafts out of the kitchen. 'Looks like Sally's up. Good girl. Time to eat, lad.'

'Mm.'

The walls

On the last day of November Willem and two of the farm hands boil up some pitch. Next spring Gregor says he and Sally are due to expand their poultry output. 'He means we're getting more chickens in,' Sally laughs when Willem looks confused.

'Aye.'

'So we need a couple of extra coups.'

They spent a couple of days sawing timber and cutting up chicken wire. They made outer walls with window slats for light. They laid wood and straw for the roosts. They made flaps so that they could get the eggs out each morning. They made inner walls lined with insulation to keep the chickens warm.

Willem and Gregor got up early. The other farmhands arrived early and now they are carrying the various sections of the new coups out of one of Gregor's barns. They load it on a truck and carry it out into the field in which the chickens will be housed.

The ground is soft. There was a lot of rain last night. It is drizzling still and the mud squelches underfoot. Willem is wearing a new pair of work boots. Sally drove to the nearest town and came back with them. They keep his socks dry. They keep his feet warm. They let him do his work uninterrupted.

'How much are they paying you?' one of the labourers asks Willem. His name is Frankie. He is seventeen and he wants to be a vet when he leaves school. His father is a friend of Gregor's and so he works on the farm during the weekends and school holidays. 'They don't pay me much,' Frankie says. 'Pocket money really, but that's all I need. What about you?'

Willem doesn't like questions. He doesn't like all this talk. He tells Frankie that they're not paying him.

'What, are you soft or something? You break your back in the cold for free?'

'They feed me. They give me a bed. They give me clothes. Look,' he says and he points at his feet, at his new boots.

'Dude, don't let them fool you. They're loaded. They're like millionaires or something. Old money. If this land didn't make them anything they would still be the richest farmers for miles around.'

'But they took me in.'

'They've got as much space and food as they do money. Do you think it's a hardship for them to spare you an old bed and throw you scraps from the table? No. Do yourself a favour and stop working for free. It's not on.'

Willem shrugs. He doesn't care too much. He doesn't really think about it.

They dig holes in the wet ground for the corner posts. They use mallets to sink the posts, they lay wooden planks as a floor. They cover the floor in tarpaulin and pin material in place. The material is rough and strong, Willem has never seen it's like before. 'Space age stuff,' Frankie says. 'Gregor likes to play around with the latest materials. It's his hobby.' They hammer the roosting planks to the insides of the inner walls. They hammer the inner walls together in place. They pin the mesh wire in the windows and they put the outer walls in place.

Both men are sweating despite the cold. The sun is far away but the air wraps tightly to their bodies. Opposite them a few more labourers are setting up coups in the same way, hammering, sweating. One of them is called Fingers. He doesn't know why Fingers has this name. He doesn't much care. It's enough to put a name to each face. All the men are stripping off their jackets and hats. They enjoy the cold wind as it soothes their warm muscles.

As the last pieces are fitted Fingers and a man called Benny bring up the truck. It gleams in the watery sun. It is muddy on the bottom but the top sparkles. It catches in Willem's eyes. It obscures the men's faces.

The boiled pitch is loaded in pots in the back of the truck. They all put on thick gloves and cover their mouths with masks. They take thick brushes, they unload the pitch and divide it between the coups. They spend the rest of the day painting it onto the walls and roofs of the little buildings. 'It'll keep it water tight and warm,' Gregor tells Willem that evening. 'It'll keep my new wee birds cosy all year round.'

The bed

He watches an owl fly past his window. He listens as it calls to its mate. The moon is large tonight. It's larger than any of us, he thinks. It picks out everything with its silver glow. In its glare everything clamours for a shadow. And the owl glides past, silent on silvered wings.

He is lying in bed, trying to dream. But he cannot sleep, he cannot stop thinking about the owl. He imagines it swooping down on a field mouse or a rat. He imagines the rodent's neck breaking. He listens to the loud snap and imagines the feel of the little bones breaking in the owl's beak. He imagines the feel of them snapping between his own jaws, his teeth tearing flesh as he flies off to feed his young.

He imagines the pain of wings sprouting between his shoulder blades. Or of feathers breaking through the flesh of his arms, growing out in layers until they are thick enough for him to glide. To catch currents and soar. His arms start to itch and he scratches them. He has thick claws from hard work and they tear away tiny ribbons of flesh. The flesh curls under his nails and little beads of dark blood trickle down his forearms, over his fleshy triceps.

This is how it starts, he thinks. This is how the wings first sprout.

His bed is soft and warm. It has feathers of its own. It is stuffed with goose feathers, Sally told him. The feathers hug his bones after a long day in the fields, in the barns and warehouses. They hug his clean muscles after he has showered, after he has scoured himself clean of the pigs' muck and the sheep's muck and the cows' muck. 'You know we shouldn't be so diverse,' Sally told him. 'Stick to pigs or cattle or sheep, but this one will never have it!' She nodded at Gregor, smiling. 'He wants it all, he wants to play with everything.' Willem likes it, he likes looking after so many animals.

The owl hoots once more. It is on the lintel above his window. Another owl replies from the trees. The trees stand sentinel along the edges of every field, green all year round. And the owls and the wood pigeons make their nests and hoot into the darkness as he tries to sleep.

The next morning Sally asks him if he slept OK. She asks him every morning. He tells her no, the owls were hooting and they kept him awake. He tells her about the last owl in Leith, about how he had seen it stuffed on its owner's mantelpiece. That it had been taken in by the police and he still wasn't sure why.

'The last owl in Leith?' Gregor asks with laughter in his voice.

'Aye.'

'Sounds like a child's story. Do you think maybe some-one was having you on?'

'Why?'

'It just seems unlikely that a taxidermist caught the last owl in Leith and that there were no others.'

'Mm.'

'How did they know there were no other owls?'

Willem shrugs. He thinks back. He remembers being scared of owls as a lad. Being scared of the dark. He had a picture book with an owl flying at night and its beak always looked so cruel. He remembers being happy when he was told there were no more owls left.

'Sorry lad, I think someone was pulling your leg.'

'Leave him alone, Gregor,' Sally snaps.

'Mm.'

The first day

There are three calendars on the mantelpiece. They are cardboard and they stand out a little from the wall. 'Here you go lad, your advent calendar,' Sally says to him while Gregor busies himself in the bathroom. She is wearing her apron, her sleeves are rolled up. There is bacon grease on her fingers and on her forearms. There is a smile on her face. She wields a spatula in one hand and is pointing the other at the calendar on the right.

'Thanks.' His throat has closed again. His legs are cold, his eyes are warm.

Each calendar has twenty four windows. The pictures on the fronts of Sally's and Gregor's show classical scenes, all snow and toboggans and gingerbread houses painted in oil. Children run about, laughing and smiling. They throw snowballs and totter under piles of presents wrapped in brown paper. 'Classy, don't you think? Dark chocolate for the grownups!' she laughs.

Willem's is dark purple. It has a CGI cartoon of Santa in his sleigh. He is in the background, his sleigh's carriage is to the left. He is facing forwards and right. The reindeer get larger and larger with each row. At the front a cartoon Rudolph flashes his nose. He smiles, they are all smiling and Santa waves from the rear.

'There's number one,' Sally points. Her fingerprint leaves a little bacon grease on the window. He opens the window and breaks the foil underneath. There is a little piece of chocolate inside. It is shaped like a bell, like a little bell from Santa's sleigh. It warms his mouth. His saliva runs as he crunches it in half. It slips over his tongue, it covers a couple of teeth. It melts and mixes with his saliva, running into the back of his mouth as Gregor comes back in.

'Thanks,' he says again and washes his hands for breakfast.

'All ready for tonight?' Gregor asks as he takes his seat at the breakfast table.

'Ready?'

'Aw, you know what I mean. Looking forward to it.'

'Aye.'

'We've a couple of friends coming over to meet you. Polly and Sam, Marcus and Seonaid, Rhona and her girls. We'll make a party of it.'

'Mm.'

Sally passes out the plates of food. 'They can't wait to see you,' she tells him. 'They've heard all about you. They're fascinated!'

He hasn't told either Sally or Gregor too much about himself. They keep digging, they keep trying to get him to open up. They know he is from the south. They assume he is from Edinburgh or somewhere in the Borders. He tells them about the last owl in Leith as Sally fetches marmalade. They suspect he is running from a gang, the kind of gang who rule the kinds of streets a man like him might call home. The kind of gang whose reach doesn't leave their own territory. Who fade into irrelevance in Gregor and Sally's community of rural farmers and suburban arbiters.

They know that he was running when they found him. They do not know to where. They have guessed that even he didn't know where he was going, only where he was coming from.

'Sally gave you your calendar then?' Gregor asks, smiling.

'Aye.'

'Been a long time since we were able to buy a young man an advent calendar.'

'Mm.'

'Speaking of which, the boys are coming home for Christmas. They want to see you too. They can't wait.'

'Mm.'

'They're also fascinated.'

The television is humming away on the kitchen counter. Sally likes to watch the early morning news. She says that she grew so used to having a houseful of unruly men that she finds it far too quiet these days. The television is the only chatter she gets now.

Willem says nothing but he hates the television. He likes the warmth and the food. He likes the hard work the farm offers, he likes the callouses newly reformed on his old labourer's hands. But he does not like the noise of the television, he cannot stand its flashing lights. He used to like it, back at his mama's house. He liked to watch shows about cars. He liked to watch the football at the weekends. But all that is gone now, it is far behind him. The voices are distractions now. Now they do nothing but inspire fear and invade his peace of mind. They cripple his solitude, they are bigger than his solitude and he doesn't know where to look.

The television invades. The newsreader says that a series of crimes in the Edinburgh area have been linked to one perpetrator. DNA evidence found in all crime scenes have been found to match, Scotland Yard has announced. This is old news, it is a recap. They heard this a few days ago. The DNA belonged to a nobody, there was nobody on any file anywhere on whom to pin it. CCTV images have shown a shadow fighting two men in a far corner in a supermarket car park in the dark. They have shown the shadow breaking a man's limbs before groping his girlfriend in the street. They have shown the shadow knocking out an attractive businesswoman and throwing two bodies from a bridge outside of town, careless.

What was the perpetrator but a mere shadow? He is an invisible man and he has been no cause for concern.

'But a man hunt started this morning for one Willem J. Gyle, resident of Leith, Edinburgh. A warrant for his arrest was issued in early September for assaulting staff at a job centre in the centre of Edinburgh. Sketches of the unknown assailant match the staff's description of this man and papers he signed at the job centre were taken into police forensics earlier this week.

'They have issued a warrant for the arrest of Mr. Gyle for triple murder, sexual assault, resisting arrest and for multiple counts of theft and assault.

'If you have seen Mr. Gyle, or if you have any information regarding this case please call the hotline number on your screen.' A telephone number flashes onto the screen in blue. Gregor and Sally have stopped chewing. They are both staring at the television. They are staring at a photograph of Gregor taken a few years ago. The photo was for a site pass. He glares at the camera, blank and ready to work.

A forkful of bacon hangs halfway to Sally's mouth and Gregor is holding a cup of tea against his lips.

'Please be warned, Mr. Gyle is considered dangerous and is not to be approached.'

They both jump as Willem stands. His ears are ringing. His eyes are hot and his legs are cold.

The dogs' breath

'Lad, what is this?' The colour has drained from Gregor's face. Sally is tight lipped, her shoulders are shaking. 'Gregor, what kind of monster have we invited into our house?' she wants to know. Her voice is a sob, it is a gasp.

'I'm not a monster.'

'Is all this true?'

'Aye.'

'You're a fucking monster!'

'Why does that make me a monster? Why do I have to be a monster?'

Before Gregor can answer Willem has him by the collar. He pulls the old man to his feet. When he first came here Willem was weak, he was shrunken from the streets, from the mountain air. Gregor is almost as tall as him and was almost twice as wide. But they have fed him well. He has worked hard and his muscles have recovered from the wilderness. Gregor is easy to move, he is easy to pick up. *The lads are all shocked at how fast you've recovered. The doctor said it's strange. Good, mind you, but strange.* But I am strong in this world, I am strong inside, he thinks. Hear me roar, watch me grow. I am too strong for any of you.

He pulls Gregor over the table. Cutlery scatters as the two men struggle. Willem head butts him, crushing his nose into a flattened pulp. His blood is bright, it is brighter than the day as Sally screams. Her scream is bigger than the day. It is bigger than anything as blood covers the old man, it covers the young man and they spin together on the kitchen floor.

The old man's head lolls forwards. He is dazed. The young man's head is working fast, faster than it has ever worked before. He tenses every muscle in his body. He lifts Gregor. His muscles scream and he bellows and he wants the old man dead, he wants all the cunts dead. The fuckers, all of them dirty fuckers. He hates them. He wants to tear them apart. He turns Gregor upside down, he drops him like a sack of flour. His head squelches and the sound is warm in Willem's ears.

He tears Sally apart. He tears her blouse, he tears her bra and her skirt. He tears her tights so that they sprout holes, deep holes. They are wide holes and they expose old flesh. Her skin quivers, it looks like cold porridge. Her breasts swing as he slaps her. He picks her up in a bear hug. He squeezes her until he can hear bones cracking. He spins around, he lets her go and she smacks against a wall.

Jacob and Marley are barking outside. They are clawing at the door, they can smell the fear and the blood. They can smell the anger, burning bright. Brighter and bigger than Willem himself. Willem takes a cleaver from Sally's knife rack. He pushes the back door open. He pushes hard and fast and Jacob flies a few feet. Marley is faster, she dodges and springs back. She leaps into the kitchen, looking left and right for the intruder. Willem swings the cleaver from behind. His aim is true and he beds the cleaver into the dog's spine.

Jacob scrabbles inside, he locks his teeth onto Willem's hand. Willem swings his arm in a wide arc, he sends the dog crashing against the oven door. Jacob climbs to his feet. His teeth are bared and foam flecks between them. It is stringy, it is rope flying from his tongue. It is his last defence as Willem grabs him. He snaps the wee dog's neck in one quick, deft motion.

Nothing else moves in the kitchen. Willem's chest heaves. He holds Jacob's body, he clings to it. He stands on his own, he buries his face in Jacob's dead fur, desperate against his own skin. It is tight against his chest and he cannot breathe deeply enough. The air in here is close, he has spoiled it with his anger. It offers no nourishment.

Sally and Gregor start to groan, drooling. They cling to life, they cling to the spoiled air in this room. Willem places Jacob down, gently. He looks at the dead dog's face, he looks around the kitchen. He furrows his brow, he squares his shoulders against it all.

The coups, the nests

Gregor's keys glint on their hook. They shine and they twinkle as he lifts them. He crushes them in his hand, scrunching tight so that they stop their jangling.

He takes an axe from the shed and tucks it into his belt. Its head is sheathed in leather but he has used it before. He knows that the steel gleams, that the edge is true. It is the truest thing he knows and its weight against his hip slows his beating heart. It is comfort, it is unthinking. He takes a hunting knife and ties its sheath to his ankle, inside his jeans.

He uses Gregor's keys to open up the gun safe. He takes a shotgun and ten rounds of buckshot. He loads two rounds into the gun. He loops the shotgun's leather strap over his shoulders. He fits the remaining buckshot into place in pouches along the strap.

He bundles his clothes into a rucksack. He puts on a fleece and a body warmer and a waxed coat over it all. He bundles a sleeping bag from the spare room into his rucksack. He takes tins of fruit and dried, cured meat from Sally's pantry and stuffs them all in on top of the sleeping bag. He takes a sports bottle, fills it with water and tucks it into a side pocket.

He can't think of anything else he might need. Nothing that he can carry.

Sally is coming around, her eyes are opening. He kicks her in the head with his steel toes. Her head snaps back, it hits the floor. He pulls her body over to Gregor's. He pulls them close and puts Gregor's arms around hers. He pulls the cloth from the table and places it over them so that they won't catch a chill. He turns up the thermostat a few degrees, picks up the dead dogs and drags them into the garden.

I drag, I drag, he thinks as he lets them go.

He reaches the garden gate and turns back. He walks across the garden, into the kitchen. He picks up his advent calendar, he folds it in two so that the cardboard pops along the creases. He stuffs it into a side pocket of his rucksack and turns his back for good.

The other workers won't be here for an hour at least. He has a little time, a head start. He throws his rucksack and shotgun into Gregor's truck. He will go off road for a few hours. He will ditch the truck and cut cross country by foot. He will head back into the mountains, he will climb as high as he can.

He revs the engine and pulls out of the driveway. Gravel crunches, it sounds like Sally's bones in his arms. Her soft flesh, her little moans. She sleeps now and brings him peace.

He drives into one of the fields. The chicken coups freshly coated in pitch are at one end and behind is a dirt track which disappears up into the forest. He drives through one of the coups, crushing it beneath the truck's wheels. As he climbs the track the trees flank him. They are strong. They are stern in dawn's half-light. An owl flits overhead, its nest is at its back. He smiles, he cries and the owl dives through the trees. Salty tears tremble on his top lip, his tongue can taste the sea. The vast deep. It calls to him.

The fast snow

He ascends. The tracks grow rough. They grow lean and bumpy as the air grows thinner.

He can see the blankets of snow above him. They fold him up, they make the going slow when he reaches them. He is ten miles from Gregor's farm, from Sally's stove. Twenty miles, thirty miles. But as the crow flies he has yet to take a step, his tread is too light. The sun is shining and it glares from the peaks as the trees give way to open slopes.

It glares from the soft snow and the distances fold him up. They fold together.

Time and sense have no meaning out here. They have no purpose. He switches from dirt track to back road, from back road to dirt track. He is thirty miles into his journey yet he might as well be five. He might as well be a hundred, two hundred. There is nothing but the tall might of the peaks. They span the world, they span time. They see infants crawling over them, gliding along their ridges. They barely feel the tickle of the infants' footsteps. His tyres grow thin as they chafe against the mountains' rubble, but nobody is here to see.

Theirs is no purpose. They are and that is enough.

'Is it, is it?' he mutters, glaring through the windscreen.

He sits forward in the seat. The heavens are opening above, thick sheets of icy rain and snow fall and falter and fall again. The windscreen wipers blur and he is tense and the mountain tracks are tense. The gear stick is hard to move up here, the truck fights him as much as it fights the dirt roads. He takes it away from the tracks. He takes it over hills and ridges who have never known roads, who have known so few tyres in all their long years that they shrug. They do not care for such a small man.

A peak looms. It is no taller than the rest. It is no older, no younger. Its feet root no less deeply than its brothers'. And yet here is a hard one. No grass grows here, no snow is allowed to settle. The crags are deep, the rocks are sharp and they chew the sky.

He turns the steering wheel so that the truck faces this peak. He puts his foot down. He churns ice and snow, he makes a cloud dance at his rear. The truck ascends, it crests the peak. The rocks are chewing, they are waiting and he snags the truck in their lines. He laughs as the metallic sound of iron shearing screeches. It screeches in his ears, it screeches from the mountains' sides. The truck leans to one side, it veers and the wheels on Willem's left buck up into the air. He fights it, he is losing. He is drowning and he is laughing.

The truck pirouettes. Up here anything can be graceful. Anything can be free. He glides before coming to a stand-still, he bows as he falls.

His boots crunch the snow as he climbs out. It is fresh and light and thin. The air is fresh and light and it burns his nostrils with the cold. He inspects the car. The front tyre on the driver's side has burst. The rear axle is in two pieces. It was shattered by the impact, by the cold.

He takes Gregor's tire iron out of the boot. He uses it to dent the windows. Spider's webs cross outwards from each impact. He strikes again and again. He hooks the iron into each hub cab, prying them off. One of the break disks is cracked, a rent splits it nearly in two. The crash performed well, the overwhelming crash. He opens the bonnet and steam blows out. It has had a hard journey and the moun-tain air knows nothing. It forgives nothing. He wedges the iron into the engine, pulling at valves, ripping them out. He takes his knife from his belt and slashes the three remaining tyres. They exhale deeply, they sag and the truck sags with them. One last sigh, one last relief.

It is not enough. He is not done. There is firewood in the boot. He lays it inside the engine. He puts a couple of fire lighters amongst the debris. He uncaps the oil, he lets it run. He uses the lighter his mama gave him, he throws sparks down and trails of smoke start to rise.

He shoulders his rucksack and shows the truck his back.

The big stir

He can hear screaming, shouts ring out. A little blood drips from his forehead and skiers on the other side of the valley have seen the fire. With a great rush the truck caught. First the engine's oil and then the petrol tank caught. They can see it, it is a black and red beacon. The flames lick red, they are angry. The oily smoke climbs high.

'Don't worry,' he tells the skiers. He mumbles. They will never know him, they will never see him. They know only the mountains and the long slopes. 'Don't worry,' he says, over and again. Nature will reclaim them all. The truck will burn down, it will rust and wither. The mountains will look on, oblivious as they reclaim the spent metal.

He hikes down the side of the peak. Three miles, maybe more. Rocks slide beneath his feet and time passes without meaning. He knows this, his bones know this and his heart knows this. He climbs another peak, every footstep taking him further into the wilderness. Farther from the chaos at his back.

Deep trees lie before him. They are below the snow line today. But they are close, they watch the snow line constantly. Theirs is a vigil of respect, of fear. They have known the snow all their long lives, they know it came before them. It will come after them. They know everything and they know nothing. They are of the mountain and they stand strong, laughing at time's little games.

The sky starts to buzz above his head. It whirs with the sound of rotors. He looks up. He squints through the sunlight, he can see a tiny pinprick in the distance. A helicopter hovers over the remains of his truck. The last of the smoke chews up the helicopter's blades. It dances and eddies, like the starlings, he thinks. It is graceful, everything up here is graceful.

The stories part IV

His mama knew he liked the fable of the wolf and the lamb. It was one of his favourites, one of the ones he asked to hear the most. He liked the picture of the wolf in the story book. He liked its shaggy grey mane and its sharp teeth. He liked its powerful haunches, always ready to pounce.

In his memories the wolf watches the lamb. The lamb is drinking at a stream. Bright blue watercolour splashes across the page, tracing the artist's brush.

The wolf wanted to devise a suitable pretext for devouring the lamb, his mama told him. So, although he was upstream, he accused the lamb of muddying the water and preventing him from drinking. The lamb replied that he only drank with the tip of his tongue. He didn't get much water this way, but the stream stayed clean.

And besides, being downstream he couldn't muddy the water upstream. The wolf's plan had failed and so he said: 'But last year you insulted my father.'

'I wasn't even born then,' the lamb replied.

The wolf in the picture smiled. He smiled with his teeth and with his hungry eyes. He said: 'Say what you like to justify yourself, I will eat you all the same.' And his mama would tickle him until he squealed.

'I'll gobble you up!' she laughed as her fingers worked under his armpits, across his belly. She laughed and he laughed and the lamb in the picture knew that his time had come.

PART IV:

THE TOILER UNBOUND

The soft earth

He scrambles the last two hundred yards over rough stone. The stone breaks beneath his boots. The stone scuffs his boots. He trips a couple of times and tears the fabric in his gloves. New gloves that Sally gave him, with full length fingers and fleecy lining. They are ruined now in his haste, but it doesn't matter. Nothing matters up here. He tears one of the knees of his jeans and he tears the skin underneath. Pale blood seeps out of the little scratches. He has to rub them to free the little pieces of grit caught in his flesh. The grit drags at him, it rips a little more.

It doesn't matter.

He crosses into the forest. The helicopter is searching the surrounding peaks but he is invisible under the canopy. He can move as he wills and the world is blind.

From the high ground to his back the forest looked vast. He could see for miles but he couldn't see its farthest edge. From under the canopy it is small. The trees around him loom large and block out all other space. The big spaces and the little spaces are all hidden. He moves through them and they move around him, they march as he scrambles.

And the world is blind.

The ground here is soft. The trees have had time to dig deep. Their roots are strong and they have churned the mountain's rock. They have hollowed it out, tenderising it. They live long, the mountain notices them. It allows them sanctuary. It allows them a place to breath and sleep and dream.

He stumbles again. He thrusts out his injured hand and supports himself on a tree's trunk. He was high when he drove, when he crashed. He was high when he defended himself against Gregor's scorn and Sally's fear. But now he is amongst the trees he is tired. Now his legs drag, his feet scrape through the underbrush.

He knows the feeling well. He used to get it when he got home to his mama from work. He would spend his days hauling bricks, churning mortar, carrying and lifting and dragging. His muscles grew strong but they also grew tired. His bones grew tired and thick. He would get home and a wave of exhaustion would immediately hit him. It would hit him behind the eyes. It would hit him in the ears, garbling any words spoken to him.

But back then he had Jap. Jap would jump and lick and scrabble. He would need taking out. So before he could sit down and give in to his tiredness he was out again. Before his eyes were closed and his ears gave in Jap would pounce and drag him back into wakefulness. And for a little while there was Celina, warm bodied at the end of the long days. She would hold him close and lull him to a sleep so deep he would struggle to wake up. Or she would nibble and kiss and drive his heart rate so high that sleep was impossible, there was too much living to be done.

Now Celina is gone. Mama is gone and Jap is gone. Charlie and the crew are gone, Gregor and Sally are gone.

His home is gone and it has taken his free name with it. Only the trees remain to support him. He takes a deep breath. He holds onto one of the trees for a second before pushing it away. Pushing himself away.

The helicopter is out there, scanning from the heavens. The police are on to him, they are baying for his blood. So he has to move. He cannot afford to be tired. He hitches his rucksack a little higher on his back and carries on, stomping through the leaves and dirt.

The hollow

His ribs are starting to push against his skin. He has lived on dried meat and soup since he left the farm. Five nights have passed and boulders and brooks have passed him and he is still in the forest. The nights bite. The spider's webs are sneaking back into his bones, crackling, cracking. A deep fog lies heavy over the forest. He sees nobody and nothing. Nobody and nothing sees him and he builds small fires at night. He huddles in close, he wakes up every few hours to add more wood. He peels the lids off soup tins and warms them in the fire's glow.

The fires are dried sticks and fir branches. The sticks crackle merrily. The firs smoke in the darkness. The smoke rises through the trees. It bolsters the fog. The fog is thick, it threads through every branch. But he is hollow. He is out of soup now. He has only a few rashers of jerky left. He has eaten Sally's tinned fruit. His ribs are starting to show as each mile he trudges strips his body of more fat. His stomach is a hole. He remembers the taste of hunger now. He remembers its weakness.

I will not give in to hunger, he thinks. *I will not let it rule me.* He finishes the last of his supplies in one evening. It is an orgy, it is a dry feast. His jaw aches from chewing, his throat is sore from swallowing. His stomach gurgles. It has grown accustomed to being left empty.

As he lays sticks on his fire he makes a decision. He is firm. Overhead the owls are waking up. Bats are starting to sweep the branches. *I will not let the land hold me to ransom.* Now that the last of his supplies are gone he will abandon food altogether. He will overcome the weaknesses of his flesh. He will wither, but that is OK. He does not want to be seen. He does not want to see. He will make a shade of himself.

As he withers his strength will become his own.

I am the shadow of my shadow, I am a free man.

The bottles, here and there

All the trees besides the evergreens are dead. Their branches stand bare. Empty nests huddle in their boughs. The songbirds have long since migrated. They have flown south and the starlings have taken their dance away. *But have they gone home or are they away from home?*

He finds a stream. It is midday and the sun is pallid in the water's bubbles. It is whisked along easily by its currents. It seeps through the bare branches overhead. It seeps through the mist and casts a weak shadow behind him.

'This is me,' he says, holding his arms wide and looking down at his shadow. The stream is noisy next to him. It covers all other sounds. The owls and the pigeons who have stayed behind for the winter hoot, they sing faint praise. They have stayed behind to stand vigil over the forest but their voices are faint. They see too far through the mist. They know what must come but their voices fall short.

'This is me,' he says, turning to the side. He breathes in. He pulls his stomach in. His shadow grows a little thinner.

He takes off his gloves and unscrews the lid from one of his bottles. It is a cyclist's bottle. One of Gregor and Sally's sons was a cyclist. He would cycle for hundreds of miles every week. 'Along the roads,' they said. 'He was never into mountain biking.' This was his bottle and Willem is glad he brought it. 'We should all see the mountains at least once before we die,' he says as he edges down the stream's bank.

The water is icy. Some branches lie on the bank, thrusting into the stream. Water eddies around them. Water is trapped by them, held in place.

The water is icy and it burns his fingers as he thrusts his hand into the water. He holds the bottle with its mouth to the current. The water is clear and clean. It is ice melt from the peaks. It will flow into a great river. It will join its brothers, it will flow for miles, picking up minerals as it flows. A large company will scoop it up. The same as Willem is scooping it up now. They will sell it in plastic bottles. They will sell it to supermarkets. And people like Willem will slip these bottles into their pockets. Or they will pay for them and slip other things into their pockets. The mountain water will be a mask, it will be sustenance as people think *fuck you* and live their lives of solitude.

'The mountain's shadow is long,' Willem says, screwing the bottle tight. 'We can all take refuge in it.' His own shadow will be lost to the mountain. Nobody will see him. And he will see nobody.

The water stings his teeth. It stings his tongue and it hurts his head. But the cold passes. The cold will always pass. It will leave everything in its wake refreshed, renewed.

The leaves

His feet crunch. The ground is slick with ice. He is following a valley. It snakes between higher peaks. It heads northwards, as far as he can tell. Though he is no expert and his head grows lighter with each passing day.

The peaks are hidden in the clouds. Below the clouds snow hugs the rugged earth. Sometimes sunlight breaks through the clouds and the snow glows white hot. The trees turn golden. He stops at such times. He stands dead still in the sunshine. He makes the most of it. He breathes it in. He bathes in it until it passes.

And then his feet start to crunch again. The floor is covered with brown leaves. Last year's leaves. Maybe the year before as well. All fallen, all decayed and frozen into place until the springtime warmth returns. Until the starlings return to dance above the canopy.

He thinks he walked about ten miles a day when he first started out. But it was up and down, it was along winding, close knit roads. Who knows how far he has come? He has no idea how long he has been walking. He has no idea how long it has been since he last ate. He survives by eating snow when his path takes him high enough. He drinks water from his stream, his teeth burn and his tongue grows numb. Now he thinks he walks five miles a day. Maybe more, but not much. His head is light and his legs are heavy.

He sees signs of civilization from time to time. Skiers flit across some of the peaks, far above. They are high, they have set themselves high and he can see their every motion. He is quiet, he is a shadow and nobody knows he is here. Sometimes he passes the noises and smells of small villages or tarmacked roads. He skirts wide to avoid them, he doesn't take the paths of man.

He passes newly forgotten campsites. They have black rings where the cook fires burned the ground. The coals are frozen over. Tyre tracks have dug the snow up and sometimes when the world is quiet enough he can hear the sounds of machinery whirring in the distance.

'What would cause a man to bring his machines up here?' he asks. 'I must be walking in circles.' The silent world offers no answers.

The cold thief

The first night he spent out here he nearly froze to death again. He built a little fire. He used fir branches. With the fog and the darkness the wet smoke from the needles wouldn't be seen. He lay close to the fire, huddled in his sleeping bag with a belly full of hot soup and dried meat. But halfway through the night he woke with his teeth chattering. His back was on fire, his limbs were solid. The ground was cold, it was frozen. It had seeped all his strength from his muscles.

He has learnt quickly. He remembers the newspapers and the naughty pictures that used to keep him warm at night. Insulation, the same as he used pump into the walls of newly built houses. 'The cold steals everything,' Charlie used to say. 'You have to be careful.' Now, each time he lies down to sleep at night he spreads out several fir branches to keep the cold earth at bay.

He sleeps peacefully now. His belly is empty but his bones are warm.

He lays his head down. He has passed out of time but the world is black and overhead the stars are twinkling. They are dead stars, shining brightest in their deaths. One of his mama's blokes told him so. They are so far away that the light you see is billions of years old. That is older than the stars themselves, so the stars are dead by the time you see them.

The same man told him about the painter van Gogh. People didn't see him until he died. He died penniless, but nowadays people sell his paintings for millions of pounds. The man bought them a poster he called starry, starry night. 'These are van Gogh's stars,' he said. 'Burning brightest in death.'

He will soon be dead. He knows it and he hopes for it. The cold will steal him away when he is ready for it.

He doesn't want to burn brightly. He just wants a peaceful escape.

'It is coming,' he says as the smoke billows next to him. It dances like the starlings. 'I will never see the starlings again. But they are in my dreams. Dance, little birds. Don't let them stop you...'

The bad moon

The wolves have been chasing him through his dreams for some days now. He heard them before he saw them. They loped through his world. They dribbled and their saliva burned the earth. It melted the snow and it dissolved his footprints as they howled cruel blood to the night.

They ate the owl. They took the meat from its mouth. They are the better hunters and this is their land. They ate the child and his rattle. Their silent paws muffled its noise. Their teeth ground it to dust. They ate his mama and Jap too, their bellies swelled. They took Celina and they ate everything up, their jaws grinding and their eyes hungry and red.

Last night he heard them, far off in the hills. Tonight as he tries to sleep he can hear them again. He wills sleep to take him but in his heart he is scared. They took so much. He doesn't know what more they can take. He is scared. He is scared for the first time since he left the one eyed man and Rosa broken and bloody and drifting in the current.

The stream is wider now. It is stronger and he thinks he can call it a river. 'It has earned that name,' he says as he huddles in his sleeping bag. It is to his back and the fire is to his front. He can hear the water bubbling, he can hear the wolves howling.

He has never seen a wolf except on the TV and in his mama's picture books. He doesn't know how big they are, how strong. He doesn't know what to expect. But he can hear them moving in the woods. He knows they can smell the warmth of his blood over the wood smoke and the water.

High above the canopy the moon is large. It is full and he imagines large half men loping through the woods. Their teeth grow long, their noses turn into snouts. Their snouts sniff him out. Their hands turn into claws and their eyes glow yellow with the moon's fever. They tear at him, they laugh and howl. They eat. They eat everything. They eat it all up.

The first shot

The first eyes begin to follow him the following evening. Dusk falls early up here in the wintertime. His shadow is swallowed. It is eaten whole by the mountains. The mountains' shadows lie long and deep. And out of those shadows the first of them appears.

He can hear his ribs rattling as he speeds up. His legs are heavy and he has to force them to move quickly. There is a small hollow in the rocks up ahead. He can make a fire there. He can keep his back to the wall and let the water pass him by way below.

He tumbles through the bushes, through bramble and hedge. He falls into the hollow and hugs its walls. It is shallow but it shares the mountains shadow. It can protect him. As his shaking hands set out his kindling and his firewood he knows it can protect anything.

His mama's lighter is running low. It takes a few clicks to get the flame started. Even then the flame is weak. It is small and blue and barely flickers. But it is enough. It has enough strength left to spark a fire. Soon he has smoke and heat and light. The fire warms the little hollow. It warms his bones. The smoke billows out, it merges with the shadows.

The bushes rustle. He can hear them over the crackling flames. There are footsteps out there, they break twigs as they close around him. They do not try to be quiet, they do not share his fear. They are circling, they are sniffing. They smell him through the smoke and their eyes light up. Two by two they light up. They are fireflies dancing in the darkness beyond his hollow. He can see one pair a hundred yards away. Two more pairs stalk behind it.

He sits down with his legs crossed and waits for them.

The barrel of Gregor's shotgun is icy. It does not share the fire's warmth. The triggers are stiff, stiffer than he thought. He brings the butt up to his shoulder. He squints like he has seen them do in the movies. He points the end at the darkness, at the mountains' shadow.

He has seen men fire guns on TV. He has heard the rocket blasts. But this is new. As he squeezes the trigger his world ends for a second. His ears cushion the force and turn numb. His head rings as it snaps away from his shoulder. He is lying on the ground. The cold rock has grazed his cheek. His forehead is bleeding again. Another gash has opened on the back of his head. The blood pools on the stone floor, it spatters a bright pattern.

He manages to sit up. His fingers find the gun. It is dusty. His hair is dusty and the cuts on his head are plastered with silt. The blast loosened a couple of small stones from the hollow's face, it showered the cave.

He peers into the darkness. He can hear nothing but the high whine of Gregor's shotgun. He can see nothing but the flame. The eyes have gone out. He knows they share his fear now. He knows they are running.

The mountains' shadow doesn't belong to the wolves. It belongs to nobody. It shelters everything and nothing. He squeezes the trigger again and the mountains ring with his gunfire.

The stumps

The signs of habitation have begun to grow more frequent. More signs of camp fires, more rubbish strewn on the ground. The roaring of machines is louder on the horizon. They roar, they shake the ground. He doesn't head north, he turns in circles. His only direction is to shy from his fellow man. The river passes down a low gorge, it separates into a few smaller streams. These cross through rocky ground before coming to a wide swathe in the middle of some woodland. His feet take him, they carry him to the clearing.

For a mile in every direction the land is bare. Trees loom on the edges of the empty space. They are tall and strong. Silver birches scratch the sky, poplars stand newly bare. Pine trees are thick with heady needles. But before them the land is dead. The streams thread through the empty space. Every few yards a stump cracks through the ground. Each one is all that remains of a once proud tree.

The cuts are straight. He has seen work like this before. The machines on the horizon are chainsaws. The shaking ground is the tremor of falling trees. The camps belong to lumberjacks, the tracks to their off-roaders. And the river will grow strong when its rivulets join up. The lumberjacks can float their finds to the next town and load them onto their trucks.

He sits down on one of the stumps. The cut is smooth but the surface is rough, sap has frozen around the split fibres. He picks at it, playing with it as it warms into glue. It warms in his hands and his fingers grow sticky.

He rolls the sap into a ball. He rolls it between his thumb and forefinger. He takes a while to make sure that all the sap is used. He takes a while to make sure the ball is completely round. When he is satisfied he flicks it hard. He flicks it as far as he can and it lands a few metres away. It lands on a half frozen leaf. It bounces, it rocks the leaf a little and falls still.

His bones creak as he stands. But his muscles go on. They have always gone on.

They carry him through the graveyard. This is how he sees the clearing. He remembers the little crosses Gregor showed him in their garden. One cross for every pet. There is one stump here for every dead tree. There were six graves in Gregor's garden. He loses count of the stumps in the clearing. He doubts that many folks will stop to count them.

At the far end great tyre tracks disappear into the forest. A wide road has been cleared. Six metres at the thinnest point and winding on down through the hills. Smoke plumes rise high over the distant hills. That is their camp. This is not his road.

He turns away. He beats through the undergrowth, he finds a little trail and forks away from the camp.

He does not want to see people. He does not want his face to be seen. He is lost, he loses himself with a will.

The cracked spindle

He counts seven deer sipping at the river. Two stand ankle deep. Their snouts are fully submerged. Five stand at the edge, licking themselves clean. The sun has broken through the morning and they bathe in its glow. They burn bright. Their ears flicker with each of his footsteps but they do not scare.

It rained heavily last night. The river is swollen. A shallow cave managed to keep off the worst but he still woke up damp through. He had to change his clothes. He pulled off his boots and his socks. He slipped out of his jumper and t-shirt. They are loose on him. His bones have shrunk. They belong to a lighter man now. He peeled off his jeans and his shorts and stood in the cold, naked and covered in goose flesh.

His cock and balls shrank. They pulled up inside his body. His lungs shrivelled, they pumped raggedly in the thin air. But even so he laughed. His laughter rattled as the rain let up. The deer heard his laughter. They rippled and wandered further down the river.

He laughed as the sun broke out. It warmed his skin. It dried his hair and beard. He put on his spare clothes. His old jeans and hoody. His old socks and boxer shorts. From before Gregor and Sally. From before the one eyed man. Before Jap got taken and his mama lay cold on a hospital bed.

He did the belt up as tight as possible. He is a lighter man these days and he has had to cut a couple of new holes. He uses the point of his knife. He digs it into the leather. He turns it one way and then the other, working through until the knife point emerges on the other side. Then his jeans will fit, then he can be his lighter self.

He counts seven deer and he unslings his shotgun. They wandered close to his camp. In the rain they didn't see him or smell him. By the time he emerges from his hollow, dry in the sunlight and fully dressed in warm clothes, they have had time to get used to him.

They are does, all of them. He learned the difference watching Bambi with his mother. A female is a doe, a male is a stag. There are no stags anywhere near. There are no antlers to tear him and the shotgun is cold. The power in his hands devastates him. It excites him. Feeling it kick back at him as he fought off the wolves excited him.

He creeps close. Their ears flicker towards him but still they stand there. He is quiet, discreet. *I am the shadow of my shadow, lost in this world.*

And the world is blind.

He brings the shotgun up to his shoulder. He aims at one of the herd. She is sipping from the stream, she stands with her rump to him. He squeezes the trigger and laughs as the world once more disappears. His ears ring and his eyes go blind and he staggers to one side.

He manages to stay on his feet this time. He blinks, he opens his eyes. The herd has scattered. The doe is limping away. She limps down the river. She bleeds into the river. Her rear left leg is scarlet, it is torn. It is a spindle cracked in the middle and Willem can see ligaments and muscle tissue straining beneath the blood.

The hunt

He catches up with the doe in a few strides. She is weak and in shock. She can barely stand. He thumps her wounded leg and she falls, shrieking. He wipes his hand on her coat. He smears it red.

Her nostrils are flaring. They are dark. She can smell her own blood. She can smell him, she can taste his excitement. She forces herself onto three legs. She lashes her head at him. Her neck is thick with muscle. Tendons thrash and tighten and knock the wind from his lungs.

His back hits a rock. It is mossy and cold. The moss is frozen, his hand slips and he knocks the back of his head. The dust and the blood sing in his cuts. The doe staggers back to her feet and manages to clamber a little way onwards. Her herd has left her behind. They fled down into a lower valley in the distance. She is alone and scared. She staggers towards the valley, but every step is a labour. Every breath is a labour.

Her leg gapes and quivers. Willem stands tall and kicks it. She squeals and kicks her good back leg, scraping into the frozen soil. Scraping skin from her hoof and shin. He holds on to her neck and squeezes. She tenses, she wriggles him from side to side but he holds firm. His forearm is locked into her throat, choking her. She slows down, she wilts. She lies still, looking up at him.

She is nearly dead. He lays her down and takes his axe out of its sheath. He looks into her eyes as he slits her throat on its edge. Warm blood flows over his hands. It is sticky and she gives one last whimper. Her muscles bunch. They loosen and she empties her bowels.

The hunt is finished.

The stories part V

A man passed a gardener on his way to work every morning, his mama told him. The gardener was watering his vegetables one day and the man stopped to talk to him. He asked him why the wild vegetables were flourishing whilst the cultivated ones in his beds were sickly and small.

The gardener said to him: 'It's because the Earth is a mother to one and a stepmother to the other.'

Willem asked his mother what this meant. She shrugged and said she wasn't sure. 'Know you're place, maybe,' she said.

'Or, it's better to be wild.'

'Mm.'

'Hey, you!' The voice rings clear in the sunshine. 'What are you playing at? What the fuck are you playing at?' Two men in felt caps are emerging through the long grass. They are wearing sturdy boots and fishing jackets over fleeces. One of them has a bow in his hand and a quiver at his hip. The other has a rifle with a telescopic sight in his hands. The men are fleshy and red and their eyes bulge from their sockets. They have a couple of birds hanging from their belts and they sweat as they chase towards him.

'This is private property, don't you know that?'

'It is god's own property,' Willem mumbles. No man owns the mountains.

'What's that? What are you, some gypo? Come on, where's your site? You bastards are always pitching up around here.' The man with the rifle is shouting, he is pacing in circles around Willem and his kill. He takes his phone out of his pocket. He points it at Willem and the doe and starts to take pictures. The grass is steaming. It is a red circle and it covers his boots. It covers his hands and his jeans and the front of his shirt. He stands tall and watches the camera.

The phone clicks as each picture is taken.

One of his mama's blokes once told him about the Red Indians. He said they didn't like having their pictures taken. The white men came from Europe with cameras and guns and shot them with both. When they shot the Indians with bullets wounds sprouted in their chests and backs and limbs. When they shot them with cameras the Indians lost their souls piece by piece.

'You a gypo then?' the man asks him, clicking his camera the whole time.

'No, no I'm not.'

'Geoffrey, call the police.'

'Sir?'

'The police, Geoffrey!'

'Sir, we don't have reception up here. The mountains interrupt the masts. We can use the satellite phone in the truck. Or we can go into town.'

'Shit. You,' he points at Willem. He glares at the blood, he stares into his eyes. The man's eyes are coals, burning and black. He is hatred and he is anger and Willem stands in the middle of it. 'You, you're coming with us. Put your gun down. Geoffrey, get the rope and bind his hands.'

Willem does not want to put down his gun. He does not want his hands bound. The man with the rifle clutches it a little tighter. The coals in his eyes burn and his knuckles are white on his lowered gun.

The man with the rifle is on Willem's right. The water is to his back. Geoffrey is circling to his left, in front of him. The mountains surround them. They circle them. They are the ground beneath their feet, they touch the heavens above.

Both men start to close in. The man with the rifle raises it to his waist. It is pointing at Willem's feet, it is ready. They are all ready.

Willem has one shell left in his gun. He swings it up to point at the man with the rifle, he braces it and fires into his abdomen. The man sinks down, his knees sink into the hot earth. They are stained by the doe's blood and by his own. The buckshot has torn through his fishing vest, through his jersey and his skin. It will be sticking out of his ribs. It will be tearing at his stomach and he clutches at the bloody hole. He clutches the floor and sinks even further. He lies on his chest, he rolls over. He is foetal and moaning and his hands are scarlet and slick.

Geoffrey is screaming. His hands are shaking and he drops his bow. He staggers backwards and Willem strides over to him. He drops the shotgun. He shoves Geoffrey to the ground and stands over him. Now Willem's eyes are coals, he is angry. His muscles are straining, they are made strong once more. He is hatred. His heart is burning, his brain is burning. He raises his fists high above his head. He brings them both down at once. They land on Geoffrey's shoulders, crunching.

Geoffrey screams again as Willem bellows and thumps his fists. Up and down, up and down. He tries to scramble backwards but Willem's fists are still falling. They fall on his arms as he tries to shield his body. He ducks his head, whimpering under Willem's fury. His fists break through and fall on his back, his shoulders. They crunch into his head.

He falls in his haste as Geoffrey tries to scramble away. Willem is walking forwards on his knees. He grabs Geoffrey's ankles and pulls. He drags Geoffrey under his own body. He straddles his chest and brings his fists down again and again. Geoffrey's nose is squashed flat. His cheeks begin to sink. His skin breaks and bleeds and his eyes disappear. His ears are ripped from his head and his gums are pushed inwards. His face is concave. His eye sockets face inwards and his teeth are loose. They rattle in his throat. They rattle as he gasps and clutches at his last breath.

Willem falls to one side. He is exhausted. His shoulders and elbows are shaking from the impact. His fists are wax, they are broken and slimy with blood and skin. He can see the tips of his knuckles poking through the skin.

There is no pain. There is joy and there is exhaustion and there are deep, gasping breaths as his lungs work to keep him conscious.

The stories' finale and the last of the strong force

There once were two men, his mama told him. They hated one another more than anything in the world. They were both sailors and one day it came to be that they had cause to man the same boat. Willem looked down at the book resting on her knee. Large text scrolled across one side of the spread. On the other side a great boat lurched through a storm.

One of these men took up his position at the stern and the other at the prow. His mama told him this meant they were on opposite sides of the boat. She showed him the picture. She pointed at the two men at either end, with the captain in the middle. A storm blew up, she read, and the boat was on the point of sinking.

The man at the stern asked the captain which part of the vessel would go down first. 'The prow,' he said, and the man at the stern made peace with himself.

'Death will bear no sadness for me,' he said, 'if I can see my enemy die first.'

He has always known the strong force. He has always been known for it. It is the strength inside him that carries on where other men give in. It is the strength in his back that carries on where others fall to their knees.

He sits in the red soil. It is red with the blood of his hunt. Two men shiver, one dead and one dying. One doe, innocent in life, sits lifeless in a pool of her own waters. Her shit is freezing. It is mixed with her blood and everything is freezing. Everything is dead or dying, but the strong force beats in his chest. He hasn't eaten for days. He doesn't know how time flows any more.

And the strong force beats on.

His hands are filthy and broken. The skin is filthy with blood. The bones are broken, he broke them against his quarry.

He is unthinking. His body is racing. Adrenaline is coursing. His limbs shake and his fingers shake and he closes his eyes to stop the mountains from shaking. With his eyes closed he drifts.

He doesn't know how time flows any more.

The man who takes

As his lungs slow and his heart beat slows he begins to think again. He cannot move his hands. They are shattered but he manages to climb to his feet. His knees creak. His spine creaks and little pops crackle along its length as he straightens. He opens his eyes and looks around. The day is ice blue, it is clear and the sky above is crystal. Red ice clings to his jeans. He has been sitting in the blood of his hunt and it has frozen onto him.

The man with the rifle is dead. His skin is blue. His lips are blue and his fingers are turning black. Willem can't look at Geoffrey. His stomach churns and his fingers start to hurt as he tries. The doe is frozen in place. Her shit and blood have wrapped her up, they have glazed her and the ice is growing thicker as time plays its tricks.

He leaves the shit and the blood. There is nothing for him here. He leaves the shotgun. He leaves the rifle, the bow and arrow. Let time and the elements carve them up as they see fit. He has no more need for them in this life.

He rolls his sleeves up. He tries to climb down the small bank to the river. His feet are slick, the ground is glass. He slithers, he slips and lands on his backside. He creaks and moves into a kneeling position. He shuffles over to the river, his knees cold in the half frozen mud. He looks like a supplicant, but he does not know this word. He does not know its meaning. He is a man who takes his worth and he leans his face towards the cold water.

It shocks him, it burns his teeth. His tongue loses all feeling, his jaw locks tight and he swallows gulp after gulp. He drinks his fill until he is refreshed, until he is as clear as the water itself.

He sits back on his haunches. His mouth is still burning with the cold. The wind whips by and stings his jaw. His beard is a sponge, it has absorbed the water. It is already beginning to stiffen with ice. 'Let it be,' he says.

The last robin's trick

As he walks away from the dead men and the dead deer and the guns and the bow and the arrows and the axe a robin flits down to greet him. It is the last robin he will ever see. He knows this and he stops. He stoops down to watch it play.

He thinks of the last owl in Leith and he looks down at this funny little creature. 'How did you survive all these years?' he asks. It chirps, it jerks its head from side to side to watch him with both eyes. 'How did the dinosaurs die out? How did the mammoths die when they were so big and you're so small?'

It chirps again, it takes a couple of steps towards him. It retreats, it advances again. It can't stay still. Its black eyes rove and flit, they take the whole world in before moving to the next image. Its breast isn't red like you see in the story books. Like he saw in the books his mama bought him. It is brown, a lighter, richer brown than the rest of its body. It is the colour of the doe's fur soaked in blood. It is bright against the cold, white earth. But it is warm and it is alive and no matter how high it flies or how far it flies it will always be of the earth.

It takes a few steps closer to him. He is kneeling down again. This time, if he knew the word, he might call it supplication. Or he might call it observance or curiosity or even just exhaustion. The little robin follows him with those beady eyes, it looks expectant as he sinks down.

'I'm sorry. I'm so sorry. I have nothing to give you.'

It flaps its little wings. It chirps one last time. The sound warms him, it makes his head light as it flits away.

It is gone. It has disappeared into the bushes. The earth has reclaimed its work.

The divergence

The road splits and he regards both routes as best he can. One of them is a walker's trail, well-trodden and smooth. In the distance he can see a thin plume of smoke. The other path is rough. He takes it, shunning the smoke plume and the heavy footfalls of his fellow man. It is thin, like walking a tight rope. 'But that is OK,' he says. 'I am the shadow of my shadow. There is room.' It bears no footprints as it takes him downwards, away from the peaks. It splits and splits again, like veins cracking the mountainside into pieces.

Men's footfalls try to dig deep, but the mountains' skins are thicker than their prints. Before they can be scratched the men will be dead. The red robin will be dead and the dinosaurs will have left a deeper mark.

'I hope, I hope,' he mumbles as he floats.

At each fork he takes the left hand side. The right ones carry on straight or climb. They climb high, they wriggle all the way to the top. They tread the mountainside to kiss the sky, but he is done with all of that.

He takes the left forks and descends. Deeper and deeper. He stumbles, he falls, he carries on.

As the sun begins to dip past the mountains' peaks Willem comes to a bothy. Grey bricks have been roughly stacked and dug into the hillside. They form a little hut. The edges are sharp even now. Even now when the moss lies deep in their crags and vines advance upwards.

'Everything climbs something else to reach the sky,' he says as he looks at the creepers. He mumbles under his breath and he coughs. His hands are aching. The exposed bone would hurt a conscious man. It would turn his head, it would burn and grow bigger than the mountainside.

He collapses into the bothy. Vines and moss are beginning to cover the logs stacked in the corner. He falls onto one of the stone pallets, a plinth built into the ground. He thinks of the trolls under their bridge, but the one eyed man has no place in this world. He cannot own this.

Willem has no place in this world. But he does not wish to own. He wishes to own nothing but himself and even that small package will soon be discarded.

The fury

As he sleeps he dreams. As he dreams he remembers.

He watched a TV show once when he was a kid. It was about volcanoes and he didn't say a word until it was finished. At one point in the programme they showed a volcano erupting off the coast of a far off country. 'There are no volcanoes going to erupt here, son, don't worry,' his mama told him. But he didn't mind, he didn't care. It could happen tomorrow, his whole world could be set on fire and he would think it was beautiful.

The volcano was an island. The island was emerald with trees. The sea shone blue all around it and the peak thrust high. It was a cone, sloping upwards out of the earth. Thrusting, thrusting. It was quiet, the world was quiet and the sky was calm at its back. And then the peak lit up, brightest orange. So bright, so quickly, so much power it made him stop breathing for a few seconds. After the light came the smoke, it unfurled black against all that pure colour. It curled outwards from the orange light and spat red and black lava everywhere. The hills ran red with a river of fire. And the smoke caught the sea breeze and danced above it all.

He sucked his thumb, he hurt his teeth sucking so hard.

The clip only lasted for a minute or so. Peace, explosion and then the reel ended. But it was enough. Its brevity was perfection. Red jewels rained from the sky, they sang and hissed. They hit the green trees and smouldered, burning black. And then three more explosions came from the island, they rained fire and billowed black smoke. One came from the side of the peak, two others came from lower down its flanks.

As the island was buried by its own power the narrator said that these little bursts were a millenia's pressure built up and then quickly released. The red rivers flowed to the sea, steam rose to dance with the smoke and the island was gone. A black smudge remained on the horizon and the reel ended.

Later on the TV show played some footage of a large brown bear loping through prairie grass. The sun shone above and the narrator said that this was Yellowstone National Park in America. It was vast, with countless ecosystems thriving in its midst. They said that every year tourists and trekkers flock in their thousands to sample its natural beauty, to bask in the simplicity of its endlessness. And beneath it all there lies a volcano with enough power to swallow it whole if it ever erupts.

Willem thought about the small island in the sea. He thought of the rubies falling from the sky, burying the volcano's slopes in fire. He thought of the rubies landing on their heads, the fury of the earth and the heavens burying everything in fire.

As he sleeps he smiles and rolls over. The mountains outside groan in the wind. It will be cold tomorrow, the fire is gone. But he burns, he will fall from the heavens and be buried. These are his dreams.

The descent

He rises early the following morning. The volcano burst too soon and the moon is still out, the stars are still out. The mountains are silver, they are their own shadows as he sets out. The fever has caught up with him. The fever from which Gregor and Sally and their doctor tried to save him. But he does not need saving. The gap between his life and his end is closing fast. 'God's speed, god's speed,' he mumbles through thick gums.

The stone hut is a hollow square behind him. It yawns, its mouth is wide. The morning is young in this old world.

The left hand forks keep taking him downwards. The air is thin at the top. It thickens as he descends. It clogs in his lungs. He coughs. The cough is wet, it sucks at his mouth. His throat rattles and his chest is heavy.

As the sun rises the earth is set on fire. Watery fire, pale gold. The clouds are on fire. They blaze, bright red to the east. 'The rising sun,' he says and ducks his head. He digs his chin into his collar and stumbles onwards.

On the horizon he can see a line of windmills. Five men in a row, spanning the hilltops. They creak in the wind, the rushing wind. It whips the grass and it whips his beard. The mountains breathe heavily, they spin fast up here.

Not windmills. That's not what the papers call them. Wind farms. They farm the wind. They cultivate it. They are moved by it and they bend it to their will. They steal power from the heavens and use it to light the cities of man, they make them burn brightly in the shadow of night.

He begins a small ascent. A last rise, unavoidable and hard. Hard on his heavy legs and his wet lungs. Dawn greets him as he crests a hill. The sun is climbing over water. His river has turned. It has come back to him in a great curve. It runs down through the hills on the other side of the valley. It runs into a deep loch. A long and silent loch.

On the far side, next to his river's mouth, a group of huts cluster about themselves. Fishing huts, with nets outside and small boats bobbing at the end of a jetty. The boats are painted white. At this distance the details are lost but he can see movement. Fishermen without faces are unloading their boats. They are carrying buckets and nets. The nets writhe, their catch isn't ready to go. It isn't ready to leave this life.

Fools. He is ready to go, and this place is as good as any other. 'Come and get me.'

The loch carries on for miles into the distance. It will end at the sea, at the vast Atlantic. 'Where the old world meets the new,' one of his mama's blokes used to say. A new world, a fresh world where every day is morning.

'Too late for any of that, Jap,' he says. 'Too late for that, mama.' And he presses onwards, down towards the loch. 'Goodbye Celina.' He thinks of the robin, flitting away. He thinks of the starlings as he says his goodbyes.

The last fall

Jap runs through the undergrowth. Willem bends down to pet him. He is soft and slightly damp, as he used to be. The morning's dew has stuck to him and mud has been squelched into his paws. His breath stinks, it stinks of dog food and mouldy socks. He puffs in Willem's face and washes the time away. He washes the hours, the days, the years. He shrinks Willem to a nipper at his mama's breast. He warms the winter breeze to a balm, a soft, warm balm.

He barks and brings Willem to. He has a stick in his mouth and the two tumble about, man and dog in a tug of war. The grass is slick and they both end covered in mud. It is clean mud, it smells fresh. It is the earth and Willem tries to laugh but there is no voice in his breath. He smiles, he gasps and Jap spins.

Willem lets him win. He always does. He is stronger than Jap but Jap doesn't know when he's beaten. He would pull until all his teeth fell out if Willem let him.

Willem finds another stick and waves it around his head like a helicopter. Somewhere far overhead a helicopter hums and soars, and down here Jap barks, dropping his stick. He jumps and jumps. He barks and whines while Willem spins in circles. Finally he lets go of the stick. Jap is in paroxysms. He is ecstatic. He runs after the stick, he runs through puddles and dives into a little brook.

He is a good dog, he is well trained. He brings the stick back. He is soaking and he presses his muzzle against Willem's thighs. The hard stones of his cheekbones bite Willem. He scrambles, he clings at brambles but his broken hands are no use. He cannot hold on. Shingles fly under his feet and his shoulders crack as he tumbles. His wet lungs are choking him.

He comes to a stop. The sun is low, it is disappearing into the hills. He can feel his voice returning to his breath. It is wet in his chest. 'Run, boy,' he murmurs. 'Don't let the bastards get you.'

The bait and the tackle

It starts to snow as he lies there. He is at the bottom of the hill. A fierce wind whips through the basin. His eyes remain closed. He is a strong man yet he cannot muster enough strength to force their lids open. As the snow falls the darkness billows through the surrounding valleys. The moon brushes him and his skin goes numb. The bones in his chest go numb. His limbs die in the snow and the muddy sand in which he lies.

He cannot move and yet he cannot sleep. He is beyond sleep. He is above it, he is larger than it. He is larger than these mountains and there is no respite from himself. With his eyes closed his ears become his sight. They show him the world. They map out the surrounding area. Fir trees line the hills. Their sap covers him and their needles stick to his hair and his skin. A couple of owls circle these pines.

Willem listens for the moon. He listens for its song. It is silver and playful as a stream. The stream before it became a river, the stream in its beginning. In its innocence. The owls' wings dance in front of the moon, they glow silver with its song. They weave through the falling snow.

The loch has its own song. It harmonizes with the moon. It is larger than the moon, it is deeper and its song rumbles far below the moon's tinny high notes. It is a song of tides and ripples and fishermen labouring to feed their loved ones. It is a song of bait being hooked and shimmering lines and nets cast to the deeps. It is a song of fishes swimming free, of fishes flying in the fishermen's nets. It is sad and it is lovely and it will last an age. There was a song one of his mama's blokes used to play, an old man sings '...and Jesus was a sailor when he walked upon the water...' His voice rumbles deep in his chest. It is clammy, it is wet.

The hills are alive. Their deep shadows house many animals. The shadows bear witness to the animals' songs. The hunting cries and the lullabies. The mountains rise through it all in chilly silence. But their silence is not absence, it is drawn out contemplation. It is conscious quiet, a restful backdrop.

The trees and the bushes spread out for hundreds of miles over the highlands. Their creaks and their shudders play a masque. The dead trees of winter sleep off the year's hangover, the evergreens stand vigil and murmur into the night.

His ears must travel a dozen leagues to find civilization. Those leagues contain fishermen's shacks and hunting lodges, farmyards and lumber sites. But they do not contain the full voices of a chorus. A dozen leagues as the owl flies and he finds the songs of a town. The creaking of doors and the snores of old men, the bells calling final orders and the bells chiming the hours. Babies cry and old women sit in electric lighting, ruining their eyes knitting sweaters which will never be worn.

And further. Cities start to spring up. Motorways busy with traffic even at this hour bring new life to their streets. The cities' stones feel the pressure of a million footsteps every hour, every single hour. They break under them. They are removed and replaced until the new ones give out and the cycle repeats. He can hear the people in the cities fighting for survival, he can hear the animals in the wild fighting for survival. 'It is a race, a race of love and of hatred,' he mumbles. His ribs are on fire beneath the snow. He is burning, he is puckered with rot.

'Love and hatred are not blind, but we have blinded them with our own passions…'

He can hear the waves crashing at the shore. At the shores of his native land and at the shores of a hundred others, 'the old world and the new and in all of it there is truly no real place...'

The animals grunt and glower in the farms. 'We think we have tamed them, but we are all tame, we have all been tamed. Small, so small...' The robin dances in front of him. It trills and it turns its head one way and the other. It is eyeing him and its eyes are burning his ribs. They are burning his lungs and making his breath shiver in his watery throat.

'I thought you were so small, so small,' he says to the robin. 'But look how big I am,' and he blocks out the noise. He listens only to the mountains' quiet thoughts. He lives an eternity in an instant as he lies on the beach. He is burning and he is freezing and he cannot muster the strength to sing.

The toiler transcends

He falls into uneasy sleep a few hours before daybreak. His bones are weary and his snores ring with the sound of the tide. The sand is rough, it is half mud. It is between the land and the sea and he is trapped in the middle. His chest closes tight. His throat closes around him as dawn repeats itself for the last time.

He wakes on his final morning with sand in his eyes. They are raw and swollen. All he can see is the red sun above and the brown earth at his feet. His trousers are wet and they cling to him, cold and itchy. His head is dry, his tongue is swollen.

It takes him a long time to take off his trousers. He fumbles to undo his zip. He uses his broken fingers to push it down. He winces as each pair of teeth opens up. He tries to slip the button through its hole but can't. His fingers open up, the skin unclenches and pale blood sticks to him. He tries again but the pain is too much and he nearly faints.

In the end he stuffs his hands down the front of his jeans. He pushes them outwards, bunching his shoulders against the fabric. The button's thread stretches, it frays. Finally it bursts and his hands fly out in front, free. They trail like two stars. They add their light to the red sun.

He sits down and kicks his boots off. He uses his toes to pull off his socks, rolling them down his ankles. He pushes them off and feels the sand and the mud between his toes. His soles rub against it, it gets caught in his nails.

He rolls onto his knees and clambers to his feet. His back aches as he straightens. It is bent. His ribs are broken and they lance him. They whimper as he shrugs his jacket off. His throaty voice hisses as he lifts his arms. His fingers tremble as he hooks them under the neck of his jumper. Through the neck of his t shirt and his vest.

Overhead seagulls circle the harbour. His eyes are opening now. The sand stings and tears stream down his cheeks. His tears blur his vision but he can see well enough for the moment. One of the seagulls dives into the water. He cannot see it for a few seconds. The others ride the air, they dance in the red sun. The water below them swirls as the seagull emerges. He cannot see if it has found its meat. 'Nothing is certain in this life,' he sighs.

He braces himself. He exhales, pulling his lungs away from his ribs. His lungs are blue and his shoulder blades are red as the sun. The world turns black as he lifts. They scorch and he sobs. The sob brings more pain, his lungs catch the red and begin to burn.

And he is standing in nothing but his shorts. The seagulls come back as he drops his jumper. His t shirt and his vest crumple in the sand. He takes out his cock. He strokes his balls. His ruined hands leave pale blood where they touch. He pulls his pants to mid-thigh, he shakes and lets them drop.

He walks towards the water. There are no last goodbyes. There is no sentiment. He discarded it already. He discarded thought and floated through his final days. Now is nothing but a full stop. A period. The end, as it should be, as he wills it.

Overhead a helicopter sings. It scares the birds away but he pays it no heed.

There is nothing left but the mud and the sand slithering between his toes. There is nothing left but the cold water seeping over his ankles. It reaches his knees as he strides, once more with purpose. His balls shrink as they too dip into the loch. His cock shrinks back, his lungs freeze as the water climbs.

His last footprints in this life are swept away as soon as they are trodden. The current and the silt rinse them out. His final footstep in this life takes him over the edge of a shelf. The water rises quickly and he falls. The water covers his eyes, it washes away the seagulls and the red sun. It chokes him. It drags him down. It shows him peace.